MW00861261

# The Haunting of Room 904

**Also by Erika T. Wurth**

*White Horse*

*Buckskin Cocaine*

*Crazy Horse's Girlfriend*

# The Haunting of Room 904

*A Novel*

Erika T. Wurth

FLATIRON
BOOKS
NEW YORK

This is a work of fiction. All of the characters, organizations, and events portrayed in this novel are either products of the author's imagination or are used fictitiously.


For information, address Flatiron Books, 120 Broadway, New York, NY 10271.

www.flatironbooks.com

Designed by Donna Sinisgalli Noetzel

Library of Congress Cataloging-in-Publication Data

Names: Wurth, Erika T., author.
Title: The haunting of room 904 : a novel / Erika T. Wurth.
Other titles: The haunting of room nine hundred four
Description: First Edition. | New York : Flatiron Books, 2025.
Identifiers: LCCN 2024029718 | ISBN 9781250908599 (hardcover) | ISBN 9781250908605 (ebook)
Subjects: LCGFT: Paranormal fiction. | Detective and mystery fiction. | Novels.
Classification: LCC PS3623.U78 H38 2025 | DDC 813/.6—dc23/eng/20240705
LC record available at https://lccn.loc.gov/2024029718

Our books may be purchased in bulk for promotional, educational, or business use. Please contact your local bookseller or the Macmillan Corporate and Premium Sales Department at 1-800-221-7945, extension 5442, or by email at MacmillanSpecialMarkets@macmillan.com.

First Edition: 2025

10 9 8 7 6 5 4 3 2 1

This is dedicated to my cousin Abner Goodbear.
The funniest, most badass motorcycle-riding,
supersmart dude of my childhood.
And to his ancestors, who lost so many
at the Sand Creek Massacre.

This novel deals with suicide (specifically as to Indian Country) and mentions of the Sand Creek Massacre, which out of respect to the descendants of the survivors, I refer to as "the Massacre." Please see educational resources at the end of the novel.

# The Haunting of Room 904

# Chapter One

I'd felt dread the minute Alejandro and I entered Cleo's apartment. Her face was sallow, stricken; she looked like a thousand ghosts had poured through her, like time itself had come for a final reckoning. I closed my eyes. I could feel something at the barest edge of my senses. Something powerful. I moved further into the ghost at my side, wanting to know more about why they were here, but they faded back into that whispering gray purgatorial world I had only witnessed in dreams.

Cleo had handed me the listing a few minutes after we'd settled in.

*Dybbuk Box for sale.*
*WARNING: This is not a plaything. It is possessed.*

*This object sat in my great-great-grandmother's closet for years. Got curious one day and decided to try to open it. That's when scary stuff started happening. I'd find scratches all down my legs, my back. I'd wake up to moaning noises, and the room would be freezing. Violent thoughts started to come into my brain, and I'm not like that. The lights in the house started flickering. I didn't connect it to the box until my mother came by and said that her mom had put it away after the same stuff had happened to her. She told me my ancestor called whatever was in the box "the cursed one." Sometimes I hear noises from the box. I just want to sell it to someone who knows what to do with it.*

*$50 OBO.*

*Per eBay Policy this object is for "entertainment purposes."*

The box from the listing she'd found on eBay was black, covered in thick gray dust—it felt sticky, cobwebby. The touch revolting. There were waxy strings holding the lid down and a large, ornate, black lock.

I glanced briefly up at the streetlights through the frosty window, the snow blowing in blue streaks beneath them. It was coming down like mad, the roads covered in gray-brown slush from a late spring snow.

"Just breathe, Olivia," Alejandro said, patting my hand.

I blinked. Glanced down. My hand was clenched around the listing. "Sorry," I said, releasing it to the coffee table. I hadn't wanted to take anything on this week.

"It's okay," Cleo said, running one freckled hand through her hair, her eyes flitting briefly to the window, then back over to me. The snow had started to fall even more rapidly, the sky a mass of white.

"So, when did all of this start?" I asked, picking up the mug she'd poured for me when we'd first come in.

"About a week after I got it in the mail. Like I said over the phone, the minute I saw it, I had to have it, there was just something that drew me—I thought it sounded neat."

"Neat," I echoed.

Most of the paranormal listings on eBay were haunted dolls,

written about in inarticulate script, clearly playing off the popularity of the Conjuring films. This object, however, was unique.

"Go on," Alejandro said. He generally let me lead the questioning. Sometimes, however, he questioned while I looked around—let my mind search. Though Alejo did a lot of the day-to-day things, like keep our calendar, I needed him with me on gigs to make sure that if I went off the edge, I had someone there to catch me. My mind was strong. But when you were clairvoyant, spirits—or anything else—could get in. And you wouldn't know until it was too late.

"Then it was little things," she said, continuing. She sipped at her coffee, and I could see her hands trembling. "I couldn't find Mousey. I got him when he was a kitten, just a tiny black ball of fur." She smiled, a small, weak smile. "Then, like in the listing, I'd wake up hearing noises. Moaning. And then the scratches started. I finally found Mousey under the bed—but I couldn't get him out. He stayed under literally all the time. I tried to throw the box out. I put it in the dumpster outside, but . . ."

"Please, continue," Alejo prompted once more.

"It reappeared. The next day—on my kitchen counter," she said, her voice shaking. "And there was a note on top of it."

I squinted, leaned in.

"It said, 'There is no escaping your bloodline.'"

That was interesting.

I sat back, still wondering if for all my instinct, I'd misread her, and this wasn't evidence of a psychic break. Stuff started going wrong in their heads, and then they'd find something to make what was happening real. The problem was, when it *was* real, sometimes it was because the entity—which was almost always a ghost—had found a vulnerability and wormed its way in.

"I have to ask you something," I said, smiling reassuringly. "And I don't want you to take offense."

She nodded, the corners of her mouth turning down, her eyes narrowing.

"Do you have a history of mental health issues?"

She went pale, then her face turned a shade of pink, then red. "Are you calling me crazy? This is *for real.* I'm scared *for real.* That thing"—she paused to point at it—"is possessed. There's like, a demon or something in it. And I don't appreciate you questioning my sanity, when it took everything I had to call you." She stood up, her legs trembling, her eyes filling with tears.

"Sweetie, sweetie." Alejandro got up and walked over to her, sat down, and patted the seat next to him. "No one thinks you're crazy, which is like, a totally shitty word anyway."

Her shoulders relaxed a bit then, and she sighed, roughing the tears from her face with a forearm.

"And like, I'm on fluoxetine? So, if anyone's crazy here, mija, it's me. Maybe it's because I majored in English, and all that poetry screwed with my head," he continued, and patted the seat where she'd been again. "Like all that Poe? Black."

She laughed despite herself, and Alejandro handed her a tissue. She sniffled and dabbed at her eyes, clutched the tissue in her fingers, sat back down, and clasped her hands in her lap. "I'm sorry. It's just. I'm not sleeping, you know?"

"It's okay, it's really okay," I said, and Alejandro patted her shoulder.

"I don't," she said after a few minutes. "I mean, I don't have a history with depression. Or like, any mental illnesses. Not that I'm criticizing," she said, her head jerking over to Alejandro.

"Don't worry about it. I'm gay. We're like, required to be a little mental, given the meathead homophobes we deal with in this world," he said, rolling his eyes.

She laughed again, her hand over her lips. Then she sighed heavily. "I did go through some therapy when my dad died. That was rough.

I was close to him—and my mom. And there were times . . ." she said, her eyes going distant, "I thought . . ."

"Go on, we're not judging you," I said.

"I thought that I, well, not that I saw him? But that I felt him in the room. I smelled him, smelled his cologne. It took me a long time to get over that." She giggled nervously. "But then I did. And I was fine. I was a cheerleader and everything. Had straight As. Went to CU."

That was how it had gotten in. That little, dark, black hole inside of her.

"I get it. My dad died too," I said.

"I'm sorry," she said.

"Cancer," I volunteered.

"Mine was a car accident," she said, one finger brushing lightly over her mug.

"Were you in the car?"

"Yeah," she whispered, the finger stilling.

We were silent for a beat.

"You want me to get you more coffee?" she asked, running one hand through her pale, greasy hair.

"Sure."

When she got back, she continued. "So, after the moaning, the scratching, the lights flickering, and then, like, this feeling. This feeling of foreboding. And I don't know how else to describe it," she said, clutching her hand to her chest, the tissue still trapped between her fingers. "This feeling of doom and darkness in my heart—and, oddly enough, guilt—that's when it got real. That's when I started to see things."

I let her go on. Alejandro took her hand, and she smiled at him, swallowed.

"I'd wake up, and I was standing in front of the mirror, in the bathroom. I don't sleepwalk?" She cleared her throat, twisted the tissue. "Then it got so much worse. I'd wake up, and behind me, I'd see him. I'd see Daddy."

She started crying in earnest then, and Alejandro rubbed her back, shushed her gently. We let her cry it out. "But it wasn't him. His eyes . . ." she said, trailing off. She shook her head. "And then I began waking up in front of the mirror—with a knife in my hand."

Jesus Christ.

"That's when I started searching for help—for, you know, paranormal investigators. Mostly what I found looked scammy. But you two, it was clear from your website that you're the real thing. Plus, you have really good reviews on Yelp," she said, ending with a small, uncomfortable chuckle.

She sniffled again, blew her nose, and Alejandro gave her another tissue from the weirdly never-ending supply that he kept in his messenger bag.

"Alejandro, could you hand me the sweetgrass? The shell?" I asked.

He nodded, pulled the flap of his bag, and handed me my materials. There was holy water as well, just in case. I never knew what I was going to be dealing with.

"Oh, the candles too."

Alejandro handed each object to me with a cloth, and I set them out, my hands folding them down in the proper way. I sat back. "I want to be clear. This is a ceremony, this is not some kind of play Indian thing. I am not a traditional medicine person, and I'm *definitely* not a priest," I said, chuckling darkly. "But this is how I know how to respectfully communicate with the dead. My family was tradish, then Catholic, then Native American Church. This is what I know, who I am."

Cleo blinked a few times, then nodded.

"And the only reason I'm taking payment? Is because I need to eat to live."

She nodded again. "Do I need to do something?"

"Just take deep breaths. Focus on something in the room that makes you happy. Focus on a memory that makes you happy."

Alejandro lit the sage and let it burn until it was creating a steady stream of smoke, and we motioned the smoke over ourselves, cleansing. I told Cleo to do the same.

I sat back. Worked hard to clear my head.

Alejandro dimmed the lights, lit the black-flowered candles—my hope being that the spirit would be drawn to the flickering light, and that the light would lead it to the other world.

I closed my eyes. At first, nothing.

"Is this working?" Cleo whispered. Alejandro quietly asked her to keep silent. To focus. To let me focus.

I could hear doors opening and closing throughout the complex. Laughter outside. I closed my eyes again. Thought about Cleo. The box. It had such strange energy. The building went silent again. And I waited. Kept an image of the box in my mind, of Cleo's guilt. There was something in that, something . . . inside. I felt a breeze, a light, cold breeze. I knew that the windows were shut. The breeze grew, and I heard distant sounds of women and children. I strained to hear what they were saying, leaned forward into the dark wind of my vision, and it came, clear, grew louder. They were screaming.

"Oh my God," Cleo said, and Alejandro shushed her quietly.

"There is someone here. Something . . . trapped in the box," I said, leaning in, opening my eyes. I stared at the box. I could feel it now. A presence. Not masculine . . . not exactly feminine. And anger. Oh, such anger and grief, it was overwhelming, my chest growing tight. I could hear whispering coming from it—desperate, furious whispering, in a language I only faintly recognized. I strained to listen, to understand. There was so much fire in that voice.

Alejandro was beside me now.

A bolt of blue light began pooling around the box, swirling. I began to pray in Apache, prayers for peace.

The blue light fired from the box and hit me. I rocked back.

"Oh my God!" Cleo squealed, standing up.

"No, no—sit down, let her do what she needs to do," Alejandro said, but I could hear the fear in his voice.

The being swirled around me, nearly inside me.

"They . . . their name is Nese. This means *two*," I said. "They were two-spirit. They were . . . a sacred person. Cheyenne. They were killed at the Massacre . . ." I focused as hard as I could, closing my eyes to concentrate. Oh, God, the images. I was going to be sick. The violence. The sheer, unadulterated cruelty. I'd read about this countless times, but to watch it hit me so far down deep, I wasn't sure I'd ever recover. My eyes flew open just as the lights snapped back on, and the box flew over to the wall, smashing into it, over and over, as if it was trying to break itself open.

Cleo began moaning, Alejandro telling her that she had to remain calm or this wouldn't work at all. The moans diminished to whimpers.

"Nese, why are you in a dybbuk box?" I asked.

Sobbing. All I could hear then as the lights snapped back off was sobbing and noises from different, dark corners of the room. Whispering, the scratch of the inhuman voice radiating fury and sadness. So much that my body physically hurt.

"Tell me. Tell me so we can help you get out," I said. "Help you to the other side."

The whispering was indecipherable at first, but eventually it came through in a language I could understand. *The white men came for us while the men were hunting.*

Oh my God, no. No.

*I am a Hēē măn ĕh h'. I was honored. I blessed marriages. I was pure luck. When they came, they murdered almost all. They did unspeakable things. I tried to protect the babies, one survived. She found me. Through her I can see outside.*

Here lights flickered again, and the sobbing turned into one long, rageful moan.

"Nese, please, we want to help you," I said. "Please. I am N'de. I know how to bring you home. I know the way if you'll only let me—"

*I can't go home.* The voice turned bitter, rageful.

The blue light fired forward again, the lock bursting open, but this time the light went straight into Cleo, who began to convulse, her eyes closing, the blue light a circle on her chest.

"Oh shit, oh shit," Alejandro said, scrambling up.

We watched, and I prayed, and finally, Cleo's body went still.

She opened her eyes, and Alejandro and I both sat back, hard.

Her eyes were black.

"Oh, *shit*," I said.

"Cleo?" Alejandro said.

She smiled.

"Nese," I said, a short, panicked warning in my tone.

Her smile grew wider.

"Nese," I repeated, Cleo's gaze turning to me in one sharp, almost robot-like motion. I shuddered. This being was angry, and understandably so.

"Nese, talk to me," I said, standing up. "Just," I said, tripping over my own feet and barely recovering, "talk to me."

Cleo's smile stopped abruptly. "You have freed me. I am allowed blood. Her ancestor murdered me, kept my hair, put my spirit in this box when I tried to stop him from doing more evil." Her voice was bifurcated, metallic almost.

She stood up, her smile reappearing.

"Cleo," I said, and her smile faltered. "Think about your father," I continued, panic rising in the back of my throat, thick and rich.

Her eyes seemed to come back then, hazel just beginning to peep through the deep, cavernous dark, but then they blackened once more, and her smile disappeared. She turned her head as if she heard something in the distance.

She headed for the kitchen.

"Your father loves you," I said, tripping as I peeled off the couch, feeling stupid, ineffectual.

"Why the kitchen?" Alejandro asked, right behind me.

"Well, it's not to bake a quiche," I hissed.

Both of us stopped at the arched threshold between the kitchen and the living room.

Her back was to us, her body against the counter.

"The *hell* is she up to?" Alejandro whispered.

I was just about to call her name once more when she turned around, a knife in her hand. She was laughing again.

My stomach dropped, and I worked to steel myself.

"This is so not good," Alejandro said, his fingertips going briefly to his forehead.

She grasped the knife tightly, laughing and laughing, lunging, just a little. I jumped back, though it was hardly necessary.

Alejandro put his arm out to protect me, shoving me behind his body. He was beefy as hell from working out. He did it to be pretty, but he also did it to protect himself from murderous homophobes—and the dead.

She went stiff, silent. "I have no issues with you," she said. "But this one needs to leave the earth before she does evil."

Alejandro pulled his switchblade out, flipped it in his hand. "I don't want to use this? I'm also like, two-spirit, but you're being a *bitch*."

I squinted. Yikes.

"I don't want to hurt Cleo. But I will if you take one more step," Alejandro said, his dark eyes narrowing.

Nese laughed, a deep, throaty laugh.

I guess they were okay with being called a bitch.

Nese put the knife up to Cleo's throat. I realized in that moment that it was quite likely we would be blamed for this. That maybe if we hadn't gotten involved, we wouldn't have made it worse.

Alejandro could feel me flailing.

"You can do this. You've got this," he said, his hand squeezing comfortingly down on my arm.

I focused. Thought of my mother. My father, gone these many years. And momentarily of my sister, grief circling my heart.

I took a breath. "Nese, you know your people have survived."

The black eyes receded. Came back.

"I know some of your people. They live all over this city. And your ancestors? They want you home."

"They would be happy that I took her blood," Nese said, the knife pulling drops from Cleo's neck.

In all honesty, though I had nothing against Cleo personally, Nese wasn't wrong.

"What if I told you that what had happened has not been forgotten? Give this girl a chance to know what happened all those generations ago."

Nese's mouth opened slowly, and a long scream of rage poured forth. She pulled the knife closer.

I closed my eyes.

"Cleo," I said, switching tacks, "think of your father—tell Nese you know you will do what you can to understand and to reckon with your ancestor's sins. Nese. You were a Roadman. Go deep inside and think about what you would have done if a spirit like yourself had come when you were alive."

Their eyes flickered. "You are N'de?" they asked, their eyes going soft.

I nodded.

"I will give you the key," Nese said. The eyes went hazel, the knife clattering to the floor.

I felt my body nearly go limp, and Alejandro's arm came up to steady me.

"I wasn't sure that was going my way," I said, listening to the sound of Cleo wailing.

"Girl, me either," he said, walking up to Cleo.

We comforted Cleo. Told her that she needed to atone. I wondered if she'd act offended, tell us that what her ancestor had done wasn't her fault, but she didn't. She said she hadn't known about any of this, that she wished someone in her family, or at school for that matter, had educated her. She said she would go to the site of the Massacre and apologize. That she would donate to the American Indian College Fund. That she would send a formal, public apology to the Cheyenne and Arapaho Tribes on behalf of her ancestor.

As I took it from Cleo, I wondered about the dybbuk box. It was perplexing. The way it had sat in someone else's closet. How it had found its way onto eBay. And then, finally, straight into the hands of a woman whose ancestor had murdered Nese, the spirit trapped in the box.

Glancing down at the box as we walked home, the snow having dissipated, I noted that the strings had been broken, the lock popped, the box opened. There was a figure in clay—what looked to be a golem, bound in more string. I closed it. When I got home, I'd call my ex Sasha. The box and the golem were certainly of Jewish origin. He was a scholar and rebel rabbi who'd left traditional Jewish practices far, far behind when a body he was preparing for a funeral came raging back to life. Perhaps he could tell me a little more about the box, so that I could store it properly.

I stopped. "What do you think Nese meant by 'I will give you the key'?"

Alejandro shrugged. "You know the dead say crazy things."

"I guess," I responded. The day was sunny now, the clouds having parted, the snow already melting on the ground. The way home was pleasant, trees lining the sidewalk, the sweet, trilling sounds of finches singing in the air. But the warmth didn't penetrate my skin. I could feel something coming, a ghost train running through the hollows of my heart. A kind of lonely whistle you hear when you're half asleep, not awake enough to know where the horn is coming from, not asleep enough to stop yourself from jolting back to consciousness with the kind of fear you don't even remember the dawning of.

## Chapter Two

*www.ghostequipmentforreal.com*
*EVP Recorders and Ghost Boxes FOR SALE*

*A useful tool for documenting activity, audio recorders are a MUST for any self-respecting paranormal investigator. A staple for ghost hunters and paranormal investigators for recording Electronic Voice Phenomena/EVP. $150.*

I turned in bed, clicked *buy* on the ghost box, and set my phone on the bedside table, the shadows in the room strange, ominous. I picked my book up, then put it down, my thoughts drifting over to my sister. Naiche and I had been inseparable since her birth, laughing at the same stupid jokes, compulsively watching the same horror movies, especially the paranormal, like *The Ring* and *The Conjuring.* We'd had matching circular tattoos inked on our inner wrists on my sixteenth birthday, illegally, secretly, drunk on the tequila we'd liberated from our mother's kitchen. I still woke up in the middle of the night laughing at something wonderful I'd thought in a dream, my finger hovering over her name in my phone, ready to text her. Sometimes, I stared at that broken circle, knowing that hers had burned away in an incinerator in a crematorium in the middle of Denver, the name of which I'd already forgotten.

"God," I muttered, switching my light on and sitting up.

The faint sounds of *RuPaul's Drag Race* drifted in from the living room, a comforting and familiar backdrop to our millennial domesticity. I closed my eyes against the darkness in my head. I could hear Alejandro's barbells clank down, hard, and then the patter of his footsteps leading up to my bedroom door.

He knocked.

"Come in," I said, attempting to smooth my hair down.

He opened the door and sloped into the frame, then walked in, his dark eyes narrowed with concern, his back to the long gold mirror on the wall opposite to me. "Saw your light on. Trouble sleeping?"

"Yeah," I said, sighing.

He sat down at the edge of my bed. "It's almost the anniversary."

"Yeah," I repeated, my voice soft, foggy.

He leaned in and hugged me, and unbidden, the tears came, Alejo rubbing my back as I cried. He was always so good to me. He always let me cry, never judged me for it, though he never let me wallow too long.

"It wasn't your fault—" he started, tipping back, but my eyes caught something in the mirror. Something that shouldn't be there.

My sister was in the mirror, her eyes two blackened bulbs, her hair electric, everywhere, her expression one of terror.

I screamed.

# Chapter Three

"Olivia?" Alejandro said, standing up, his hands going to his chest in a reflexive, defensive gesture.

I blinked. She was gone.

"What the hell was that?" he asked, one hand reaching tentatively out to my arm.

"I . . . thought I saw Naiche. In the mirror," I said, my heart still racing, one finger pointing to the offending object. I was used to dealing with the paranormal, but my sister's ghost was something else altogether. I shuddered.

Alejandro turned around. Peered into it. After a moment, he asked me if I wanted him to get some equipment.

I nodded.

We hit the mirror with the EMF meter, Alejo running it carefully from one end to the other. I watched him, my body rigid, my mind locked in a state of confusion and anxiety.

The meter stayed silent. Not one beep.

I closed my eyes. Sighed deeply. "I think I'm just overwhelmed."

He nodded. "You haven't been sleeping. And this is a shit time for you anyway."

"I'm sorry if I scared you," I said, but Alejandro shook his head and left to get my sleep meds. I'd already taken my usual singular pill, but apparently I needed a double dose tonight. He brought me a cup of water, and I let him tip it toward my mouth like I was a child, or like I was taking sacrament, a ritual my sister and I had participated in whenever we'd spent Sundays at Alejo's house.

He asked me if I was okay and I nodded, though both of us knew that I wasn't. He smiled uneasily. He closed the door. I turned, my book in hand, and thought of my sister's face. Not the one I'd just seen in the mirror, but her true face, her doll's face, the one that stared at me shyly from beneath lowered lids whenever my mother and I would laugh loudly over red wine. The one that had been just two years behind me watching as I danced with my father, his face red and happy. I shut the light off. The shadows in the room began coalescing into something like a human figure, my mind playing tricks on me. I tried to not look at the mirror, though it felt like it was pulsing in the dark, my heart racing and slowing down, racing and slowing down, the image of my sister in the mirror haunting me, chasing me through the corridors of my mind as I finally, but not blissfully, slipped into a troubled and nightmared sleep.

## The Massacre, Part I

The soldiers had told them to stay here, to wait until negotiation resumed, but Nese knew that Vó'kaáe Ohvó'komaestse and Mo'ohtavetoo'o were nervous. And if they were nervous, men who had proved their worth, who carried the Sacred Arrows after many ceremonies, many of which Nese had led, taught by Sweet Medicine, things were grim. The medicine should have protected them, should have protected the entire nation, but the morning felt still and ominous. Deadly. The birds weren't singing. There was silence across the plains, except for the strange, lonely sounds of the wind whistling hollowly across the crust of the snow.

The Heévâhetaneo'o had only been hoping for peace.

There was a shadow over the plains. Nese glanced up, their hand over their eyes. An owl. A shudder pierced their flesh like a Sun Dance scar. What was an owl doing flying over the encampment when the sun had barely risen? Though their men had left hours ago with the owl's feathers attached to their arms, a vision of the owl could mean death.

Nese glanced at the women who were tending to the children, and their heart rendered into a million sharp pieces, each one cutting at the meat of Nese's spirit listening to their cries. The people had been battling the Vehoc for many years, and they were hungry, and they were broken. They had tried to negotiate. They had failed.

Of the men of the Vehoc, Nese liked the thin one with the kind eyes the color of the sky. The bigger one, however, had a shadow on his back—a hungry, sick shadow that clawed at his flesh. Only Nese could see the shadow. It made them sick. It made them need ceremony.

The morning was cold, and there was snow on the ground, in the air, the tiny white stars floating down and down, making Nese feel like they were in a dream. They pulled their meager skins around them and tried to see into the future, but the trail had gone as cold as the air. The men had gone to hunt, though their grounds had been decimated through reduction of their lands, and there was little hope for game.

Nese felt a tug at their robes. "Nese?"

It was the boy they had begun to train to become a medicine person. Nese reached down and caressed his hair, and the boy smiled. That was what Nese loved the most about him, his ability for joy in the midst of such great pain.

"Yes?" Nese asked. The boy was a close relation. They had held him in their arms as a child; they had sung to him.

"Do you know when the men will return?" the boy asked, looking up at the sky. Nese wondered if he had seen the owl too. The boy was special. Intuitive.

Nese sighed. "They said they would return when they had news or food."

The warriors had decided to stand their ground on their lands; here, there were only old men. It unsettled Nese to think of it.

The boy looked off in the distance and frowned. "I feel strange."

Nese's stomach turned, and they tried to shadow their fear, but it was hard. The boy saw so much. Nese put their hand on his shoulder and squeezed.

Nese was about to say something, to pull something from

somewhere inside to comfort him, even though they had nothing, had felt empty inside for longer than they could remember, when at last the silence was broken.

The entire camp heard it: the noise of hoofbeats and the small, sad sounds of gladness at the thought that buffalo were around the corner. Mo'ohtavetoo'o's wife, Ar'no'ho'wok, originally of the Ponka, looked up, a tiny smile on her sweet lips. But it turned sour.

It was the Vehoc. And even from this distance, Nese could see the monsters tearing at their backs.

# Chapter Four

The escape room was a gothic dreamscape, with ornate black chandeliers, old books, and black-framed paintings of ancient-looking people whose eyes followed you as you moved. The owner and our guide for the day, Laurence, was dressed like a B-rated Vincent Price, in a much-worn black-and-red velvet smoking jacket that looked like it'd been purchased on sale at Spencer's—complete with a pair of plastic vampire teeth, which he had trouble talking around. Finally, he asked if it was all right if he just took them out.

Laurence was also playing bartender.

"This place scares me," Sara said in a hushed little whisper, breaking me from my morose reverie. Her eyes were on a large gothic cuckoo clock in front of the bar.

Victoria rolled her eyes. "*This* place?"

Sara huffed.

I had convinced Victoria and Sara to go on a job in an escape room housed in an old mansion. Alejandro was helping an ex-turned-friend adjust to his HIV meds, and I never went on a job alone—it was too dangerous. A few jobs ago, I'd almost run off a cliff, I'd been so immersed in the memories of a woman. The owners of the escape room, two college friends—Laurence and Seamus—

had structured the story around the *actual* story of the ghost who allegedly haunted this enormous hall. It was a hit. Until patrons started to experience things—sometimes violent things—not of the owner's design. They'd brought in priests of all denominations, and nothing had worked. Finally, one of them had suggested me.

Though I'd been skeptical, I could feel it the second I walked into the hallway, which also served as the front desk, the back of my brain spiking painfully with visions. Mainly a singular, very female presence—which did match up with the legend around the place. I'd asked Laurence to let me go on a regular, run-of-the-mill tour, as that's when the phenomena occurred.

The place was smooth, though, the lighting dim, the bar dark and marbled, with tall black candelabras and ornate charcoal mirrors covering the walls. The last gave me a chill. Ever since my sister had suicided right next to one, I had been simultaneously thrilled and terrified by them.

"Earth to Apache," Victoria said, snapping her fingers in front of my face. "What are you doing in there? Dreaming of murdering my ancestors?"

"Very funny, Victoria," I said, "and yes." She'd never let that in-joke about Apaches versus Navajos die down.

She laughed and ordered us another round. "When is this thing going to start? I'm bored."

"Just drink your drink," Sara said, pulling her glass to her lips and sipping. "I'm guessing our vampire host wants us to get good and soused before we enter the Murder Hotel."

"Because it's going to suck," I said.

"No pun intended," Sara said, giggling.

"I don't know if he really wants me getting drunk," I said. "I *am* on the job."

Laurence had been scrolling on his phone, leaning against the bar while we talked, but hearing something to do with him, he paused and looked up. "What?"

"Don't worry about it," Victoria said.

He looked back down at his phone.

"You know how much I hate this kind of stuff," Sara said, pulling her rebozo tighter. "Back home in New Mexico—"

Victoria interrupted her. "Back home, I was told everything I did was wrong, okay?"

I smiled sadly and took a long sip of my drink. I promised myself I was only going to have one. My sister had been deeply enamored with escape rooms, her face flushed with excitement every time she found a new one. We'd all—Sara and Victoria, Alejandro and myself—been to an escape room with her a few years before she died. A haunted escape room at that—one that had subsequently closed. My sister had been halfway through when she'd stared at a portrait of a child, her face growing pale. She'd insisted we leave and, no matter how much I pressed her, wouldn't talk about why. *You wouldn't believe me anyway,* she'd said, my body going hot with guilt, *you never do.*

"Are you guys ready?" our vampire guide asked, his head out of his phone.

"Give us a few minutes to finish these," Victoria said, pointing to our glasses of wine, "and yes." She'd gotten herself and Sara another round, despite the fact that Sara was still working on her first.

"Uh, okay," he responded, and sat down on one of the black velvet divans, his head once more in his phone.

"Think he's scrolling for victims?" Victoria whispered, and Sara giggled.

"I'm not sure he's effectively puncturing anyone's neck with that shit," I said, meaning the plastic teeth. He looked up from his phone, frowned, and looked back down. Sara giggled again, her hand in front of her mouth, Victoria laughing with her head thrown back.

A few minutes later, we were ready, and Laurence led us to a doorway that appeared only when he pulled a hardback book out of its place on a large, antique-looking bookshelf.

Victoria *ooh*ed as it slid back, and the inky, almost elven tree trunk–ish doorway was revealed. I had to admit, I was impressed. I was also feeling the presence I'd felt when I'd first come in—and right behind me. I took a quick, circumspect look, but there was nothing visible. At least not yet. It was just a breath on my neck, a tingling at the back of my brain.

"Cool," Victoria said, Sara's nervous "I guess" echoing behind us, and we followed Laurence into a room that did, honestly, look like an old dusty office in some mysterious gothic mansion; the scent of old books, patchouli, and something else, something I couldn't pin down—but that was deeply satisfying, almost like the smell of water rushing over rocks—permeated the room. A quiet sigh reverberated throughout as we entered, followed by an oceanic sadness sinking into my skin. I took a deep breath.

There were typewriters on every surface amid old buttons, armless and legless dolls with cracked faces, end tables and desks covered in musty-smelling hardbacks, decks of cards, and, of course, a good number of gothic mirrors.

Faintly, I could hear blues—the tenor of the music scratchy, as if it were being played on an old record player, and I looked to a few I'd seen scattered throughout, wondering if they were the source. But they were still.

"So, like, you just want the regular tour? Like anyone?" Laurence asked, one hand reaching around to rub the back of his neck. He was nervous. Most people had at least some sensitivity, and from what he'd said on the phone, he and the other guy had seen some shit. In fact, the other guy—Seamus—wouldn't come into the mansion anymore after a typewriter key had flown out of the machine, narrowly missing his eye, one night when he'd been working late.

I nodded. "That'll give me a sense of what's happening here, and why."

"Okay, well, then," he said, shrugging and pulling at his velvet jacket, "have a seat, and I'll tell you a tale." Laurence gestured to two frowsty red velvet couches, settling into a chair not far from us.

He took a deep breath. "When Denver was new, and the gold rush had just ended, there was a young woman named Carlenna who lived with her father in this mansion. She was half Indian, and her mother died during childbirth."

"Convenient," Victoria whispered. "And I thought this was supposed to be a haunted hotel?"

"Mansion *turned* hotel," Laurence retorted, then continued with his story. "She was beautiful, and her father was rich, and old, and she had many suitors. But she wasn't interested in marriage. She was interested in staying in her father's mansion, caring for him in his old age, and reading. She had a true love of books."

I closed my eyes. There was something, almost a low humming, somewhere in the house. The presence I'd felt behind me earlier intensified, heightened. And that tidal feeling of sadness hit me so hard, I had to work to not feel overwhelmed, to pay attention to the story.

Laurence continued. "One day, she was walking in the hills near her house—remember, this is before Denver as we know it now existed—when she tripped and, fearing that she'd broken her ankle, cried out for help, as she could not stand. Some time had passed when she began to despair, hoping that her father's servants would come looking for her. Dark began to fall, and that's when she heard wolves howling, she was sure, for her blood.

"Glowing eyes peered out at her from the distance in the darkness, and as they came closer, she knew it was her time. She closed her eyes, prayed to her Lord and Savior, and as one of the wolves came up on her, its breath hot, she hoped her father would not suffer long upon learning of her death.

"Nothing happened."

Laurence, despite his goofy attire, could tell a tale. Sara's eyes, in particular, had gone large and round as a child's.

"She heard soft, masculine laughter and opened her eyes. Above her, holding his hand out, was a dark-haired man with streaks of silver threaded throughout his mane. His was a sharp, lean, handsome face, a scar lining one of his cheeks."

Victoria started laughing. "Cheek," she said, and Sara shushed her.

I opened my eyes long enough to glare at Victoria. Why did people with super-high IQs have the most juvenile sense of humor?

"Sorry," she said.

She was not sorry.

Unfazed, Laurence continued. "He took her hand, and then hefted her onto his shoulder and got her to her father's house. He visited often, near dusk, and they talked as she recovered. They had much in common—their love of books, their fondness for silly humor—and as the time passed, they fell in love." He paused here. I knew why. They'd told me that it was at this point that the paranormal activity often started.

My eyes closed again. I started to reach out. I could feel her, Carlenna—her agony, her great, welling sadness. I began trembling then, and Sara's hand shot out, took mine.

There was a gentle, almost scraping noise, something you could miss if you weren't looking for it. I was moving now, into Carlenna's memories.

"It's starting," he said, and I could hear Sara's sharp intake of breath, the sound of something being pushed off a table.

"Just continue," I said.

He took a deep breath. "But one day, as Carlenna was almost completely healed, her love confessed a secret: he was a wolf-man. A shapeshifter. He told her that he could not eat her when he first saw her, as she was too beautiful. He had kept his pack at bay and shifted. At first, she did not believe him, thought him mad, but he changed right in front of her eyes and leapt out the window.

"She mourned for days, but came, eventually, to the conclusion that, for better or worse, she loved him. When next he visited, he told her that there was a way that they could be together, that he could make her what he was. She consented.

"The very next night, her love came through the window and bit her."

I was there. I was Carlenna, though there wasn't anything that I'd call a werewolf. Just a man and a woman, neither of whom looked anything like her, chanting above her bed, the woman holding what looked to be a dagger.

Sara yelled, and our host paused. I was pulled out of the memory. I struggled to keep my eyes closed, but I couldn't.

"The . . . typewriter moved! On its own!" Sara said, her face going pale.

"It really likes that typewriter," Laurence said, unconsciously rubbing at his eyes.

"It's okay, Sara, let's just be here for Olivia," Victoria said, her voice firm.

Sara squealed. "There's a shadow . . . that's not . . . it shouldn't be there." She started wailing.

I told Laurence to keep going.

"Just—just . . . as she could feel the change afoot, the door opened," Laurence continued, one eye on the typewriter. "It was her father. Her father screamed and pulled the firearm he had at his side up—he'd heard a commotion and had come up to check on his daughter, worried for her safety—and fired at the beast. Carlenna leapt into the way of the bullet, and as she lay dying, her love changed back into a human and held her as her eyes closed."

Sara began sniffling. "The shadow is moving towards me," she said in a voice so terrified and small I had to work to stay in the vision.

I felt a chill. It was Carlenna. She was beside me. And she was furious.

I was Carlenna. I'd leapt from my bed. I was lying in the man's arms, the life draining from me, a mirror above me, the woman still chanting. I could hear other voices. As I died, I felt power briefly surge through me, and a feeling as if I was twisting that power.

I could hear whispering in the room now, loud, angry. I reached out to Carlenna and she retaliated by pushing me, hard. I fell to the floor, my eyes snapping open, Laurence and my friends staring down at me. I scrambled up, pulled the chair into place, and took a breath.

"I'm okay, finish."

Laurence hesitated, then went on. "The father, confounded and terrified, finally came to his senses and aimed. The wolf went out the window, never to be seen again."

The shadow . . . Sara had said there was a shadow moving toward her. But she was on the other side of the room, practically. And Carlenna had pushed me over. Was there another presence in here?

"But they say," Laurence continued, to my great surprise, "that you can still sometimes see a wolf roaming Capitol Hill at night, howling for his lost love, Carlenna eternally searching for him, so that she can beg his forgiveness."

"Damn—" Victoria started.

At that moment, a window blew open, and a bolt of lightning flashed, there was thunder, and the piercing, haunting sound of a wolf baying echoed throughout the room. And I could feel the other presence—evil, skulking, full of hate.

Sara screamed.

## Chapter Five

"Dude! Dude! It's okay," Laurence said, rushing over to Sara's side. She'd crawled up to Victoria like a child woken from a nightmare and buried her head in her neck, wailing in terror. "That part is like, fake! Well, not the window? But like the wolf howling."

Victoria laughed nervously and forced Sara to look at the window—there was a wolf there all right. A wolf on a high-res television screen. It howled again.

"I'm sorry," Sara said, going red in the face, her sobs downgrading to hiccups. "This is really hard for me."

"I'm proud of you for doing this," Victoria said, and Sara peered up at her, her dark brows knitted.

"Do you guys," Laurence said, shuffling his feet, "want to not do this? Me and Olivia could just—"

"No, no—" Victoria said, cutting him off, "she's *fine*."

I looked over at Sara. "Are you?"

"She's—" Victoria started, but it was my turn to cut her off.

"Sara?" I asked. "I really appreciate you coming with me, but I would understand if you needed to go home."

She took a deep, shuddering breath. "I'm fine. I'm thirty-three years old. I need to face my fears. And you need me," she said, tipping her chin my way. "I'm fine," she repeated, rubbing first one elbow, then the next.

"See?" Victoria said, petting Sara's long, wavy hair. "Fine." She smiled. "I want to say it again: I'm proud of you, Sara."

"Thanks," Sara responded, bathing in the glow of Victoria's approval. They'd had a little thing in college that Victoria still relentlessly teased Sara about, which in my opinion was cruel. It was clear that Sara wasn't over it.

"Cool, okay, like, sometimes people freak out. It's," he said, rolling his eyes to the side, "meant to freak you out. And with the real stuff," he said, his eyes skirting once again over to the typewriter, "you should freak out."

"Right," Victoria said, sitting up straighter.

"I mean, when stuff started floating or getting shoved in people's faces—or people started vomiting because they felt something bad in the room, that's not part of it. And also? I really hate cleaning up barf."

"Let's just attempt to get back on track," I said, trying to reorient.

"Yeah, yeah, gotcha. Okay." Laurence settled back into his chair. "So, your goal is to free the spirit of Carlenna. If you can escape from the room, then you've freed Carlenna's soul, got it?"

"Got it," I said, trying to relax, to allow Carlenna into me again, though that sadness, it hurt. And there was something specific about it, something familiar that felt like a word you just couldn't think of, one right on the tip of your tongue.

"This is usually when I go. Do you want me to stay?" Laurence asked.

"Let's just keep to your normal routine," I answered, smoothing my hands over my knees, a nervous tic.

"Good luck," he said with obvious relief, and left.

The lights dimmed, and one of the princess phones started ringing.

"I'll get it!" Victoria said, shooting up off the couch.

"You're having way too much fun with this," Sara said.

She picked up the receiver and we watched as Victoria cradled the phone into her neck and narrowed her lovely, sharp, dark eyes in concentration. Faintly, I could hear a voice on the other side, though I couldn't make out any words. Victoria listened for a few minutes, then hung up.

"What did they say?" Sara asked.

I closed my eyes. Carlenna's presence felt very distant, and I wondered if bringing Sara had been a mistake. She was a good balance to Victoria's crafted irreverence, but this part of my life wasn't exactly her kind of vibe.

"They said, 'Tomes are the key to release the tomb.'"

All of us went silent.

"'Tomes are the key to release the tomb?'" Sara repeated.

I took a breath. I could feel it again, that familiar something, some dark, untenable mystery. Something to this story that was causing Carlenna—and someone else, her lover?—to stay on this earth, to rage. Also, keys . . . Nese had said something about giving me a key. I had been dreaming of them, dreaming of the Massacre.

"Yeah," Victoria said. "Stupid. I don't get it."

Sara stood up and started pacing, stopping at an end table piled high with books, her hand resting on the top. "Wait. Tomb . . . tome?"

"That's like, the same?" Victoria said, her eyes flashing large in indignation.

"No—so, *tome,* with an *e,* is another word for books. It's even pronounced differently," she said, smiling and looking down at the pile of dusty hardbacks her hand was resting on top of.

"Oh, like there's a clue in one of the books!" Victoria said.

"You got it," Sara said, pulling at a strand of her hair and rolling it thoughtfully between two fingers.

At the periphery of my consciousness, I could feel Carlenna's presence creeping back. Victoria stood up, and it was as if she was moving underwater, so quickly was I taken to a dream state. I watched my friends' limbs nearly ripple as they walked around, shadows flitting onto the surface of the room, overlaying reality, kaleidoscoping. Carlenna and her father, his light brown eyes. The mirror. There was something about her father. A kind of excitement. Something that terrified Carlenna to her core.

"But there are so many books . . ." Sara said. Through the haze of my vision, I scanned the dusty blue, rose, and graying titles littering the room, the formal lettering gold, silver, ornate.

"Okay, then we've got to look through all of them," Victoria said, one fist tightening at her side. She walked determinedly, plucking a book from a shelf, and flipping through.

She and Sara thumbed through the books stacked on the end tables, on the bookshelves, some of them piled on the floor, against the walls. I was hoping there was something in one of them. Victoria was putting a novel in its place when I felt eyes on my back, the hair on my neck prickling sharply. I took a breath, turned. There was a mirror behind me. I looked into it, wondering if this was part of my vision, or part of the act—if a wolf or ghost would appear—when the mirror seemed to grow black and smoky, as if it was . . . compiling into something.

Carlenna appeared, weeping, her trembling hands around a box that looked eerily like the box Nese had been trapped in, the rest of the mirror black, impenetrable.

"I just thought of something," Sara said, pausing with one slender finger in a book. "We're merely looking through books—but we're not thinking about the story." She looked down at the book and then shut it, placed it back on the shelf. "We should be looking for something do with Natives, and we should also be looking for something to do with wolves."

"Why didn't you think of that earlier?" Victoria sounded annoyed, but she was beaming.

"Look!" Sara said, thrusting a book up into the air. "*The Hound of the Baskervilles*."

Victoria plucked it from her hands and opened the first page. "This isn't *The Hound of the Baskervilles*."

"Yeah?" Sara asked, taking it back. "Oh . . . yeah. I mean, not that Brit lit is my specialty. I know more about *Borderlands*—but this is definitely not *Hound*."

"I know," Victoria said, stealing it back, "because my dad got a copy for me cheap at Barnes and Noble when we were visiting Albuquerque, when I was thirteen. God, I loved that store. I used to sit in those armchairs in the back, in the kids' section, all day while he went and traded for his jewelry. I read the whole damn thing in one sitting."

"What does it say?"

"It's a weird little phrase, repeated over and over," Victoria said. "'Find the keys, and you'll find THE KEY.' The rest is just a bunch of blank yellowed pages."

"Cool," Sara said, scanning the room. "Okay, keys—find all the keys."

They began rummaging, ignoring me as I'd instructed. After a few minutes, Victoria found a key in a cigar box, one sitting in a lock, and another inside a book called *Colorado's Indigenous People* that had been hollowed out: three keys.

"Okay, what now?" Victoria said. "I'm losing my buzz, and that sucks."

"Mommy can get a cocktail soon, okay?" Sara said, and I struggled to keep my focus.

While my friends began searching the room, wondering what the three keys could possibly fit into, I asked Carlenna what tribe she was. I felt a surge of backbreaking emotion, so strong that I doubled over.

*I am Heévâhetaneo'o.*

Another Cheyenne? So soon after the incident with Nese, the two-spirit. And from the same band that had combined with the Arapaho, even . . .

"Guys, look," Victoria said, walking over to a painting of a particularly sad-looking dark-haired woman, and pulling me temporarily, and partially, out of my vision. "Keys," she said, pointing to the three obscured keys standing by the woman's hands, scattered among dead maroon flowers and coins on a table.

She ran her fingers along the frame, stopping at something on the left-hand side. A latch. She pulled at it, and the painting swung outward, revealing three keyholes. "Okay, that's cool," Victoria said.

They placed the keys inside the keyholes and turned. But nothing happened. "That's weird. What are we missing?"

"Wait. There's writing above the holes," Sara said, tracing her finger along the words. "It's faint." She squinted. "This . . . isn't in English. Or Spanish. Or like, any language. It's—what the hell?"

"Let me see," Victoria said. She looked at it for a good, long time. Then, "I think I get it. We have to push the keys in and turn the keys all at the same time." She leaned back, looking satisfied.

"How did you . . ." Sara asked.

"Letter recombinations. Like I said, bored on the Rez. Gives you a lot of time to use your brain. My dad was into these. Had whole books of brainteasers.

"Here goes," Victoria said, and they turned together. The wall moved out of the way, and another screen appeared—with the ghost of a woman, smiling, and then floating away.

My heart leapt into my throat. I understood.

*I have visited the great-granddaughter of one of the men who slaughtered your people. She has atoned. She has admitted their sins. She is bringing honor back,* I told Carlenna.

Her eyes closed, and the feelings of joy and sadness and relief that flooded through me were so electric I thought I might pass out from the intensity.

She smiled. *I honor and thank you, child of the N'de,* she said. But her expression faltered. *However, I have a warning from Nese.*

Her image in the mirror began to waver, a great light behind her. She turned to look, and I could see, just behind her, shadows in the light. They were the shadows that had stayed with her, the shadows in the room I'd seen—they were her family, and their love for her was bright, boundless. They were waiting to welcome her home.

*The two-spirit?* I asked, wanting to make sure. *Who was trapped in the dybbuk box?*

*Yes,* she answered. *They say to beware the Heávohe. He charms.*

## Chapter Six

*For Sale: "Sally." Play Hide-and-Seek with the Soul of an Innocent Child Trapped in a Doll.*

*Sally's EMF reading is off the scale. EMF meter stops at 10 V/m and bounces. Sally the girl was a child with a rare heart condition. Favorite doll also named Sally in her arms when she died. Parents started to notice strange phenomena with the doll after the death of the child. Crying. Whispering that she wanted her hair combed.*

*Give her attention like she was your own child. Or else.*

*Per eBay Policy this object is for "entertainment purposes."*

The innocent screams of children playing outside in the sprinklers on Grant Street below ricocheted into my office window, echoing the much darker ones in my head.

I pulled my fingers off the handle of the window I'd just finished opening and stared at the army of creepy dolls in front of me. I'd bought a ton of them off eBay, but Sally was the only one with potential, with her cracked porcelain face, her eyes two dulled green orbs, her hair a lusterless grayish brown. Even her outfit was off-kilter, a faded white pinafore folded over a pale pink dress, something from another age.

I'd pulled my EMF meter from the equipment room—a small closet adjacent to the haunted objects room—and was about to turn it on when I heard a knock.

I put it down on my desk.

"Sasha's here." Alejandro was at my door in his favorite blue-and-cream tracksuit. He said working out in it inspired him.

"Great, tell him to come in," I said, rubbing at my temples.

A few minutes later, my ex-boyfriend-turned-friend Sasha Teyf sauntered in, a playful smile on his little pink lips. I smiled back. I'd texted him not long after I'd gotten the dybbuk box out of Cleo's apartment and freed Nese's spirit. Sasha was a little under six feet tall, with rich black curls—a little sophisticated gray at the temples—and wide green eyes. He put one hand to his yarmulke as we hugged, his bulging arms tight around my shoulders. He drew back and narrowed his eyes at me thoughtfully, a sharp electric charge in the air. There was something simultaneously self-possessed and a touch insecure about him.

"So, freed another spirit? Made a little cash?" Sasha asked.

"Yes, and yes," I answered.

He laughed and took a seat on the couch, splaying his long olive arms out either direction.

Sasha and I had gone out when I'd first begun in the paranormal community. It had been an instant, extremely intense attraction, but it'd cooled once he'd realized that I was not into relationships. Sasha was *very* into relationships—marriage. Or at least the idea of them, as he was, as of yet, unmarried. I was still wildly attracted to him.

Alejandro came in a few minutes later, a latte for me, a cup of black coffee for Sasha. Alejo closed the door after letting me know that he was off to the grocery store, a knowing smile on his lips. I sipped.

"New equipment?" Sasha asked, eyeing the meter.

"It is. An updated EMF meter."

"Don't you have five of those?" he asked.

"It's updated. Better."

"Well," he said, sighing, "you always loved your equipment."

I snorted.

"You want to show me the dybbuk box?" he asked, leaning forward and resting his elbows on his knees. His gaze migrated to the line of dolls. "God, those dolls are creepy."

"I know," I said, smiling. "But if I don't buy them, someone else will—"

A massive honk from the street, and then the sound of a man yelling from his car interrupted me.

After the noise ceased, I continued. "And much as I like making money off the pain of others, every once in a while, it occurs to me to give back and take something I think is spooky as hell right off the market. Plus, they're cool."

"Gross," he said.

"You're pretty squeamish about the dead for a guy who makes his living off the dead," I said.

"Just get the box. I can at least tell you what I know, and you can turn your equipment on it."

I stopped myself from making a flirtatious, sarcastic aside, and got the box.

"Huh," he said, holding it, revolving it around and around, then setting it down and flipping it open to reveal the golem. I noted he didn't touch it. "Do you know about the origins of the dybbuk box?"

I shook my head.

"It's actually quite strange," he said, his fingers splaying out artfully. "The golem, well, that's certainly tradition—tradition that goes way back to the Kabbalah, the code of Jewish mysticism. An artificial being, created by magic, usually to protect people. But the box . . . that's controversial. Some claim that it *also* goes back to Jewish mysticism. Some say that it was a rumor, for lack of a better word, created on the internet. But this looks old."

He was silent for a time, lost in his thoughts. After a minute, he looked up. "And you say this spirit that you freed in the escape room—what was her name?"

"Carlenna," I answered.

"Ah, yes," he said, snapping his fingers, "she gave you a warning from the spirit originally trapped in the box? Wasn't it . . ." His eyes went distant. "'He charms'?"

"That's right."

He nodded thoughtfully. "You are being called to something. Something to do with the Massacre."

"Yeah. And somehow, it all connects to my sister. I don't know how, or why, but it does." I rubbed my knees.

He nodded again. "Turn your . . ." he said, gesturing with one finger like a conductor at the EMF.

I switched the instrument on and immediately it began to beep.

"There's something else here," he said, turning the box around in his long fingers. "If you freed the spirit, why is the meter going off like that?"

"Kind of part of why I brought you in," I said.

Sasha opened the box, revealing the ancient golem. The meter pulled farther upward, hard. And that's when I began to feel it. The shadows in the room lengthening, becoming blacker, the hair on the back of my neck spiking in response to a growing presence. An angry one.

"Is it me, or . . ." Sasha said, his words tapering off, his eyes flitting to the corners of the room.

"I'm seeing it," I said.

He took a breath, closed his eyes, and, after hesitating for a moment, put his hands on the golem. We watched it expectantly, my heart beating so loud I was sure Sasha could hear it, the ticking clock on my desk the only sound. Sasha lifted the golem gingerly. He looked at its strange little face and then turned it around, running his finger down the clay. He turned it back around. "Ruah tum'ah—" he started.

It jerked to life, one arm twitching violently.

"Shit!" Sasha said, dropping it.

It hit the ground and scrambled around until it was on its feet.

I blinked. I'd seen a lot of weird stuff in my time, but this was racing to the top of the list. "What the . . ." I started, backing up toward my desk, one hand behind me grasping blindly for my sage and sweetgrass and missing.

It turned slowly at the sound of my voice, and spotting me, its lips curled into a snarl.

"Hell, no," I said, reaching again for my sage and sweetgrass and this time managing to pick a strand up.

Sasha stood up.

It began screeching, a horrible keening sound.

"Diablo, be gone, back to where you came from. Grandmother, help me pull this demon back," I started, grabbing now for my lighter and only managing to knock it to the floor, the tiny clay golem growing close, my prayer having no effect.

It began running straight for me.

## Chapter Seven

Sasha stood up and, coming around to face the golem, screamed, "Dai! Dai!" It stopped dead in its tracks, and stared up at him expectantly, as if awaiting instructions.

"Sage it," he whispered fiercely.

I bent to the floor, grabbed the lighter, got back up, and lit the strand, praying over the little clay creature as I did. It moaned, vibrated, and then went still. After a second, Sasha toed it. It toppled over as if it had never come racing for me in the first place.

"I need to do more research," Sasha said, his lips curling in disgust. "Golems, as I said before, were made to protect the good. This thing? It was made to protect something evil, though I'm not sure what. Someone, I assume, who tasked an Ashkenazi mystic to trap Nese in that box."

I nodded, my heart rate beginning to return to normal. I placed the sage and sweetgrass on my desk. "Odd how it reacted to you. And to me."

"What do you mean?"

"Well, first of all, it came to life and tried to attack me. And then it clearly responded to your speaking Hebrew. You were like, the boss."

He furrowed his brow momentarily, then said, "Well. If someone used Hebrew in the ceremony to trap it in the box, it only makes sense that it would respond to Hebrew." He shrugged. "Like I said, let me do a little more digging. I need to see if I can find anything that would connect a golem, a dybbuk box, and the Massacre. I have my doubts, but I'll contact you if I do."

I sighed. "Thanks. I know that's a tall order."

He squeezed my shoulder affectionately, a charge moving from his hand to the rest of my body. I turned into him, and the charge increased.

"I'm back from the store—" Alejo said, cracking the door open. And, seeing us in a near-embrace, muttered, "Sorry," and closed it again. But the moment was gone.

I put the golem back in the box, placed it in the room with the countless protection ceremonies I'd put in place, and closed the door. Sasha told me again that he'd contact me if he found anything, but both of us were mystified. Mystified as to why the thing had been drawn to the woman with the ancestor at the Massacre, mystified as to why it was coming after me—and even more mystified as to what Nese, the spirit I'd freed from the box, had meant by "I will give you the key." My guess was that they'd meant some sort of clue. But if so, I wasn't getting it. Not yet anyway.

Afterward, I was tired, and as Alejandro made us gin and tonics in the living room and I put my equipment away, Naiche's face came, unbidden, to my mind. It had been fragile, rounder than mine, which was wide too, but also long and angular. Her face had been a heart. I remembered her hands, so soft, like a butterfly's wings—tiny, beating lightly on my arm when we were children. She'd always been angry, rebellious, her fury much more overt than my sarcastic, I'll-work-within-the-system-though-I-hate-it thing. But it had gotten far worse after Dad died. Something buried came loose in her. She came undone.

I came out into the living room, took the glass Alejandro handed me, and plopped down, hard, onto the couch. I sipped thoughtfully.

"I'm tired," I said.

"Me too, girl," he said, and we clinked glasses, sipped again. "What are you thinking about? Sorry I wasn't there to help with the miniature man attack. I ran out of protein powder," he said. "But I got us the ingredients for a lemon pesto risotto."

"It's okay, we handled it," I said, sighing. "I was thinking about my sister. About when she went catatonic." I stood up and went over to our shelves of books, leftover from Alejandro's and my time in college. We'd gone to Fort Lewis together—that's where I'd met Sara and Victoria, where my sister had followed when she graduated from high school.

"God, I remember that," Alejandro said, crossing one leg neatly over the other. "That was spooky."

It had been spooky. She'd lain on her bed, her eyes red, sleepless, staring up at the ceiling. My mother spoon-fed her soup, half of it drooling out of her mouth. But though it killed me when Dad died, I bounced back. Naiche never really did.

"Then, when she came out of that . . ." Not finding what I was looking for, I sat back down on the couch. I closed my eyes. Shook my head.

"I didn't even recognize her," he said, turning his glass in his hands.

None of us had. She'd been like an animal, feral beyond belief, tearing our furniture and lives apart. She'd left my mother's house when she was sixteen, living with people so gone from speed, weed, heroin, and every street drug you could imagine, they looked like zombies.

"The thing I can't get over—well, one of the things—is how rehab worked. Like, it *worked*. And she got better. And she went to college. And for what?" I ran one finger along the edge of the glass.

"I guess," Alejandro said, interrupting himself with a sigh, "something inside her wanted to live." He went over to the shelves I'd been staring at and fingered a book out.

"That's the worst, I think. Remembering that," I said, my voice breaking.

He came back over and hugged me, a book in his hand poking at my shoulder.

"I hate the Sacred 36," I said, feeling real venom entering my voice. "Fucking shit cult."

At first, it had been just a little comment, something she'd found on the internet. Something she and Mom had bonded over, while I rolled my eyes and pored over the newest article in *Psychology Today*. They'd look at the Sacred 36's page on the internet, taking in their stories of haunted houses, the ghosts of the bodies never removed from Cheesman Park on Capitol Hill, their long, pseudo-theological rants.

"Do you think she'd be alive if it weren't for them?"

"I know she would," I said, bitterness lining my voice.

Naiche had been going to Sacred 36 meetings for two years before Mom and I started asking where she was all the time, why she suddenly wasn't available for pedicures or dinner on Sunday evenings. I'd been far too deep into my dissertation to really think about it until it was too late. The thing was, before my sister's death, I hadn't believed in an afterlife or ghosts. I'd rolled my eyes whenever my mother or sister would say they'd seen something paranormal: a round, glowing light or a voice late at night. But much as I hadn't believed them about seeing the dead, I was terrified Naiche would tell me she'd seen our father. And on the night of my graduation, Naiche had called. She'd told me that she needed me to come to the Brown Palace. That she was scared.

I'd dismissed her. And she killed herself.

I stopped giving two shits about research. And I couldn't leave my mother—she was out of her mind with grief for years. Alejandro got HIV. My research became old. I hadn't gotten on the job market, and I hadn't published, and now the best that I could do was adjunct at a local college for pennies.

To make matters worse, my visions, my premonitions, my ability to talk to the dead that had flipped on like a switch the night my sister died got stronger and stronger, overwhelmingly so.

And one day, after a couple of years of living with my mother and trying to help her pick up the pieces, I came across a degree one could get online. One that certified someone as a paranormal investigator. I don't know what made me do it, beyond instinct and desperation. And then I set up a website. And I was called. And I bought equipment. And I was called again. And I hired Alejandro to help me.

"I'm going to get on Tinder. Is that cool?"

"Of course," I said. "Sara and I were going to read at a bar tonight. But now I think I'm just going to drink this," I said, holding my glass up, "drink another, and go to sleep."

Alejandro laughed. "She still working on that book?"

"Oh yeah," I said. "And I could stand to do a bit more research on this new camera I got on ghostequipmentforreal."

"Don't you have enough ghost cameras?" he asked, standing up. His eyes were crinkled in that way that I found so sweet, so familiar.

"Never. And this one's full spectrum, infrared—"

"Whatever. The only thing you love more than dresses or pretty furniture is new ghost shit."

I nodded, shrugged a little defeated shrug, and told him to have fun.

"Bye, bitch," he said, shutting the door.

I drained my glass and poured another. I went to the window, leaned one hand on the frame. The children I'd heard earlier were gone. All that was left was the growing darkness, the outlines of buildings in the orange streetlights, the lonely whisk of the cars rushing by in the streets. I narrowed my eyes, sipped. The Sacred

36 were secretive when it came to their members, but what they had online was compelling. A beautiful, gothy aesthetic: pictures of sharp-nailed women scrying over haunted-looking mirrors, stories of everlasting life, ghosts crying out from the beyond on Instagram, YouTube videos of glowing eyes in the distance, in spooky, dark woods. It wasn't just gorgeous; it was emotionally spellbinding. It promised another world.

With the apartment empty, the graying shadows fell over the furniture like a dream. The darkness enveloped me, and the image that I worked to push away most nights came, unbidden: the image of my sister's body on the silver metal slab. Pale. Drained of life. She had been darker than me. I was a pale yellow, she a warm medium brown; her hair had hints of gold, mine was black as the glossy goth shoes I'd worn during my tween death cult phase. My mother and I had stood over her body in the coroner's office, Mom's face crushed to my neck, her hand squeezing my arm so hard it felt bloodless. The *swoosh* of the sheet being pulled back. The shock of my sister's face, her expression a terrifying mix of inexpressible sorrow and horror, her eyes and mouth cracked unnaturally wide, her grayish skin a confluence of black veins. The brief flash of her arms, cut all the way down, from elbow to wrist. My mother's cry, like a scream.

## Chapter Eight

"So, I got a call while you were out," Alejandro said, pushing the barbell up with a grunt and then letting it down with a clang. He sat up, wiped his face with a towel, hung it around his neck, and turned to me.

"A job?" I asked. I'd been out shopping. I walked over to the couch and put my packages down, a bright blue bag with silver lettering falling to the floor. "Sorry, you know I don't answer the phone when I'm buying things."

He laughed, pulling his hands through his hair, a gesture I knew he only made when he was flirting, or nervous. "I know. But anyway, it's big. But also . . ."

"Just tell me," I said, pulling out a maxi-length white eyelet dress I'd been watching for a month and holding it up to my body.

"Nice," he said. "Do you want to talk about this later?"

"No . . . I'm good." I set the dress down on the couch, my pulse lifting.

With one last swipe at his face and arms with the towel, Alejandro set it down on the bench and retreated into the kitchen. "Sit," he said, a bottle of sauvignon blanc in his hand. He poured me a glass.

He sighed, and poured himself a finger, sipped, a bit tipping over the rim as he did. "The Brown Palace called." He took a tissue and wiped the droplets that had fallen over and onto the base of the glass.

I could feel my mouth go dry instantly. I sat down on the couch as commanded, setting the crystal down first so that I wouldn't spill, then picking it back up for a large sip. The Brown. Where Naiche had suicided.

"And?"

"They were super," he said, snapping his fingers, clearly searching for the right word, "circumspect?"

"Circumspect," I repeated.

"They just kept saying that you needed to come in. That they wanted you for a big job, but that they understood that due to the situation with your sister," he said, rubbing the back of his neck awkwardly, "that they'd understand if you didn't want to."

"Okay . . ."

"But they also said to tell you that you'd want to. That there was a reason that they'd called. That basically, you were their only hope."

I blinked hard.

"I didn't say yes. I told them that I'd tell you, and that I was sure you'd need time to think it over."

I set the glass down again after another large sip and slid one finger up the fabric of my new dress thoughtfully. "You know, I was just googling the Sacred 36 last night."

"Oh?" He was watching me closely, the towel around his neck, a hand clenched around the fabric at either end, his glass also on the end table.

"I'd nearly forgotten. They were obsessed with the Brown. No wonder that was where she called me from." I pulled one hand through my hair, a nervous tic.

Alejandro's eyebrows lifted, and there was a flicker of guilt at the edges of his large amber eyes. I knew he felt responsible too. We all did.

I felt my stomach roiling. "It would just be nice if they hadn't called barely a couple of weeks before the anniversary."

Alejandro sighed again, heavily.

I leaned back into the velvet, turned my head. The shitty part was every year, I nearly forgot—or was trying to, subconsciously. I'd feel horrible, despondent. And then I'd remember. I'd go into a monthlong depression, culminating in a blackness so large on the anniversary, I often wondered if it would swallow me.

I sighed, gathering myself and leaning back up, and drained the last of my wine. A few minutes later, the first few bars to Beyoncé's "Run the World" floated through the air via my iPhone. Victoria—that was her song.

*BITCH,* it said.

I laughed despite myself.

*WHAT?*

*NEW JENNY ARTICLE JUST DROPPED.* She included a link.

I rolled my eyes.

Jenny Kunza was an ambitious reporter for the *Colorado Sun*. She'd made her small reputation calling out corrupt businesses, though most of her sensationalist methods left people feeling queasy, and she was a little too excited about busting on people who didn't, upon further examination, seem to deserve it. Though my mom and sister got a kick out of making fun of her, I hadn't thought much about her articles until she'd gone after me. The first time she'd written a piece, I'd called. She'd answered immediately, and when I'd asked if she'd be willing to talk more about the issue, consider an interview, she'd told me in her breathy upspeak that perhaps it might be hard for me to *understand*? But that there were those who believed in science and felt what I was doing was *dishonest*? I'd sighed and told her I'd gotten a doctorate in psychology and that I was a big believer in science. She'd paused, as she'd clearly not factored this in, told me to have a nice day, and hung up.

"What is it?" Alejandro asked.

"Jenny's going on about me again," I answered.

"Oh, God, just don't look," Alejo said.

I clicked.

"I'm about to slap that phone out of your manicured hands," he said, sighing dramatically, throwing the towel into the leather laundry basket he kept by his set for just this purpose. "What if she's published a new—"

"Too late," I said, reading.

"Olivia, stop." He paused. "Okay, what's she saying?" Alejandro asked, a smile creeping onto his lips.

"It's totally about me, and it's hilarious."

It's true that her op-eds used to get to me, but after seeing how little impact she had, and how dull she was, I'd stopped caring. Still. I had to read them, as she was always trying to get people to stop patronizing my business. The thing that amused me was that she always hopped into the comment sections of her own articles, pushing her book *Fake, Faker, Fakest,* published with an obscure press out of Vermont.

**Paranormal Fauxvestigator Strikes Again**

In the latest in a series of "investigations" into the paranormal, Mexican "investigator" Olivia Becente victimized yet another local, who wished to remain anonymous. The victim, who has historically suffered from mental illness, reached out to Becente after experiencing a series of "phenomena" subsequent to purchasing an allegedly paranormal object—nicknamed a dybbuk box in internet

> forums. In interviewing the victim, she described a series of obscure—and even perverse—rituals, including sage burning, black candles, and a long, drawn-out performance of de-possession. While the appeal of such theater is understandable, the damage to those with clear issues with mental illness is incalculable. At best, it's a cynical ploy for money. At worst, it delays necessary treatment. Although Becente claims to have a doctorate in psychology, this way of making a living damages our growing city. I ask the larger community of Denver to consider whether their money isn't better spent at Meow Wolf or Disneyland, where at least the businesses are clear about the fact that what they're offering isn't science, isn't helpful, but is merely harmless entertainment, unlike Becente's "Fauxvestigations."

"She's in love with me," I said, rolling my eyes again and putting the phone down.

"I don't know, Olivia," Alejo said after reading the article on his phone. "She seems willing to go right to the edge of making shit up about you. She's dangerous."

I sighed. "I guess. She just seems desperate to make her career, and for some reason sees me as a good way to do that. No one cares about some obscure pseudo-journalist."

"Just keep an eye on her, okay? This is her third article about you this year. And all kidding aside, I don't like the way she's using the word *Mexican*. Which, you're Indigenous, and she knows that. But it's like she's trying to delegitimize that, and at the same time, hit that racist, anti-Mexican thing hard."

I nodded. Then, "What are you in the mood for tonight?" I asked, then paused dramatically. "*Mexican?*"

"Girl, you need to take this seriously," he said, laughing a little anyway. He went back over to the kitchen to put the bottle away, and I sat down to check the messages on my phone. There were five, all from the Brown Palace.

I went into my room, plopped down on my bed, smoothed the white-on-white star quilt my auntie had made for me, and listened. It was the last one that got me.

"Dr. Becente, please. It involves your sister."

# Chapter Nine

*Yelp Review: Avoid the Brown Palace at ALL COSTS!*

*As a full-service vacation planner, it's my job to make sure every customer's experience is perfect. I'd heard the Brown Palace Hotel and Spa was one of the most luxurious hotels in town, and I'd put together a package for tourists from California thinking about moving to Denver. Staying at the Brown Palace was the second thing on our itinerary. I was just settling in for the night when I heard a crash. I'd asked for a suite—suite 904. I ran into the living room. There, in the mirror, was a woman, weeping. I screamed. Ran out. I asked for my money back, told them I'd never take anyone there again. They offered to move me and comped me the room—and I decided to take them up on their offer, but I couldn't sleep a WINK.*

The lobby of the Brown Palace was filled with opulent colors, deep blues, the atrium stretching out in filigreed lamé and green layers as far as the eye could see. There were old-fashioned, intricate gold sconces on each of the pillars, and my heels echoed on the tile floor, muffled mainly by the sounds of guests milling about, a few of them wearing masks—evidence of the lingering, if diminished, pandemic.

I glanced over in the direction of Ship Tavern—the bar that my sister and I'd spent so much time in when we'd first come of age. We'd had wine at the bar, old-fashioneds in the booths, my sister's head tipping back to roar with laughter, her short, slightly wavy hair shimmering red in the dim bar lights. I hadn't, of course, been back since they'd discovered her body.

"Thank you for coming, Dr. Becente." The concierge, Mark, was showing me around. He'd told me that he'd worked there for twenty years, that the owners trusted him implicitly, and that he knew everything there was to know about the hotel. "Is it true you have a doctorate in psychology as well as expertise in parapsychology?"

"Parapsychology is the study of extrasensory human ability. My specific expertise is in the paranormal," I said. "But yes, I do have a doctorate in psychology. And I am degreed in paranormal investigation. And trained, if you will, in a number of spiritual traditions."

"I see," he said, but it was clear he needed a more thorough explanation.

"I can hear and see the dead, tap into their memories," I continued, feeling a shudder pass through my body. Before everything, I'd found the hotel's haunted history compelling, fun. I'd loved the stories of the train conductor who disappeared through walls of the Brown Palace, the mysterious piano playing.

"I'm sure you know the room's history, Dr. Becente," Mark said, flicking an invisible piece of lint off the pant leg of his impeccably tailored suit, two golden keys crisscrossed at the shoulders.

"I know a bit," I responded. "My sister's—the occult group that my sister was a part of was obsessed with the room." I knew more than a bit, actually. I knew that one Mrs. Luella Stillwell had lived and then died, supposedly of a broken heart, in the room my sister had suicided in. Room 904. "And just call me Olivia."

"Olivia, then."

I smiled.

He continued. "Of course, you know your sister died in the room."

My smiled faded. I nodded soberly. "Of course."

"In fact," he said, quickly recovering, "we had many members of the Sacred 36"—and here, he paused to roll his eyes—"stay in 904 over the years. But your sister was the only one who died in that room, though many of them"—he stopped, his upper lip curled in disgust—"expressed the desire to."

Good God. There were so many reasons to hate that cult.

"In any case," he continued, "I'm very sorry. And sorry we felt it necessary to call you in. But all of this is relevant, I promise."

"I see," I responded tightly, not seeing at all.

"You'll understand when you view the footage," he said, clearly noting my confusion.

"Footage?" My stomach did a turn.

"Why don't we speak in Ship Tavern?" Mark asked.

I hesitated for just a moment, and then gave in.

The dark wooden doors to the bar were saloon-style, with large iron anchors set on the front. The concierge noticed my expression of amusement, curiosity. I'd forgotten how incongruently sea-themed the place was for a state that was landlocked.

"The owner of the Brown, from 1920 to . . . ah, I think somewhere around the eighties, loved Cape Cod and decided to bring back a plethora of décor from the area and make the bar motif nautical—as you can clearly see," he said, chuckling.

All that had stayed with me was the name of the tavern, the neon sign bearing the moniker of the establishment alongside bright neon ships. It was, like a lot of things from that time, something my mind had grayed out.

He gestured and I followed, taking in the toy ships and salty captains' faces in metal topped by candelabras adorning the wood-paneled walls.

He gestured to a booth with rope-and-cage-style chandeliers, and we sat. Above the booth was a stylized map of the "New World," complete with cartoonishly large, romantically painted crustaceans, stars, sun, and moon, and, of course, all varieties of boats—every single one of them pointed in the direction of the Americas. I shivered, thinking about what those boats had brought.

"Can I get you something to drink? Pinot? That's what I'm having."

"Sure," I answered, and with a nod from Mark, another employee came up and took our orders.

Mark's cell rang, and he smiled apologetically, pulling it out of his front pocket, and took the call. I stared at my own, resisting the urge to scroll social media. After a few minutes, he hung up.

"As I stated over the phone," he continued, clearing his throat before he went on, "there is always a suicide, or murder, in room 904—we're never sure."

"You're never sure?" I asked, taking my drink and sipping.

"Let me explain. We've kept a camera in room 904 from the minute that technology came available."

That was a surprise. Kind of an invasion of privacy, I thought. Maybe even illegal.

"The thing is, Dr. Becente—"

"Really, just call me Olivia," I reminded him.

"Olivia," he continued, "is that there has always been a pattern to this room. Every five years, a woman dies in 904. Over the years, we've brought in the police, private detectives, mediums—"

"Really?"

"Oh yes. Because no one has ever been able to solve the mystery of room 904."

I blinked rapidly. "Why don't you shut the room?"

"We've tried. We've shut it, and a woman checks in a different room, and we find her dead in 904—three weeks after her stay. These women appear in the room the night they check in, and then they reappear, only to die. We suspect that even if we shut the entire hotel down, it would still happen."

I ran my finger along the edge of the table. "Three weeks?" I asked. That was strange—the whole thing was strange.

"Three weeks to the hour. To the *second*, even. It's awful, and we've been powerless to stop it. Do you know of the story of 904? When it came to be haunted?" He shifted in his seat.

"Luella Stillwell," I said, thinking back to the woman with the broken heart.

"That's right. We assume that time frame has something to do with her story. And of course, women began appearing—and dying—after she was found in 904. But whatever the case, we never know who it's going to be."

"Can't you . . . post a guard?"

"We do. Every year. Every year. We keep the door open. But every year, in that five-year cycle, a woman appears as if out of thin air in the room, confused as to how she got there. And every year, in three weeks, she reappears and cuts her arms open." He finished his wine. "And every year, the footage shows Mrs. Luella Stillwell in the mirror when the women, well." He paused. "Reappear. And die."

With a short sigh, Mark pushed his glass away and pulled a small iPad out of his briefcase, complete with a set of earbuds, which I found puzzling. He set the iPad down, briefly pausing to look around before returning his attention to the tablet. There were few patrons this time of day—a couple of men in suits who looked like they were guests, one of them wearing an expression of sour cynicism as the other monologued; a few women in fancy, old-fashioned hats and dresses.

I realized in that moment what I was about to see.

He turned to the iPad and swiveled it around, tapping on the glass presumably to return the image to the screen. He then spun it back around so that I could view what was on the screen. "Something you should know. The footage always fritzes off and on during the event. This particular year, there was a lot of fuzz. And every year that we've had this technology, when the women reappear, Luella appears in the mirror. She smiles sadly and then dissipates when the woman expires. It's as if . . ." He looked out the window behind us, then back. "As if she doesn't want them to die alone." He handed me the earbuds, and I wound them into my ears.

I clicked. There was fuzz.

Then, as the picture began to clear, the room came into slight motion, not in a way that was easily discernable—perhaps a breath of air from the vents on the lush orange curtains, a flicker of light across the ornate gray-filigreed wallpaper. Distant, haunting piano and saxophone filtered in from what seemed like another room; a soft, sad bluesy voice, the song was eerily familiar. And then.

A scream ripped through the room as my sister appeared out of thin air, her back to the camera, a blade in her hands. The footage went out, replaced by white noise and TV snow. When she reappeared, she was in an entirely different part of the room. I couldn't tell how much time had passed. She went over to a coffee table, picked up an old black metal dagger. She slashed one arm with it, then the other, her body wilting on the bed set beneath the ornate black mirror, blood pouring out of each meaty slit.

I flinched violently. I could see her face now. Tears began streaming down my cheeks, and it took everything I had in me not to squeeze my eyes shut.

And then, as if what I was witnessing wasn't horrific enough, as the life faded from my sister, Mrs. Stillwell watching from the mirror above, suddenly Mrs. Stillwell faded. And Naiche's visage appeared in the mirror, looking down on her own cold, still body, her mouth frozen in a grotesque scream of fear.

# Chapter Ten

---

It had been two nights since I'd visited the Brown and I'd barely slept. My eyes would close, but the moment I'd begin to drift into that other world, my sister's face would come to mind. Her sad, soft smile. The sound of her voice in hysterics over the phone the night she'd called. The image of her on the iPad, cutting herself. Her ghost in the mirror.

"Go on," I said, trying to focus on the two women in front of me, but they wavered like eighties video cam footage, the backdrop of their apartment pale woods and tapestries, lamps in browns and creams and blues. They'd called because, as usual, they'd bought something on eBay for fun, and it turned out to be anything but.

"I just . . . I don't know. I've never seen anything like this, and I wanted to. But it's ruining our lives." Regina began crying then, and her girlfriend laced her hand through hers and squeezed. Regina wiped at her tears with the sleeve of her pastel sweatshirt.

I nodded sympathetically, but my mind drifted almost immediately, despite my best efforts, back to Naiche. I knew she'd died in the Brown. But I'd had no idea she'd replaced (or joined?) the ghost of Mrs. Stillwell. Or that there was a mysterious cycle of suicide.

And that the Brown wanted me to figure out who was next was too much. I'd told them I'd need some time to decide.

My eyes burning, I took a deep breath to clear my head, and glanced down at the listing.

*For Sale: Haunted Book.*

*This book is haunted AF. I'm not kidding. This was part of some old estate. I just liked the title:* Ghostland. *I love occult stuff, big goth here. I've tried every ritual in every book I've ever bought from a metaphysical shop or from here—nothing ever did s***. Until now. The minute I opened to the first page I could hear howling in the distance. The first night it was nightmares. Then it got worse. I don't even want to say some of what I dreamed. What I did. Open only if you're ready to have ghosts and shadow figures haunt you every night of your freaking life. If you're ready to wake up doing crazy stuff. Had to call a priest in to get right. Not sure it worked. Has keyhole. No key.*

*$200 OBO.*

*Per eBay Policy this object is for "entertainment purposes."*

"It's just like the guy said in the listing we showed you." Regina shifted on the couch, her pale hand on her girlfriend's thigh.

"I feel bad," Latonya said, shaking her head, her eyes dark, intense. "I told her to go ahead, to buy it. I like encouraging her. She has fun with this jazz. Spells, witchy things, it's cool. Part of why I was so attracted to her in the first place." She ran her hand over her short curls and sighed. "To be honest, I just didn't believe in any of this stuff. I'm—well I was, an atheist. You can imagine how hard it was to grow up in a Baptist home as a lesbian."

Alejandro leaned forward. “Oh, I can imagine.”

Theirs was such an interesting story. One, I’m sure, my little article-writing nemesis Jenny wouldn’t believe. To be fair, before Naiche’s suicide, I wouldn’t have either. I had always aligned with my father, and against my sister and mother, when it came to their near-unshakable faith in the paranormal.

I rubbed my knees. If I pursued this thing with the Brown, my mother could find out. She’d wanted to see my sister, but to know that your daughter was haunting a mirror? Was trapped inside it even, and had been for years? It could break her.

“You know?” Latonya was saying.

I blinked, and felt the sharp, bony jut of Alejandro elbowing me subtly in my ribs.

“I’m so sorry—haven’t been sleeping lately,” I responded, feeling like a jerk. “I can absolutely help you. I’ve just got a little bit of personal stuff on my mind.” I ran one hand through my hair.

“How about some coffee?” Regina asked.

I relaxed a bit then, relieved she wasn’t insulted. “I’d love that.”

“Girl,” Latonya said, standing up and smoothing her white polo over her hips, “let’s just say, lately? The coffee’s been flowing in this house. We aren’t sleeping either.” She squinted down at the book on the coffee table in front of them.

“I’m scared to sleep,” Regina said. “That fucking thing.”

“That’s what I’m here for,” I said, smiling in what I hoped was a reassuring manner. I had to get it together. This couple needed me. My eyes flickered over the leather-bound tome. I hadn’t touched it yet. It was a fairly innocuous-looking book—a weathered blue-and-silver cover, a landscape with a moon and stars, rolling hills, and a depiction of what almost looked to be a chest with ghosts of all kinds flooding out of it. But there *was* something about it. I could hear whispering gathering around like a cloud of gnats. The odd part was I couldn’t discern what any of the voices were saying, or how many of them there were, whether they were angry or afraid. I couldn't tap into any memories or sense any specific entities—human or non. Perhaps I was too tired. Hopefully the coffee would help.

Alejandro and Regina chatted while Latonya made the coffee, Regina sharing that her parents had been hippies who loved all things natural and pagan, and that her interest in the paranormal had formed from hanging with her parents' pagan community.

"I mean," she said, laughing, "they were more into trees and granola, but let's just say there were friends of theirs who claimed they could do magic. Or talk to the dead. That really piqued my interest—and I've been chasing that idea ever since. I've joined every coven, gone to every psychic in this city and any city I've ever visited, scoured the internet. I'm sad that the only time I found it was in something so . . . frightening."

I nodded sympathetically. This was often why I was called in. There was plenty about the world that was beautiful and mysterious and strange—and not evil. But evil was powerful. And it stirred parts of the other world up faster than good. And it often stirred up the sick parts of the self—especially in the very naïve or very ill-intentioned.

Over the phone, Regina had described her nightmares. She said that sometimes there were people screaming, dying, but that mostly, each night seemed to correspond with a story from the book.

"Describe the stories," I said.

"Well, they're short. Really short. More like poems. The first was about a magical box full of trapped souls. The second about a woman in love with a monster. There are three sections."

I nodded, narrowing my eyes.

"But then . . . I woke with a knife in my hand in front of the bathroom mirror."

That *was* familiar. It was exactly what Cleo had said—the woman whose ancestor had been part of the Massacre.

"After that, I was done," she said, cutting the air with her left hand. "I tried to sell the book back on eBay, but every time I posted, the post disappeared without a trace."

I narrowed my eyes. "Really."

"Yeah, and I guess . . . I just thought of it as a glitch in the system. So, I tried to take it to booksellers to sell, but every time I arrived at the bookstore, the book was mysteriously absent from my bag. I'd search and search, go back to the car, look on the seats, under them. Nothing. But here's the kicker. When I arrived home, it was always sitting right on my coffee table," she said, hitting the table with her index finger several times. "That's when I got really scared. When I realized I had found something magical all right. Magically evil. Latonya told me to throw it away. I did. Twice. It reappeared on the table the day after both times."

"Regina, this is going to sound random, but did you have an ancestor who participated in the Massacre?" I asked.

She closed her eyes, briefly. Then, "Yes, to my shame."

That was weird. Why was I being brought to the Massacre, again and again?

I looked down at the book. Perhaps it was my imagination, but I felt that the whispering wasn't just growing louder, but that it was increasingly directed at me. And faintly, I thought I could hear laughter. I shuddered.

Latonya returned with the coffee in a blue ceramic French press.

"Thank you," I said, taking mine and sipping. After a cup, I did feel better, focused.

"I'm going to try something now," I said. "Try not to react to anything you see or feel or hear. It will help me to communicate with whatever is alive in that book and hopefully resolve what's going on here, one way or another."

There was fear in Regina's amber eyes, but a kind of steely resolve as well. Latonya squeezed her hand and nodded. "We'll try."

I took a deep breath, closed my eyes. I visualized clouds in a sky with little blue—a ball of cacophonous light somewhere in the distance. With my breath, I pushed the cottony white clouds out of my way, one by one. I asked my ancestors for help. I could hear Alejandro opening our work bag, pulling out sweetgrass and sage. I opened my eyes, briefly. He placed the combination in a shell, and gave it fire, guided the couple as to how to cleanse themselves. I did as well, and then I closed my eyes again. Focused on the smell, the sound of the voices—the ball of light I was growing closer to.

After a few minutes, there was the sound of wind rushing through the curtains in another room and the whispering intensified. It was complete discordance at first, and I struggled to get anything out of it beyond white noise. Eventually, however, I felt like one of the voices separated from the jumble of light, of sound, and I felt, as I had earlier, that there was a singular voice scrambling to speak to me—that the reason this couple had been unable to get rid of this book had to do with me. The sky inside my mind darkened, and though I had not called it, a thunderstorm began, and the ball of light I'd called forth to help me visualize what was happening darkened. Distantly, I could hear a storm outside, in the real world. There was something urgent about the voice that had broken from the herd—distinct, almost familiar. I leaned into the storm, trying to invite it into me. I asked the voice to tell me what was happening, why it was so full of fury and rage. I could feel that anger now, like a white-hot sun. I could also feel . . . urgency. Desire. Desire for power.

"It does not like that sage," Alejandro said, a nervous flutter to his voice.

I opened my eyes.

I felt, for a moment, as if I must be hallucinating. Much as there had been in my mind, a small thunderstorm was gathering around the book, the wind and rain blowing strongly in the direction of the sage. I felt, then, that there was something I could not touch, something hidden, and I knew in that moment that the book wasn't carrying a misunderstood spirit but something malintentioned. Or, in a word, evil.

"Oh my God," Regina said, scooting back against the couch, her legs pulling up and her arms circling them. "That's a rain cloud. In my living room."

"Remember what she told us. Keep calm," Latonya said, squeezing Regina's hand tightly. I was glad she was working to reassure her girlfriend, but her eyes were growing larger by the moment.

"There's no water—it's an illusion," I said, holding my hand under the cloud. "Whatever is in that book is trying to scare us."

"Well, it's working," Regina said.

One of the small bolts of lightning struck out, but instead of a white light, it was dark. It arched out into a corner and spread, a darkness growing, consuming the fluorescence of the standing lamps, creating a hollow in the corner of their small house that looked like a portal to another world.

"Dear God," Latonya whispered. Faintly, I could hear her murmuring the Lord's Prayer under her breath.

Trying to connect with whatever entity was in that book was useless. The only thing I could do was banish it.

"You aren't welcome here," I said, standing up, motioning the two women to stay behind me.

I heard a low, inhuman cackle come from the black and then a voice. I had been wrong. It wasn't a singular voice. It was countless voices, speaking as one. I struggled to understand what it was whispering. I leaned in, Alejandro sighing fearfully as I did. After a moment or two I realized it was saying a single word over and over, the lust in its tone so palpable I felt like I could hear its mouth working, its tongue salivating: *Power. Power. Power.*

"I have a way to get rid of you, but you won't like it," I said. I motioned Alejo to stand by me. We had to recite this together. "You can choose to leave this place on your own."

I could hear it laughing again. The corner of blackness snaked out farther, and peering into the corner, I could see what almost looked like another world. I leaned in farther, Alejandro putting one hand on my shoulder to caution me, and saw a further blackness, and more than that, something alien, disjointed, unnatural figures moving in the dark.

And something peering back at me.

I could hear Latonya and Regina whimpering behind me, Alejandro comforting them with small sounds.

I picked the sweetgrass and sage bundle up, Alejo with the lighter at my side, relighting, words a curandera from Idaho Springs taught me in my mouth, words of banishment, of calling up healing to seal the rift whatever had possessed this book had created between worlds. There was a thread of obsidian leading from the corner of the house to the book.

Suddenly a thread sped out of the black, shooting toward Regina. She screamed and jumped off the couch, narrowly avoiding the charcoal bolt. It retreated, snapping like a whip as it did.

"What the fuck!" Latonya said, leaping off the couch and moving toward Regina. She thrust the both of them into the corner opposite the portal and pushed Regina behind her.

It was trying to get to one of us—get *into* one of us.

I prayed louder, my stance firm, Alejandro's hand on my shoulder, calling the prayers to his ancestors in echo to mine. "Ancestors, hear me. I call on you for protection. Mimi, Grandmother, Siichoo, I call you. I call you to help me push this thing back into the hell, to Xibalba, al infierno—"

I heard hissing, more sounds of thunder. The thread thinned but didn't evaporate. The corner still opened wide to another world. And the figures seemed to be growing closer.

I put both hands out in front of me. "I will burn this book if you don't leave," I said, and I could hear squealing from the portal, feel the fury emanating from the rift.

My eyes darted over to the book on the table. It was turning red-hot, and I knew if I touched it, my hands would scorch.

*You are nothing but a source of POWER.*

I opened my mouth to continue the prayer when a bolt of black lightning shot out and struck me in the head.

"Olivia!" Alejandro's hands moved underneath my arms to catch me as I buckled, my eyes shutting in a movement that felt simultaneously as if it was happening in slow motion and quick as a gasoline-fueled fire, as if I'd never seen light at all. Noise came up around my ears like a muffled thunderstorm. There was only black.

Inside the black was an ocean. In the ocean I swam, seeing thunder beings dancing in the distance, massive trees above endless caverns, my father. He smiled and tried to take my hand. His mouth swelled. Blackened like a diseased root. He laughed soundlessly through the rush of the water, his red hair a flame, and I pushed back against his body, which was pale and bloated. I could feel the pressure of the water all around me, moving up into my nose, my mouth, drowning me. Distantly, I could hear my father calling me, and I swam away from him, knowing it wasn't him, that it was something else. Something inhuman. The voice continued, and this time, I could hear it above me. I could see light—

I opened my eyes. I was standing. All was calm. An unnatural silence pervaded throughout the room.

There was no blackness, only Alejandro standing in the corner where the portal to another world had stood. His eyes were closed, his mouth trembled.

"Alejo?"

His eyes shot open, stricken with fear.

"Come," he said, his hand extending outward, his face wet with tears.

"What just happened?" I asked, my head swimming, my eyes feeling waterlogged. I rubbed them, trying to regain my balance.

"Olivia, *come here,*" he hissed insistently.

I heard the women whimpering behind me. "Olivia," one of them whispered, I couldn't tell who.

"Olivia, it's about to pull me into hell," Alejandro said, his voice breaking, his arm outstretched, blackness reopening behind him. I took a step toward him, regaining my equilibrium, my arm moving out toward his. His fingers flexed.

That's when I heard Alejandro's voice.

Behind me.

# Chapter Eleven

"That's not me, Olivia," the Alejandro behind me said, his voice steady. Unnaturally calm.

The hair on the back of my neck spiked upward rapidly, and the Alejandro in front of me shook his head. "I'm right here. Please, Olivia. It's right behind you." The last sentence a whisper.

I closed my eyes. Thought of the Alejo I knew. The man who was a survivor of five years and counting of HIV. The man who lived with me, who was an expert bowman, who loved Dante, who made frittatas for me when I was too sad to move, the man who'd grieved so hard over my sister with me it was as if she was his own sister.

"That's—that's not him!" Regina said, her voice small, filled with terror.

I didn't know which one she meant.

"Olivia, I'm behind you. Just back away."

I took a deep breath.

"Olivia, that thing is evil," the Alejandro in front of me said. "It's going to kill us all."

I heard an exasperated, snotty breath behind me.

I closed my eyes. Let my powers move outward. My eyes flashed open.

I had to be sure.

"Are you saying he's a liar?" I asked the Alejo in front of me.

"He's—the one in front of you is the thing!" Latonya yelled. "At least . . . I think so?"

The Alejandro behind me stomped his foot. "It's me, you pendeja!"

I looked at the Alejandro in front of me. "They're calling you a liar, you know that?"

His eyes narrowed, and he cast an angry glance in Latonya's direction.

"She's the liar," he said.

Now I was sure.

I floated my hands out in front of me, palms up. "Alejandro, put your hands on my shoulders."

I felt his hands.

I began to pray again.

The Alejandro in front of me snarled. His face turned black, his teeth long, and the blackness began to spread down his neck, thread into his arms, hands. "Quiet!" he said, his face distorting like an overfilled balloon, then bursting into black.

I pictured the thunder beings I'd seen dancing in my vision and called them forth by name.

The thing that had posed as Alejandro collapsed into a floating cloud of darkness and zipped back into the book.

"Quick, Alejandro, run the smoke over it."

He came over, relit the bundle, and ran it over the book. It seemed to shudder, its pages flapping preternaturally. I watched it until it was still. Until there was nothing inhuman left in the room. I sighed. The book was evil. It would never be completely cleansed. But it was contained, for now.

"I can take the book," I said.

The couple collapsed into each other's arms and wept.

I shook my head at Alejandro, who handed me the book. "Pendeja?" I said, taking the book from him.

"You were being a pendeja," he answered, cocking his head at a jaunty angle.

# Chapter Twelve

I stood outside the Stillwell Mansion, contemplating whether I should go in. It was an imposing white French Renaissance–style building with sizable brass sconces framing the front door, three stories high, with an embellished iron fence surrounding the entire structure. I'd made a call to what was now a law office that the mansion hosted, telling them a more palatable version of the truth: that I was working as an outside consultant with the Brown Palace on a series of murders that were entangled with the original resident of the Stillwell Mansion, Mrs. Luella Stillwell. They'd been very kind, stating that whatever they could do to help, they would.

"Dr. Becente?"

I blinked, coming out of my reverie.

"Yes," I answered, "and please, call me Olivia."

I walked up the large stone steps to shake the hand of a man who seemed to be in his midforties. He smiled genuinely, squinting in the sun as he shook my hand. I supposed my moment to back out had passed. But it seemed to me that if the ghost of Mrs. Stillwell had been replaced by my sister, if I decided to go forward with this investigation—and I still wasn't sure about that—going to the house she'd spent so many decades in only made sense.

He told me his name was Troy Robyns. "Thank you for doing this," I said, turning my white buffalo turquoise cluster ring around and around on my finger nervously.

"It's no problem. It's a day where I'm stuck looking at piles of briefs, so I welcome the distraction," he said, his smile disarming.

He opened the door and gestured for me to go in first, his pale, freckled hand ushering the way.

"Wow," I said. There was a large, curved wooden staircase in the foyer, leading up to an orchestra balcony. The tile was black-and-white—checkered and glossed to a high shine. It was bright, airy—but there was a kind of historic weight to the place, a sense that the people who had occupied this mansion, who had lived and loved and hated, were merely around the temporal bend and might just pop right back, their hands clasping a glass of bloodred wine, a silvery pale martini, a fireplace poker, another ghostly hand.

"Twenty-three rooms, nine fireplaces," Troy said, running his fingers over his carefully coiffured dark hair. "We feel strongly about keeping it close to what it looked like when it was built in 1904."

"It's something." I peered up at the orchestra balcony, picturing Luella standing there, looking down at her guests. I shuddered. I could feel something here already. A low hum of activity bubbling beneath the surface.

He looked around. "I like it. I like the vibe, if you will."

I laughed. "It's giving dark academia."

It was his turn to laugh.

"Come with me," he said, leading me to a set of white French doors off to our left. He swung them open, and I followed.

"This is where we often meet with clients—initially." The desk and modern glass-and-copper chandelier were clearly new, the desk a pale wood, grand enough to accommodate the four large office chairs surrounding it. I thought for a moment about the conversations that must take place around this table. I could hear a few faint echoes. Mainly, it was the dead I could hear and communicate with. But if there was intensity around a memory, especially if a memory contained a tremendous amount of emotion, I could often see it as if it were my own.

"Sorry about the mess," he said. There were files on top of files, boxes surrounding them. "I have an office upstairs where I usually hide the majority of the chaos, but like I said—no meetings today, so I decided to work downstairs."

"You should see my office," I told him, and one side of his mouth curved up.

A long, very modernist painting was hung on the wall above the desk, and built into another wall was a fireplace, with a large square wood-framed mirror above. There were bookcases set into the corners, the molding ornate and winding. And in another corner, what must have been an original mirror, large and golden and occupying the entire wall. I peered into it and felt a chill.

I sighed. "Beautiful. Do you know what this room was used for when Mrs. Stillwell occupied it?"

He nodded thoughtfully. "From what I understand, this was a drawing room, a fancy living room of sorts, where they entertained smaller groups." He squinted. "Lots of drama went down here, I assume. She had a social group, called . . ." He looked off into the distance, trying to remember.

"The Sacred 36," I said, smiling. The 36 had taken their name from Luella's original social group, the Sacred 36.

"That's it!" he said, snapping his fingers. "There was so much junk we had to get rid of when we took it over. Rotting furniture, weird paintings, countless old books we sold off. Anyway, would you like to see the rest of the house?" he asked, the corners of his blue eyes crinkling charmingly.

"Sure," I answered, following him out of the drawing room.

Much of the building was shut up—bedrooms with little use, with the furniture covered in thick sheets coated in dust, or rooms with more piles of boxes and files—and then a number of working offices, a few occupied by sweaty-looking men and a few women on the phone or computer, almost all of them white, or white-passing, except for one lone Asian, all looking tired and overworked and fully immersed in whatever projects were occupying them.

As we went, we chatted, and I told him a little bit about myself and he about himself. He was born in Louisiana, law school at Tulane, and then, after an internship in DC, he was offered a position here, in Denver—a city that was being built up and away from its former, much grittier incarnation quickly. I'd only seen bits and pieces of the old Denver, being in my midthirties, and in all honesty, preferred the new, the sparkly, the co-op, the opulent restaurant Denver to the dives and old amusement parks my mother adored, like Lakeside.

After climbing another set of stairs, we moved into a hallway that was darker than the ones we'd visited below, and Troy told me that there were fewer occupied rooms on this floor. It was almost completely shut up, except for two rooms: the children's room and Mrs. Stillwell's.

He pushed open a door to the children's room. There were two sweet matching beds—with white-checkered blankets, little white pillows, and tiny decorative pillows on top, embroidered with what were once certainly brightly colored animals and raggedy dolls, now faded. There was a set of dolls on the little matching dressers at the other end, staring back at us with flat button eyes.

"Dolls always give my ex Sasha the heebie-jeebies," I said. I pulled my jacket closer. "They don't get to me the way they do him. But I understand. It's the way they seem to stare at you, even though they're not alive."

"Oh, I get it," Troy said. "I had two sisters, and they loved dolls. And sometimes they'd leave one in my room. And the eyes seemed to watch me all night."

I laughed, and we moved on.

"Do you know much about Luella Stillwell?" Troy asked, as

we crossed the threshold into a room that felt and looked very different.

"I'm just beginning my research," I said. "I've started with Google—and I've talked to the concierge at the Brown Palace. I have an appointment with the on-site historian. That should be illuminating. I do know Mrs. Stillwell died of a broken heart in room 904 in the Brown Palace after a lifetime here."

"That's . . . Who told you that?" he asked, his eyebrows knitting.

"The concierge at the Brown Palace—it seems to be common knowledge."

"Well—this is—was—her room," he said, gesturing to the immense four-poster bed, the large mahogany writing desk, the tall windows that should've let in light but somehow didn't, leaving the room murky, like it was underwater, waiting, the furniture almost waving in deep ocean winds. Some of the furniture was draped in the same thick white sheets I'd seen in the other rooms. "We try to keep this clean, dusted—sometimes people want to see it and the children's room for research purposes, and . . . it just feels right. But it's expensive enough to keep the place up, so as you can see, we do keep some of the more extraneous pieces covered—most of the mirrors, the armoire and such."

I nodded, glancing over at the large ornate golden mirror above the desk, not entirely unlike the one in the drawing room downstairs.

It was uncovered. And though I was sure that it was certainly my recent experience seeing my dead sister in a mirror, I found the mirror . . . disconcerting. Looking at it, I felt dread. Anticipation, too, almost like I had to keep my eye on it. I squinted, feeling like something would appear in it at any moment. The echoes were strong here.

"Why isn't that mirror covered?" I asked.

Troy laughed uneasily. "It, well. It won't stay covered. When we try to drape it, when we come in, it's undraped. Every time. So we leave it be."

I felt a strong shudder pass through me. "Jesus," I said.

"I know."

We were both silent for a beat or two, and in that silence, I heard a kind of soft, ominous, silvery whispering.

"So, as I was saying, that idea that you had," Troy said.

"Idea?" I answered, blinking.

"Yes, or rather—idea that some folks have about Mrs. Stillwell. That she died of a broken heart. It doesn't seem quite right."

"Why is that?" I walked over to a few of the more ominous-looking objects. There was something about the fact that they were covered, something about the room. The dark, dank chill of it. The way that it felt frozen in time—but at the same time, darkly alive. It felt as if Luella had left moments ago and might return at any moment. Maybe in that mirror.

I glanced over at it.

"You see, she was quite the party animal—even up into her sixties. And, though she did have a lover, her husband didn't seem to mind."

"Really? That's progressive, for the time." I put my hand on a sheet. "Mind if I . . . ?"

"No, not at all. Just put it back when we're done."

"Sure," I said, sliding the sheet off what almost certainly was an armoire. It was sitting at the back of the room, swallowed in shadows, many of which seemed to gather at the top, giving the illusion of a figure crouching. Waiting.

I took a deep breath and continued pulling.

"I think the wealthy have always had . . . different rules," Troy continued. "Additionally, she was a powerful woman."

"Oh?" I said, the sheet falling in dusty folds to my feet. I opened the door, unlatching the metallic catch first—and peered inside. In my periphery, I swore I saw something in the mirror and glanced behind my shoulder at it, then back at the contents of the armoire.

"She was also—in her bourgeois way, I suppose—an eccentric woman," Troy said. "She went through a séance phase."

"Really," I answered, not wanting to interrupt with what I knew. I ran my hands over the silken dresses and woolen coats, pulling them back, my heart in my throat. There were still enough items left that the back of the closet was obscured. I felt . . . dread, curiosity.

Despite my fear, and perhaps even because of it, I thrust my hand slowly, inch by inch, into the folds of the clothing, my heart beginning to thump as I did. I stopped a few times, the cold edge of a sleeve spooking me, but I kept going, expecting a stiff, icy hand to grab mine back. Finally, I felt something. I gasped—but it was just the cold back of the closet, and maybe a metallic catch? But as I pushed my hand back, I thought—I could've sworn—I felt something cold, but alive.

"Her lover," Troy said, continuing his thought, "married another, younger woman—when Mrs. Stillwell's husband died."

"Ouch," I said, shaking my head to clear it, closing the doors to the armoire, and moving to the next object. It looked to be a full-length mirror. Behind it were a number of tall, person-shaped, sheet-covered objects. I shuddered.

"She got her revenge, though," he said, laughing.

"Is that so?" I answered, pulling at the sheet on the mirror. "How?"

"As I said, she was quite influential, quite powerful. She met with his investors—and persuaded them to pull out. He died a pauper."

"When did she die?" I asked, curious. I'd already, reticently, started my own research, but that detail had escaped me, and I couldn't remember if the concierge at the Brown had mentioned it.

He squinted. "I think . . . in 1955? Don't quote me on that, though," he said.

I went to turn around, impressed, when his phone began ringing, startling us both.

"Sorry," he said sheepishly, and shoving his hand in his pocket, plucked it out. He stared at the phone. He gave me an apologetic look. "I have to take this," he said.

I nodded, and he stepped out of the room.

I turned back to the mirror in front of me, pulling the sheet the rest of the way off, trying to tune into whatever was here. It was a beautiful golden mirror—it looked as if it and the mirror above the desk had been styled by the same artist. I ran my fingers over the pattern. This was certainly "New World" gold—ripped from the earth and utilized as an excuse to genocide and remove and assimilate Native people. My mother had told me that there were Apache who still wouldn't wear gold. I wondered if Mrs. Stillwell had ever had any involvement with Native people, or at the least what her opinion had been on them. Most certainly not good, considering her status.

I went to look in the mirror again, lost in my thoughts of colonization, marveling at the infinite mirror-within-a-mirror effect, as there was a mirror positioned directly in front of it on the wall opposite, when the whispering grew sharper, and then a sound, like someone drawing their fingers to their lips and shushing.

Then I saw it.

I screamed and stumbled back.

It was a long, dark figure with a maw full of long white teeth staring at me from the mirror behind—I could see it reflected in the mirror in front of me.

I fell back, hard, its fury covering me like a blanket, on the floor, squeezing my eyes shut, Troy suddenly at my side, asking what had happened.

I opened my eyes. There was nothing. The thing I'd seen looked just like the thing I'd seen in Regina and Latonya's apartment, the thing attached to the book, *Ghostland*.

"I'm so sorry—I thought . . . there was—" I said, sitting up and looking directly into the mirror in front of me, then the mirror it had appeared in, and shook my head. "Something . . ." I finished lamely.

"It's okay, that happens in here sometimes. Great room—but spooky. The light's no good, and it creates shadows. At least, that's what I tell myself. I never go in here alone—wouldn't have let you except for the call, it was from my client. And it's a big case—they were panicking. I'm so sorry."

"No, no—I'm the one who's sorry," I said, my cheeks flushing. "God, I'm embarrassed."

"Don't be. I squealed like a little girl in here one time. Could've sworn I saw something in that mirror," he said. "Let's go back downstairs, I could get you a glass of water—or something stronger," he said, rubbing the back of his neck.

"Okay," I answered.

I closed my eyes. Took a breath.

As we crossed the threshold into the hallway, I couldn't help it—I glanced back. From the angle I was at, the mirror above the desk reflected the human-shaped figures behind the full-length mirror. I sighed. And then the head of one of them moved. Just a little.

# Chapter Thirteen

My heart was still hammering, my mind a blitz of barely receding terror, when I saw him. It took me a minute to realize who it was. He was leaning, his long, muscular legs propped one in front of the other, against a large, flowering tree directly in front of the Stillwell Mansion, right outside the gates. My chest went cold, and I froze in my tracks on the deck—I'd just said goodbye to Troy. He'd made sure I had a glass of water before I left. Made sure I drank the whole thing. My hands had been shaking so badly I'd barely been able to hold the glass, positive it was going to slip out of my fingers the entire time and ruin the lovely oriental rug beneath me à la horror movie cliché. Obviously, on the regular, I was able to keep my shit together when paranormal activity went down—I wouldn't be able to do my job if I didn't. But not only were the beings I was encountering lately evil as shit, versus the usual ghost merely looking to tell their story so they could leave this earth, there was something different about that spirit in the mirror. Something to do with my sister. I'd been too embarrassed to tell Troy what I'd seen right before he'd shut the door—or what had appeared in the mirror when I'd screamed.

I closed my eyes, took a breath. I willed my limbs to unfreeze and began walking toward him. He didn't look up until I'd passed the gate. I considered moving right past but knew that if I didn't confront this head-on, he'd follow, and it'd be even worse.

"What are you doing here?" I asked, pausing in front of him. I stood with my feet apart, my hands on my hips. It was something they'd taught us in self-defense. Take up space.

"Oh, hey," he said, looking up from his phone and smiling, acting like this was a casual run-in.

"Josh, we discussed this."

As much as Alejandro and I made fun of Josh, the fact that he'd been essentially stalking me ever since we broke up was, in reality, terrifying. Honestly, I should've known from the get-go: he'd love-bombed me with flowers, jewelry, and dinners at trendy, upscale restaurants. And went wild with any mention of exes: he'd been especially jealous of Sasha, as he knew the both of us worked together in the paranormal community.

"Olivia," he said, his smile flickering. "Chill." He ran one hand down his cream-colored tracksuit—one I was sure cost more than most folks' business suits.

"Don't gaslight me," I said, narrowing my eyes.

He laughed. "Don't give *me* your TikTok psychology terms."

I ran my hands over my knees. "Josh, I *told* you I wouldn't file a restraining order *if* you stopped showing up places where I was. I told you and you didn't listen."

He ran his fingers over his perfectly coiffed hair. He was so *American Psycho*. "Let's just have a calm, civilized talk? In fact, I have a great idea. Why don't we have brunch? You know you love the Matchbox. Or Belga? Babe, I just got out of the gym, and I had a major workout. I'm hungry."

"Calm? *Calm?* You're the reason I got a gun," I said, burrowing my hands farther into my hips to stop the shaking.

I hated guns. Beyond hated them. But I'd decided, after a few incidents involving obsessed ex-clients, one break-in, and a whole lot of Josh showing up wherever I happened to be, to bite the bullet as it were, and get one. I kept it in a safe, and only I—and Alejandro—knew the combination. And I checked it nightly.

A look of rage blossomed behind his handsome, placid exterior. "Who were you with in there? I saw a man—you dating this guy? No one will ever be able to satisfy you like I can," he said, his hand jetting out lightning fast, one finger stroking my arm.

I jerked away. "Satisfy me? I wasn't 'satisfied' *once* when we were together. You were too busy looking in the freaking mirror to watch your quads flex as you thrust."

He laughed. "You're just negging me."

"Josh, I'm not in love with you. I was *never* in love with you. Even if that had ever been a possibility—as I told you, I don't see relationships that way. I live with Alejandro. He's my life partner."

"Alejandro." Josh's eyes narrowed.

"See," I said, laughing, "this is exactly what I'm talking about. You were even jealous of a gay guy!"

"Let's be honest," Josh said. "He's into you."

I rolled my eyes.

"Here's what I'm going to do, Olivia, as I'm a high-value man," he said, chuckling affably.

I snorted.

"I'll give you one more chance, because for some reason, you get to me. Move in with me. If you'd just moved in with me in the first place, it would've been different," he said, shaking his head.

I slapped my forehead. "No, it would've been worse. And I've told you this—we've gone over this a thousand times, you creep. You would've been after me everywhere I went. You already were—are! Showing up at every job I had."

"Olivia—"

"Wait a minute," I said, trailing off. "How did you know I was here? I know Alejo wouldn't have told you shit."

"Alejandro." His eyes narrowed once more.

"Not that again," I said, exasperated. "Did you . . . did you follow me?"

He looked down at his feet. "Of course not. I would never—"

"You did. You fucking followed me."

"Olivia, if you just had a normal job," he said, clearly trying to manipulate me into changing the subject—a tactic he pulled a lot, "this wouldn't be an issue. I don't have a problem with your advanced education, which is," he said, pausing to sweep a strand of escaped hair out of his eyes, "pretty progressive. Something I like to pride myself on. But going to strange men's houses to find ghosts? I have to be honest with you, Olivia. About how it looks." And here he lowered his voice. "It looks slutty."

I stared at him for a moment, and then I started laughing. "I am a slut. I'm slutty—in fact, I don't hunt ghosts, Josh. I *fuck* them. I'm a ghostfucker."

His hand shot out and caught my arm, his eyes filling with rage. "Don't say that, don't—"

"Is there a problem?" It was Troy. I hadn't even heard him walk up behind us.

I tried to pry my arm out of Josh's muscular grip. I'd been planning on a hard chop to his solar plexus when Troy had come up.

"I think the lady would like her arm back," Troy said.

I closed my eyes in humiliation.

"She's my girlfriend, whatever she told you."

Troy was silent for a moment. "I don't think so."

"I have a restraining order against him. He's not my boyfriend. I went out with him for a few months, but he was . . . like this," I said, gesturing with my head.

"Let her go," Troy said.

"Let's just talk," Josh said. "And really, what can you do here?" His face was a mask of coy sophistication.

"I'll call the cops. And if you have a restraining order, and they show up? You're off to jail, my man," Troy said, raising his eyebrows.

Josh's nose curled, and an almost-snarl came out of his mouth. He let my arm go with a violent twist, and I massaged the already-bruising spot where his hand had been.

"You think you can take me?" Josh said.

Troy rolled his eyes. "I'm not interested in fighting you."

Josh looked off to the side and then swung.

Troy saw it coming and ducked. "Ten years karate, my dude."

"Fucking pussy!" Josh yelled and swung again.

Troy ducked and stepped back.

Josh tripped and fell, one knee coming down hard, his meatiness and overconfidence working against him. He got up, his face a mask of animal rage. "I'm gonna kill you, man."

"You sure you want to say that to a lawyer?" Troy asked. "Especially considering you've got a restraining order on you?"

"Oliva's *my* girlfriend!" Josh screamed, coming at Troy like a bull.

Troy ducked again, stepping out of the way.

Josh fell flat on his face this round, and I couldn't help it, I giggled.

That's when we heard the sirens. I'd texted 911 once Josh had been distracted by Troy.

"Shit," Josh said. He turned to me. "Babe?"

"I'm still babe?" I shook my head.

"She's so not your babe," Troy said.

"I'm . . . This is Alejandro's fault," Josh said, dusting himself off with his big, beefy palms.

"Alejo's?"

"Pretending he was gay, just so that he could get close to you. Push everyone else away. He'll pounce once he knows he has you in his grip," Josh said, grinding his teeth.

I went to retort but instead burst out laughing.

Josh clenched and unclenched his fists. "I have proof, you know." And with that, he leapt over the fence and was gone.

# Chapter Fourteen

*For Sale: Ouija board haunted as hell. With demon attachment.*

*This board attacked my boyfriend. It's that active. Sigil indicating which demon on back. I won't say, for fear of retribution. Sick, terrible smells fill the air when used. THE DEMON ATTACHED TO THIS BOARD WILL HURT YOU. Use extreme caution.*

*$100 OBO.*

*Per eBay Policy this object is for "entertainment purposes."*

"Do you believe in ghosts?" I asked the table.

I'd picked the Ouija board up at a McMansion in the Highlands from folks who wouldn't even answer the door. They'd emailed me via my website, told me that if I'd bless their house with my "Native American shaman powers" and take the board, they'd PayPal me $5,000. They'd forwarded me the original listing. It was a deal.

Alejandro looked over at Sara, the sound of crickets softly

overlaying the evening. "I mean . . . I know my mom does," Sara said. "Told me the La Llorona stories. Mainly, I think, to scare me into going to sleep. Needless to say, it didn't work." Sara laughed. "I just read with a flashlight under the covers, so much that I wanted to get a degree in like, reading."

"Mine too," Alejandro said. "But"—he paused to get up and pour everyone another round of rosé—"I always thought it was kind of sexist. Also, I think playing with that board is a horrible idea, Olivia. Because after what I've seen with you? I believe all right."

I sighed. "I think that what a lot of white folks—or Christian folks, or Catholic for that matter—what they call demons *are* nonhuman. And just like the Warrens—"

Here Victoria and Alejandro moaned in unison.

"Just like the *Warrens*," I continued, "it's my job to figure out the difference between a ghost and a nonhuman entity—or bullshit for that matter. But the problem with their way is that when you assume every nonhuman spirit is evil, has to do with the Christian universe, and can be solved with the power of Jesus Christ, you miss that some of these entities are powerful Native gods that still exist on this continent. And they're not going anywhere because some holy water was sprayed on them. That said, some of them are demons that need to go straight back to their homeland. And of course, most that are real—which is rare—are ghosts."

"You're not exactly filling me with confidence," Sara said, slapping at a mosquito. I had set citronella around the table, as I loved dining outside—but the bugs often got through my aromatic defenses.

Alejandro picked up the mainly empty dishes and headed for the kitchen, me holding the sliding doors open for him.

"Shit," Victoria said, taking up the mantle. "Not to be a Diné traitor or anything, but everyone on the Rez was always talking about skinwalkers and witches, and I'm not saying they were lying, or that it wasn't real, but I never saw any of it. I'll play with that board. I don't care. And even if that stuff's real, I know Olivia can handle it."

"Really?" Sara asked.

"Really. I mean, don't get me wrong. All that shit from back home can be dangerous, and I'll tell you why. People are witches. They do evil shit to gain power—whether the Great Creator's behind any of it or not."

Alejandro returned and sat down.

"My guess?" I said, crossing one leg over the other. "This thing's just a run-of-the-mill board that spooked two kooky rich people who were probably high as hell on some expensive, high-grade weed. The other half of the time, billygannas don't know that it's just a G'an."

Victoria giggled. "I hate that word in English."

"Right?" I responded. "It's pretty much the same word in Diné Baazad as in Ndé Bizaá."

"What's a Gaaan?" Sara asked.

"It's little people."

"Like leprechauns and stuff?" Sara asked.

"This is why I hate that word in English," Victoria said, putting a hand to her forehead and rubbing.

"Sort of," I said. "I mean, my Celtic pagan friends say they're kind of similar. They pick stuff up—like wallets or wristwatches, put them other places. They like to fuck around and find out. I have an irresistible treat for them that gets them to leave people alone. They especially seem to like couples with kids. Sometimes there's a reason though, and I have to call social services."

Sara drew breath.

"Yeah. But anyway, if there *is* something evil attached to the board? I know how to deal with it, even though I've never encountered anything I'd consider irrevocably evil. Lately though, I have to admit, I'm encountering beings that don't want redemption, or to be understood. I know folks say hurt people hurt people, and that's often true. But sometimes, human or not, there are beings that just enjoy harm. And other paranormal investigators have told me that they've encountered what they consider pure evil," I said, thinking of what I felt, saw, in the Stillwell Mansion—I'd been scared in a way that I hadn't been in a long, long time. "But in any case, because this is a communal object, your presence will help me to determine what's going on with it and *how* to deal with it—if it's even haunted."

"Should we be drinking if we do this?" Sara asked. "That seems wrong."

"Think of it as communion wine," Alejandro said.

Alejo left and came back with my equipment. I wanted my EMF and EVP meters. My sage. Sweetgrass. Holy water. The only time I stumbled was when I came across African, African American (though I had some connection and familiarity there), or Asian traditions—but I had people I could call who were from a variety of backgrounds in that case. Many of them had flown in, and I had done the same.

We cleared the table and set the board down. It was old, almost amber in color, a sun on one side and a moon on the other, a picture of a woman presumably sitting around and playing with a Ouija board on either side of the piece.

"Everyone clear your minds, as much as possible," I said. It was advice I needed to take myself. "Everyone think about the most peaceful place you've ever been. And stay there for a minute."

"This is stup—"

"You too, Victoria."

She clapped her mouth shut.

We were silent, and after a minute, after Alejandro had lit some black and Virgen de Guadalupe candles and we'd set some sweet-grass to burning, everyone's breathing slowed, calmed. We were in the right space.

I ran the EMF meter over the board. Nothing. Not a blip. I ran it again.

"See? Two kooky rich people," I said.

Sara took a shaky breath and sighed. "Sorry, Catholic over here."

Alejandro patted her hand.

"Let's take a look at that sigil," I said, flipping the board over. It was burned into the board, a symbol that was a star, with the sign of what looked like eternal life overlaid.

"If I'm not mistaken, and I have a friend in town who could come over in a heartbeat if shit goes down, that's a European pagan symbol meaning women's body fluids," I said. "Or, wait—"

Victoria started laughing uproariously. "Dude. At home that would get that board banned for life. We have ceremonies—"

"You're like a Navajo frat bro, I swear," Sara said.

"You loved it when I—"

"Oh my *God*, ladies, and I'm supposedly the gay one," Alejandro said.

Victoria only laughed harder while Sara turned her usual shade of red.

"Anyway, can we get back at it?" I asked. I realized I'd been wrong anyway. Upon further reflection, that was the sign of the demon Mammon.

"Whatever," Victoria said. "I just wish the wine hadn't run out. This is going to get boring fast."

"Just everyone, focus. And put your fingers, lightly, on the planchette," I said, and they complied. "Spirits. I respect you. If you're here, tell us what you need."

For a long time, nothing.

"I'm so bored," Victoria said. "Isn't there an app for getting more—"

The planchette began to move. Circles upon circles.

"Did you turn the EVP on?" I whispered to Alejandro. He nodded.

"If you're here, give us a—"

The board began vibrating.

Sara whimpered sharply and leapt up from her seat, the chair falling backward with a large clang. Victoria caught her by the arm. "No. We have to deal. Wrap it up. Or shit will go down. For us." For someone so cynical about the occult, Victoria sure knew how to keep her cool in the face of it.

Tears were running down Sara's face. "Okay," she whispered. "Okay." She sat back down. I held my hand out. She took it, and everyone around the table followed suit.

"Everyone, chill," I said, the board vibrating so hard it was clattering on the table.

I closed my eyes. Tried to move into the mind of the spirit. I could almost see it . . . it was a feminine presence. I could feel overwhelming grief. It hurt to take it into my body, like there was a blackness at the center of my being, feeding the pain.

"Everyone, put your fingers back on the . . ." I searched for it, one hand holding the board down, the other patting the ground. "Planchette," I said, closing my fingers around the triangular piece of wood. It had fallen due to the vibrations.

"I'm so sorry you're in pain. I want to help. What's your name?" I asked, hoping my tone carried the respect I'd tried to inflect it with.

The board stilled.

Slowly, hesitantly, the wood began to move, spelling out *Luella*.

I drew back. "Wait. No."

I had to center myself. Take a breath. "Luella . . . Stillwell?"

The EVP began to crackle. I thought I heard weeping.

"My God," Sara said.

"Is that . . . ? The woman from the mirror? From the Brown Palace?" Victoria asked. "Man, now I want one of those self-righteous NAC dudes from back home."

I knew the entity could be lying. That's what the Warrens would say. That it was demonic. That it was *learning* me. Learning how to get inside me, manipulate me. I had to ask it a question only Mrs. Stillwell would know.

"What was the name of your lover? The one that broke your heart?"

The board moved again. Just a little.

"It's okay. We're here for you." Something must have led the board to me—just like the dybbuk box with the Cheyenne two-spirit, Nese, to the woman whose ancestor had trapped them.

The planchette began to move. It took a minute or two to spell what it was trying to spell out, all of us whispering each letter as it did.

*Bulkeley Wells.* That was right. That was the name of Luella's lover. Shit. Just shit. I took a breath. Centered myself.

"What can I do to release you? Help you move on."

The wood began to move again. I could hear the soft evening noises around me as it did, the EVP meter silent now. The scraping sounds of wood against wood. Then.

*Y-O-U. H-A-V-E. T-H-E. B-O-O-K.*

"Book?" I said. "What the hell—"

The weeping on the meter grew loud, then shut off. After a moment of silence, Alejo announced that he was going to have a few more bottles delivered.

"Wow," Victoria said.

I rubbed my knees. "Yeah," I answered. I genuinely wasn't sure that had been Mrs. Stillwell on the other end of the board. But if it hadn't been her, who *had* it been, and why would it want to pose as Luella? I put my head in my hands, and Victoria patted me on the back. "You know—" she started.

"Hold on," I said. I could hear my phone going off in my bag. I rifled through until I found it, conversation beginning to pick up around me.

"Olivia?" It was my mother. She sounded hoarse, upset.

"Mom? Are you okay?"

"Olivia . . . I . . ." I could hear her swallowing, then, "The strangest thing just happened. The strangest thing that's ever happened to me in my life."

"Okay," I said, working to keep my voice steady. "Do you need me to come home?"

She was silent for a moment. Then, "Yes. Is that okay?"

I nodded, realized that she couldn't see me, and then answered in the affirmative. "What happened?"

"I went to the Brown Palace—"

"Mom, no!" I said, closing my eyes and bringing one hand to my forehead. My stomach began to swim with unease. Oh Jesus, Jesus Christ. "Just—tell me that you didn't check in, tell me—"

"I did, okay? Don't be mad at me, listen. I know you've told me I need to move on. And I have, but I had to do it. I checked in—I tried to get room 904, where she . . . where she killed herself."

"Oh, Mom, no . . ." My eyes flashed open. This was a nightmare. My worst nightmare.

"Just let me finish! You never let me finish!"

My eyes closed again with resignation. I knew what she was going to say.

"They wouldn't give me that room. Said it was closed for renovations. But then . . . I went to sleep. And when I woke up, I was in room 904."

# The Massacre, Part II: Prelude

Before the soldiers, before the blood, before the screaming of the women that would haunt Nese through the years as they haunted, Nese remembered the day the sun shone through the boy's dark hair. His soul had been light with the sound of airy Maiyn dancing around them both, blessing them with their immaterial presence. The boy's small, sweet fingers had reached up to Nese's, handing them the medicine. The Ve'eve-shestoto'e, which they had been gathering that day, was one of the most powerful medicines the Heévâhetaneo'o had. It aided in salving colds, in creating flutes for love medicine, and it connected the heaven Heamahestanov to the underworld Atonoom; the in-between Blue-Sky Spaces so bright, so beautiful, Nese felt as if they could see all the way to Ma'heo'o, could call on them to bless what Nese feared was coming for them all.

The boy would make such a good medicine person, Nese thought, their stomach turning and trying not to turn. It was spring, and green, and fresh, and beautiful. The flowers dotted the plains: red and pink and purple, all moving in the soft wind like they were dancing to a kind of music only they could hear, the grasses following in the symphony. There had been game. The Vehoc had been kept at bay the last few weeks.

"Why are you sad?" the boy asked, his face tilting up. It was such a sweet, good face, full of the joys of childhood. Nese had watched the boy play with other children, his tiny, nimble fingers shaping leathers and quills into dolls.

Nese pulled a branch of the silvery-white juniper they were plucking to their nose and inhaled its sharp, unique tang.

"I fear for the future," Nese responded.

The boy nodded. He looked off into the distance, into the east, where they began their prayers in the morning, when the sun first rose.

"There is no future. But I'm not afraid."

Nese paused at this. "No future?" They moved forward, grasped a branch, and carefully removed a piece so as not to damage the plant for growth.

"I mean, for me."

Nese blanched.

The boy seemed unconcerned.

"Your road will be hard," the boy said, turning to Nese, tenderness in his eyes. He took Nese's hands and squeezed them.

Nese's stomach flipped again. "My road?"

"Yes. But you'll meet her. She's the future."

Nese pulled a piece of dried meat out of their bag and handed a section to the boy before eating some themselves. They chewed thoughtfully, then showed the boy how to pluck the branch, though he barely needed instruction.

"Don't worry," the boy said, turning his small hand in Nese's. "There is so much beauty coming for the people. After the pain."

Nese's head reeled. They felt desperately that they needed to sit down. The boy was more powerful than they had understood.

"Just remember," the boy said, concern in his eyes. "You'll know her because her people have been enemies of the Heévâhetaneo'o, and she will have a two-spirit by her side, helping her. You will enter her dreams, give her visions. And this is the most important part," the boy said, looking west, where the sun was just beginning to set. "You must give her the key."

## Chapter Fifteen

I was sitting at Mom's dining table in Aurora, my head in my hands. The dining table, a sparkly retro Formica we'd had since I could remember, was dotted with cups of coffee. Mom liked to meet with other retired newspaper writers, novelists, artists. She'd written for the *Denver Post* for thirty years, ever since she'd finished her master's in journalism at Columbia in New York and come home. She still had her editing side gig. Sometimes, however, I had to fill in the blanks financially. Thank goodness she'd bought her house before the big real estate boom. I lifted my head and began to turn the cup she'd given me when I'd come in. It had her name, Monique, in big, cursive letters embossed on the front, a parting gift from friends at the *Post*. She was unnerved by what had happened but didn't understand why I was so upset with her for checking in. She had no idea her life was in danger. She had no idea that she had three weeks.

"Just talk to me, Olivia," she said, one short, elegant hand on my arm. "It can't be that bad."

I closed my eyes. Images of the footage of my sister in the mirror blossomed forth in my mind. Memories, cloudy and indistinct at first, then forming into concrete, flooded into me. Naiche and

I sharing a cone of pink gossamer cotton candy when we were children, arguing over who had gotten the most. She and I laughing at our father dancing around the living room, banging his head to his favorite, AC/DC. She and I watching *The Ring* for the first time, her hand snaking over to mine for reassurance the moment the ring of light appeared, the strange, poetic images flooding the screen.

"I just want to say one thing before you get started, Olivia. I'm a newspaper writer—I deal in facts. Tangible, provable facts. When Mom used to go on about ghosts and spirits and devils, it used to drive me batty. It's part of why I left Houston, to get away from her, from her obsession with those things—some of that shit I guess came from Catholicism, but other parts were tradish. Either way, I didn't care. But then it started happening to me. Dreams I couldn't explain. Things I'd seen in my sleep would come true—down to the absolute last detail," she said, tapping her finger on the table with each word, her nails a bright pink. We'd gotten manicures together a few weeks ago. "And now you've come into it. So you have to believe me, you just have to."

"Mom that's not—I know, you've told me this."

My mother got up from the table and went over to the counter to pour herself another cup from the French press my father had bought for her a few years before he'd passed away. She blew at the steam and then sipped and leaned against the counter.

The phone—a yellow rotary she'd kept, another holdover from my childhood—rang with a clattery zing, and she glanced at it and let it sing until it stilled.

"Anyway, I didn't sleepwalk, if that's what you're thinking," she said. "I swear to you—and I don't do that anyway—that I went to sleep in room 412 and woke up in room 904. Unless someone drugged me and somehow got my unconscious body up five flights unnoticed, I reappeared in that room, like magic."

"Yeah," I said, "I have to tell you—"

"I've been dreaming of your sister," she said, looking out the window. I followed her gaze. Mom had planted tomatoes; soon she'd plant corn. Every year she planted corn. Sometimes blue, like her mother's. Sometimes Cherokee corn—a few of her friends were citizens of the Nation and had given her seeds that had been issued to them.

"I dream about her too, you know," I said, letting her derail me. "I miss her. Every day I miss her," I continued, my heart feeling like physical weights and pulleys were attached to it. If I was honest with myself, it felt like that all the time, especially around the anniversary of her death.

"I know. You two were so close. Only two years apart."

I rubbed at my knees.

I knew I should've listened to my sister when she went on about the Sacred 36. It had all just seemed so cheesy, so silly. I figured they sat around chanting and playing with Ouija boards—which at the time I'd found to be nothing but kiddie shit—and spooking each other out. Naiche had been an accountant, and like my mom, I'd assumed that she'd needed something fun in her life when her everyday existence had been essentially bland. And like my mother, she'd always claimed to see things—see dolls move, see ghosts in mirrors, see things appear in the sky that were supposedly omens—and have prophetic dreams.

I'd seen nothing.

"Did they tell you anything about 904?" I asked.

"No—there was someone outside my room when I appeared. He asked for my room number and then told me the Brown would be in touch. I tried to get something out of him—I'm a reporter for God's sake, and I'm usually pretty good at that—but his lips were sealed. So I just . . . went back down to my room, packed, and left. But I did some googling. Apparently, a high-society woman lived in that room for many years and died there. I have to assume that what happened to me had something to do with that." She ran one hand through her thick black hair.

"Her name was Luella Stillwell," I said.

"That's right," Mom said, smiling at me uneasily. "Interesting story."

"Right," I said. I sighed. I had to start somewhere. "So, the Brown Palace called me."

She blinked and readjusted, her back still to the counter, her long, dark eyes, so like mine, narrowing in confusion. My sister's eyes had been lighter, rounder, another nod to my father's side.

"They revealed something. Every five years, a woman checks into the Brown, and regardless of which room she starts in, she appears in 904. You appeared in front of the mirror? In the living room?" I ran my fingers along the edge of the mug in front of me. I wasn't sure if that detail mattered, but I wanted to know.

"Yes," she said, surprised. "You're saying that this happens every five years? Did I hear you right?" She blinked and straightened, put her cup down.

"It does."

My mother took this in, and I let her have a moment to process.

She blinked once more, rapidly. "Why?"

"They don't know. All they know is that it started when Luella Stillwell died, and they've done everything they can do to prevent it—including keeping a camera on the mirror in the living room in 904—but nothing stops it from happening."

"That's so strange."

"It gets worse. So much worse," I said, my voice hitching.

"What's wrong?" For the first time in our conversation, fear entered my mother's voice. Another thing we shared—our deep alto. "You need to tell me—and I have more to tell you."

What did she mean by that? I took a deep breath.

"The woman who checks in and reappears," I said, shifting uncomfortably in my seat, "well, Mom, as far as they can tell, three weeks later she appears in the room out of thin air, and she kills herself. Just like Naiche, five years ago."

My mother blanched, grew pale. She closed her eyes.

I got up, walked to her. Put my arms around her.

"I wouldn't . . . I wouldn't do that," she whispered finally. "I'm not like Naiche. I know I was distraught when she died. But I'm not like that."

I leaned back, my arms still around her. "I know. The people at the Brown don't understand. All they know is that Mrs. Stillwell—the woman who died originally in 904—appears, well, used to appear, in the mirror to watch as the woman dies. In Naiche's case, it was the Sacred 36, I'm sure, who pushed her to check in at the right time."

Mom shuddered, and I could tell she needed a minute.

I was quiet for some time. Then, "I'm scared, Mom, and . . . it gets even weirder."

"I think I know what you're going to say," she said, her eyes snapping open.

"I don't think so," I said.

"I need to sit down," she said.

We settled back at the table, and my phone went off. My God, it was Josh again. I was flooded with irritation, which quickly turned into fear. What he'd said about Alejandro had been so creepy.

"It's Josh, isn't it?" she asked. "You need to watch that boy."

I nodded silently, blocked the number. "Anyway, Mom, finish what you were telling me."

"There was a reason I checked into the Brown—it was the anniversary of your sister's suicide, and I'd heard things. But it was more than that."

I cocked my head, my heart hammering.

"I'd been dreaming of her. But not just the usual dreams. She was in the Brown Palace, yes. I'd dreamt that before. I'd dreamt of her dying in there, so many times. You're not the only one who thought she was under control." Her eyes were sharp suddenly.

"I know, Mom. I'm sorry if I haven't listened to you more," I said, fingering the edge of my mug. "It's just that it's so horrible. It's so sad." I paused. "And ever since she died, I haven't been right. I know I need to work on that." My mother only had an inkling as to how "not right" my behavior was sometimes. Occasionally, Alejandro would threaten to tell her. That would often throw me into shape. The only other person I loved as much as Alejandro was my mother. And the thought of causing her any more pain was unbearable.

"She's been appearing in the mirror, isn't that so?" Mom said, her hands to her eyes. "And not just to me?"

It was my turn to take a sharp breath.

"That was what was in my dreams. Your sister, in the mirror, at the Brown. She's haunting the Brown, isn't she?"

## Chapter Sixteen

*www.ghostequipmentforreal.com*
*Perfect Ghost Camera FOR SALE*

*This is the highest-tech camera for detecting visual anomalies related to paranormal activity that money can buy. High-quality images guaranteed. Infrared light, full spectrum, night vision camera designed to see into the other world. $400.*

The hotel stood on the bisection of two of the most major streets in Denver, a slim, oblong shape cutting straight into the meat of the city. I looked up, wondering if I could spot 904 from here. Wondering if my sister was in there right now, somehow living in that gray, liminal space between worlds. Just what *was* the story with that mirror? How did it trap people? Why? And why, after all these years, did it trap my sister? And where was Mrs. Stillwell? Had that really been her attached to the Ouija board?

"Ma'am?" It was the doorman. "Are you all right?"

I blinked and looked back down, feeling a touch of vertigo as I did.

"Yeah," I answered, and though the doorman only looked mildly reassured, I smiled at him and walked through the revolving doors. I was greeted by classical music inside, the sound of idle chitchat, the sight of women in fancy dresses, all dolled up for tea. Some of them looked blissfully buzzed. I was jealous.

The concierge looked up and smiled, one eyebrow crooking upward. "So, you've decided to take the case?"

I nodded.

"Come with me," he said, moving out from behind his station, a model of efficiency. "We've closed 904. Not that it matters." He sighed. "However, I have some names for you. Might help." He led me, again, to Ship Tavern, and we sat. He didn't even ask if I wanted a drink, he just ordered two glasses of white wine.

"You know, it's funny," he said, as we waited for our drinks. "Didn't believe in this kind of thing at all before I started working here. Didn't believe in ghosts, demons, magical mirrors—you name it. I was an atheist." He laughed.

The bartender set our drinks down, and we sipped. "When I applied for this job, everything I read online was positive. It *is* positive—the job. The staff is wonderful, the environment is—as you can see"—he said, gesturing—"beautiful. It's a lovely place to work. All I found online about anything ghostly, if you will, only amused me. I read that when they were refurbishing 904, they got calls at the front desk. But no one was in there."

"Really?" I sipped. It was nice. A crisp, appley sauvignon blanc.

"And there was no phone," he said, laughing. "Allegedly, this is true. This story. But they waited a few years to tell me about the mirror. About what happens every five years. Apparently, many employees stay for the long haul. For example, the hotel historian—you'll see her books for sale in the gift shop if you go—has been the historian for twelve years. But some go, move to other cities, end up with better opportunities. And they figure why burden them, unless they must? But I liked the job. So they told me."

We drank in silence for a while, and then I cleared my throat. "You said something about names?"

"Ah, yes. I have the names and footage of the women who died in here, going back as far as you need, though I'm assuming the event relating to your sister is most relevant."

"Can you give me a copy of all of the footage?"

"Of course. Though you should know, we've tried to clean your sister's cycle up, but our people have had zero success in that department."

"I'll give it my best shot," I said.

"Wonderful," he responded. "And of course, you have the run of 904—of the whole hotel, if you need it."

I nodded. "My assistant and I will be setting some equipment up in 904, if that's okay. We'll start with cameras. And we'll be spending some time in the room. And yes, email me the list too. I can try. I'm also going to attempt to find some members of the Sacred 36."

"I think I can help. A woman on that list—Catherine Lambert—she was a friend of your sister's, and she was a member of that cult," he said, his lips pursing.

I searched my memory. In the back of my mind, faintly, I remembered something about a woman named Cat. A woman my sister had been very close to before she died. It was pretty likely that Cat was Catherine. I sighed. Naiche had been deeply entrenched in a cult that was turning out to be far more dangerous and influential than I'd ever imagined.

# Chapter Seventeen

I hung up the phone, and Alejandro handed me a latte. I sipped, drank it a little too fast, and sputtered, wiping at my face as I did.

"Slow down, girl," Alejandro said. "Take a breath." He went to make himself a cappuccino, and I could hear him scrounging around in the kitchen, shuffling pots and pans to different—and, to his mind, better—locations, wiping the counters down, and in general being the high-maintenance friend I loved.

I sat with the phone in my hand, listless, my brain running a mile a minute, working at this whole thing, wondering at the strangeness of it, the puzzle. I had to put aside the sheer, unadulterated panic I felt when it came to what might happen to my mother and get to work.

The first thing I'd done was call the number the concierge, Mark, had for Catherine Lambert. It was still her number—her voicemail made that clear—but so far, she hadn't answered, or called back, though I'd left several messages. I'd been able to get ahold of the mother of the woman who'd died in the Brown two cycles ago. She was sweet. Sad. But when I told her the history of the Brown, she'd said that I was horrible for trying to exploit her grief and hung up on me. When I asked Mark what the woman had thought about materializing out of thin air in 904, he'd just said that apparently, she'd decided she'd had too much to drink—then three weeks later, just as the women before her had, she'd reappeared and suicided. I'd hung my head in frustration. The things people did to convince themselves that this was a rational universe.

We'd set the equipment up in the room, and we had a direct video link so that we could watch what was happening at all times from our apartment; so far, nothing. It wasn't surprising. From everything I'd learned, the activity mainly took place every five years, when the women appeared, reappeared three weeks later, and died—though there were exceptions. The real key was the Sacred 36 and its connection to Mrs. Stillwell. I'd been doing my research.

The Sacred 36 was originally—or at least as far as anyone knew—an elite group of thirty-six socialites who gathered for lavish parties or for bridge. But what was less known was Mrs. Stillwell's interest in the occult, in psychics, the paranormal. She had held séances in her mansion on the hill that a core group of the 36 participated in. And the year of her death—1955—was the year the Sacred 36 officially became an organization whose main interest, publicly, was in the occult, while the rest drifted off into the squeaky-clean Blue Book, Denver's own "who's who" listing that lasted for several decades.

I'd also updated Sasha, my rabbi ex, on the newest development with my mother, but he told me that, unfortunately, there was nothing new or relevant that he could find on golems or dybbuk boxes that he hadn't already told me, though he wanted me to keep him up-to-date with the hope that he could help. He said that he'd keep researching, that he had a few people he could still ask. I wasn't surprised. Sasha was a good person and I often suspected that he was still interested in me, but in addition, he and my mother had gotten along well when we were going out. She'd been upset when I'd broken it off, telling me that I was throwing an opportunity away.

I'd told her that he wanted more than I could give. She'd hung the phone up on me.

I sighed heavily and went to join Alejandro in the kitchen. I stopped at the counter, looking down at the full rack of clean dishes, the sparkle of the ridiculously clean sink.

"It was my turn," I said. He was Windexing the glass above the kitchen table.

He spun around and cocked his head sarcastically. "I know."

I smiled at him sheepishly and pulled the window cleaner out of his hands. "It looks immaculate."

"Damn right it does," he said. "I'm going to check the monitors."

I nodded distractedly. I knew he was worried. He loved my mother almost as much as I did.

My mind wandered again to Catherine Lambert. Maybe I'd attempt calling her for the fifth time. I'd even tried texting, but there had been no response to that either. I'd googled around. Wealthy. Strange. Big art freak. If I could ever get her on the phone, if she was willing, I wanted to meet up in person. I knew she was the most important—not only because the concierge had said she'd been a part of the cult, and not only because I was pretty sure she was the Cat who my sister had talked about, but mainly because my gut told me so. I was still a tremendously fact-based creature. Like many in my field, I held myself to rigorous standards, and there wasn't a creak, branch scratching spookily against a window, or otherworldly hoot I hadn't investigated thoroughly—and more importantly, objectively. From the beginning, I'd bought state-of-the-art equipment, and I kept my equipment clean, well-maintained, and current. However, I still trusted my gut. I still peered, with all my heart, into the unknown, fully expecting nothing but a squeaky board where someone thought their dead father was—but knowing that at least some of the time, it was something from the beyond, something that had taken up residence in our world.

I was sitting on the divan, the list in front of me, my finger on Catherine's name, when Alejandro interrupted me.

"Whoa. Wait a minute. Uh, Olivia, you better come here."

I went over to the desk and set my palms on either side of one of the monitors, leaning in. "Yeah?" I didn't see anything at first. I sat down so I could take a closer look. "I was just about to try that Cat—or Catherine—person again."

"Look," he said, pointing to the icon that reflected the temperature gauge in the room. "It just went down—and I mean, within seconds—from a comfortable sixty-eight degrees to fifty. And look at the mirror."

"Wait, what?" I squinted. Rewound. Sure enough. There seemed to be a smoky presence beginning to coalesce in the glass. "Let's get the shit over there," I said, standing up abruptly and almost knocking my chair over.

"Agreed."

The rooms at the Brown were beautiful, opulent. A marriage of dark academia and modern, with white lamps, beige tufted headboards, fluffy white duvets; the bathrooms were white tile and dark wood. I looked up at the framed plan of one of the rooms of the Brown on the wall—it was right next to the temperature control. The plan was large, elaborate, and blue with white lettering the same cream color as the walls. Though we were on the ninth floor, the print was of the fourth, which I found strange and idiosyncratic. I peered at the hotel's temperature gauge, while Alejandro checked ours. Both of them were at fifty. I'd wondered if it would stay at that temperature long enough for us to get here—we hadn't been far, but traffic was bananas in this city the last decade. But it had. And really, we'd hardly needed to check—the minute we walked through the door, the chill had hit us both. It was spring, and a temperate seventy-some-odd degrees outside. The difference was clear, beyond clear, and I was glad I'd brought a sweater with me. I pulled it out of my briefcase and put it on. But the mirror, for now anyway, was clear.

Alejandro and I checked the Olympus VN-541PC digital voice recorder—nothing there. But the TriField EMF recorder was going wild—and, according to the cameras, had been for a while. I went back over to the gauge on the FX camera and then the digital thermometer—we had both to measure temperature—and tapped the thermometer thoughtfully. They matched up. I was about to turn around when I began to sense what I'd feel sometimes walking late at night. A heaviness on the back of my neck, like moist, hot breath—the echo of not-so-distant footfalls—the feeling that someone was there. And that they meant me harm.

I took a breath, realizing that my back was to the mirror, and felt the temperature move downward even more. That was when it hit me: my sister's perfume, a sweet lavender and vanilla combination I hadn't smelled in years. She'd bought it in a store on Broadway that didn't even exist anymore. I closed my eyes.

"Olivia," Alejandro sang in a low voice, and my stomach dropped hard. I didn't want to turn around. I opened my eyes, trying to steel myself, trying not to picture her as a little girl, crying because she'd gotten what she felt was the smaller piece of birthday cake. Trying not to picture her telling me, with hysteria lining her voice, that I had to come over to the Brown *right now*. Trying not to picture her dead body laid out in the morgue, her eyes cracked unnaturally wide.

I turned.

What I saw hit my gut like an electric bolt of lightning. It was her. In the mirror, holding an elaborate black candelabra. My sister, looking just like the day she died, her eyes closed and swollen as if she'd been weeping for decades. I put one hand to my throat and took in a sharp breath. I went to call her name, but nothing came out.

Her eyes flashed open, and I stumbled back.

She was staring at me now, her eyes black and burning holes into me, her skin paler than it had ever been in life. She began to snarl. To scream, a high-pitched wailing noise. She raised one finger and pointed, straight at me.

I stumbled back farther, hitting the gauge.

"Naiche?" I whispered, finally finding my voice.

The smell shifted then, from perfume to something foul, rotten—like a festering wound.

"He's behind me," she said, hissing each syllable, then just like that, her mouth snapped shut and she was gone.

## Chapter Eighteen

Catherine. Catherine Lambert. I'd tried her so many times, and no dice. But after what had happened in room 904, I was desperate—I'd already lost three precious days. I'd gone through the list of the relatives of those who'd died in the Brown, and just as I'd suspected, most of them remembered that their female relative had been involved with the Sacred 36. Some of them just said "that cult" and some didn't have any recollection of anything like that, though I suspected they just hadn't known. And of course, some had been as furious with me as the first person I'd called and hung up on me. The only other relevant thing was that one of them, from a recent cycle, thought their family was, in their words, part Cherokee. The thing was, the Cherokee Nation of Oklahoma, like a number in that state, had no blood quantum requirement for enrollment—if you were able to find a relative on their rolls, no matter how far back, you became a citizen. So, when I asked if they were citizens of the Nation, and they'd responded with confusion, honestly, perhaps they *did* have a relative on the rolls and just didn't know it. Or genuinely were of Cherokee descent, which was more than possible, considering how large the tribe had been and still was. It was something to put on the brain's back burner to simmer, to see if it had relevance. But Catherine Lambert was the one person I absolutely had to talk to.

I dialed. After a few rings, I began to despair, but just as I was about to hang up, someone answered.

"Is this Catherine? Catherine Lambert?"

"Yes." The voice was feminine, strong. Almost smoky.

"This is Olivia Becente." I tried to keep the desperation out of my tone.

"Okay . . ." It was clear she wasn't making the connection.

"Naiche Becente's sister."

There was silence. Then, "Oh. Oh, my."

"I want to be clear: I'm not blaming anyone for anything. In fact, if there's anyone at fault here," I said, with an uncomfortable chuckle, "it's me."

She was silent. I wondered if she'd hung up.

"I'm wondering if we could meet?"

"Why?" She was still on the line.

That was rather blunt.

"I'd rather tell you more in person. I've been, in short, hired by the Brown Palace, and it has something to do with my sister."

I could hear the click of a lighter and the intake of breath. "Oh, I don't think so."

"It's pretty urgent."

There was a pause. Another intake of breath, smoke. And with the next sentence, my heart began knocking against my rib cage, hard.

She sighed heavily. Then, "I want nothing to do with all of this. But just to clear my conscience, fine. I have something that I want to get off my chest. And I'm sure it's relevant. It's about your sister."

## Chapter Nineteen

I knocked on the gigantic double doors of the wildly gothic charcoal-black Victorian mansion using the left of the two ancient, though well-maintained, darkened brass knockers. The face of the knocker on the left was of a fantastical wolf, the one on the right a goblin-faced human with short, sharp-looking horns. I couldn't help but watch them with each swing, waiting for them to come to life and take a bite. Catherine—or Cat—had given me the address. And I'd known it had to be something; it was in Cherry Hills—the priciest neighborhood in Denver, and one of the oldest. But this was so on-brand for someone who'd been a part of a cult called the Sacred 36, it was almost silly. The porch was wraparound, the overall design of the building complete with flying buttresses, pointed arches, and, I was sure, vaulted ceilings on the inside; the awning was an ornate series of carvings in intricate designs, clinging to statements in Latin. There were gargoyles on the turrets, looking out at me—almost appearing as if they might take off and fly toward me with the express purpose of scratching my eyes out.

"Wow," I muttered.

"Right?" Alejandro said.

"Thanks," came a voice from above.

I nearly jumped out of my skin.

There was laughter. "I'm sorry. I knew you were coming, and I turned the camera on—it has a microphone component. I'll be right down."

I waited in surprised silence.

The door swung open to reveal a tall, thin, seemingly white woman with a distinctly retro, 1950-ish aesthetic—but with multiple piercings in her ears, face, and, I had to assume, tongue. Though she looked to be no older than her midthirties, something about her sophisticated demeanor led me to believe she was probably in her late forties or early fifties and was either genetically gifted or had a great surgeon, or both. Probably both.

"Please, come in—Olivia and Alejandro?"

I nodded.

"I was just enjoying a gin and tonic, if you'd like one," she said, gesturing. "And," she added, stopping to chuckle softly, "I'm so glad you're impressed by my house. I am too. I inherited it—but not from family. From a husband who died." She yawned. "Unexpectedly, of course."

"Of course," I responded, taking the gothic dream of an interior in. There were rococo black chandeliers dripping with Edison bulbs, more gargoyles, black-and-teak end tables, and a large, winding black wood staircase in the foyer. Almost every piece of furniture looked antique—divans, couches upholstered in black velvet, and, of course, numerous mirrors of all sizes in burnished woods or ceramics.

Alejandro ran one finger across the alabaster sculpture of what looked to be a tall man of African descent—but in Greek style.

Cat observed him appreciating the sculpture. Then, "He almost looks like you. Though you're a touch more . . . exotic."

"I'm Mexican and Black," he said with a sigh, preempting her inevitable question. We were both used to it, and the word *exotic.*

"Ah. Well, please, come this way—why don't we talk in the drawing room. I love that phrase, don't you?" Cat asked.

Before I could open my mouth to respond, she added, "Mind if I smoke?" And without waiting for a response, she pulled a silver case out of the pocket of her slim black skirt and lit up with an equally old and ornate lighter.

"Want one?"

"No, but thank you. I've always admired smokers."

Alejandro snorted.

She cocked her head, clearly sniffing for sarcasm, and, not finding any, laughed pleasantly. "Aren't you an entertaining one. Unlike your sister, if you'll pardon me for saying so," she said, taking a breath of her slim cigarette and opening a set of art deco double doors. "She was wonderfully smart, but a bit morose for my taste."

I nodded curtly. Alejandro gave me a look, and we sat on the settee that she gestured toward. I wondered at the kind of person who would decorate her house like a vampire but find my sister to be morose.

The smoke wasn't unpleasant, as the cigarette was a sweet-smelling clove, and the windows were open, allowing the scent of the lavender and lilac planted out front to waft in. I felt a buzz in my pocket and glanced down at my phone. I frowned. It was Josh, texting from yet another go-phone, asking if I wanted lunch. I blocked the number and apologized. He was worryingly persistent, but I couldn't think about that now.

Cat went over to a fancy art deco copper-and-black drink tray, and after turning to get the okay from both of us, began the process of putting our drinks together.

"I have so much to tell you about your sister, but you first," she said playfully, after handing us our drinks and sitting down. She cocked her head at me thoughtfully. "You're cute, by the way. Like girls?" She crossed one long leg over the other, shifting her skirt with a finger in a smooth, sophisticated motion.

That was fast. "Sometimes," I responded. "But okay. I'll go first."

This woman was tricky. I wasn't sure she was hiding anything per se, but she liked to fuck with people, that much was clear. But it was also clear that she knew something. That she was worth the risk.

"The Brown Palace called me not long ago."

Alejandro settled back.

Cat nodded, took a few more puffs, and twisted her cigarette out in the ashtray. "Do tell."

I told her everything, even though I'd signed an NDA with the Brown. I knew that she wouldn't give anything up if I didn't.

"Can't say I'm surprised," she said, lighting another cigarette and sitting back. "People made fun of the Sacred 36 but he—they, I mean—they were powerful. I saw things . . ." Her dark eyes grew distant. "That you wouldn't believe. Things I'd certainly never believed in before my involvement. You know the Sacred 36 believes the Brown sits on a sort of nexus?"

I had known that. The nexus was once a sacred Cheyenne site.

"And if you don't already know, Mrs. Stillwell was involved in the occult—that's how the Sacred 36 began. She also had a real interest in Native Americans, despite her very wealthy New York pedigree. She believed—and they do too—that the original inhabitants of this area knew something about where the Brown was built, that it had energy from another world."

There it was.

"The Sacred 36 believes that Mrs. Stillwell was able to move," she continued, ". . . if you will . . . into a world adjacent to ours, and that's why we can see her in that mirror."

"Wow," Alejandro said.

"That's a lot to take in. I'm not sure if I believe that," I said.

She shrugged. Then, "You've seen your dead sister in a mirror. I'd think you might."

I sighed, the guilt pushing up inside me, piling into my stomach. I pushed it back. Sipped at my drink. "Ghosts are one thing. But other worlds?" I knew she was telling the truth. But I also knew that subtly doubting people made them tell you things they wouldn't otherwise tell you, in order to prove their point.

"Even physicists believe in other worlds."

"It's all theory, though."

She shrugged again.

"Will you tell me now? What you wanted to tell me about my sister?"

"Can't you guess?" she answered.

I sighed. Slippery. Playful. But in a way that made me very, very uneasy.

"Look, I'm not trying to be insensitive here, but we conducted a ceremony—your sister had been picked to try to break the curse, break into the other world. Obviously," she said, looking into my eyes as she drew smoke, "it worked."

# Chapter Twenty

I stood up. "Picked?" I could feel my heart hammering in my chest. It almost hurt.

Cat looked up at me. "Didn't you hear what I said?"

"Did you dumb bitches kill her?" Alejandro said, standing up with me, a note of aggressive hysteria in his voice. He was really leaning over her, his eyes narrowed. Alejandro and my sister had been close. So close that they'd gone out in high school, before he admitted to himself that he was gay. So close that he'd called me up whenever Naiche and I had fought, helping us to reconcile. So close that except for my mother, except for me, the only one more eaten up by guilt and remorse and pure, unadulterated pain over her death was Alejandro. He had loved her.

Up until now, I had never wanted to punch a woman more than I wanted to punch Cat.

Cat went silent for a moment, looking up at us. "Perhaps there's a misunderstanding here. In addition to the fact that I have security of my own. So . . . sit back down," she said, two large, beefy men appearing at the door to the drawing room. "And we can continue our civilized discussion. That's the first option."

Alejandro looked at the men. He was big. I often joked about his guns being more like cannons. And I was no shrinking violet. But they probably had weapons. Not that I didn't own weapons myself, but did I really want to start that kind of thing? And when it came down to it, I wanted to hear what this woman had to say. I took a deep breath.

"Mrs. Lambert?" one of them asked. The bigger one, if you could say that—they both looked like if skyscrapers weightlifted.

"The second option is you leave," she said, going over to the drink cart and pouring herself another gin and tonic. "There is no third option, I'm afraid."

She turned to us. "Another drink?"

I sat. "Yes, thank you." I motioned for Alejandro to sit as well. Reluctantly, he did, and Cat nodded at her men. They left.

"Look, I have a certain deadpan manner," she said, turning back to the cart. "I don't mean any harm. I liked your sister, despite her lack of a sense of humor. And what you need to understand is that I'm no longer in the Sacred 36," she said, artfully clasping ice cubes with a pair of delicate silver tongs and placing them in cups. "I didn't like what happened to your sister—to Naiche—one bit. It's why I left. They're dangerous. I don't want a damned thing to do with them, ever again. But I was willing to talk to you. Because I admired your sister, like I said. I think they wronged her, though to be fair, you should know that technically, at least, it was her choice." She paused. "Or at least she felt it was. Dorian—well, he can be very persuasive."

Dorian. That rang a bell.

"I can see you recognize the name. His full name is Dorian Stillwell. He's the head—if you can call him that—of the Sacred 36. He organizes everything. He's savage—if you'll pardon the term. He nearly got me killed on a number of occasions. And of course, he was responsible, even if indirectly, in my opinion, for your sister's death. And yes, he's *that* Stillwell's descendant. The one and only original haunt of room 904."

She handed us our drinks, and I took mine gratefully. She sipped at hers, sat back, one arm draped casually around the top of her couch, one finger stroking the velvet thoughtfully, her gaze somehow piercing yet managing to appear relaxed. Her eyes were brown, but there were sparks of green throughout.

"The thing you need to understand about Dorian is that he's clever and funny—you don't even realize he's manipulating you until it's far, far too late. I was just lucky that, despite my obvious charms, he found me, in all honesty, to be quite boring."

I found that hard to believe.

"Oh. And he looks like if Edgar Allan Poe and an Abercrombie and Fitch model had a baby," she said, tittering, her eyes narrowing thoughtfully. She almost looked sleepy in that moment, but it was clear she was assessing me. Assessing if I was worth the trouble, if I was interesting enough. "The thing is," she said, "I can tell you where he hangs out—or where he used to hang out."

I sat up. Surely he would know something about how to reverse the whole process—move my sister out of that other world—pull the curse off my mother, if he'd been the one to replace Mrs. Stillwell with my sister. If he'd been responsible for trapping her there in the first place, which was quite a feat, considering how long Mrs. Stillwell's tenure in the mirror had been. Well, unless they were in there together. Wherever "there" was.

"Yes, please," I said.

She smiled. "Isn't that phrase appealing? Especially coming from your pretty mouth."

I had the feeling this woman had heard "yes, please" many, many times in her life.

"You could show me?" I asked. "Take me around maybe?"

"Oh, sweetie, like I said, I don't want anything to do with the Sacred 36, and specifically Dorian, ever again. I understand why you need to pursue this, what with your mother and all—not that I can relate, I never cared for mine—but I can't do this with you. Though your company would certainly please me," she said, pulling a finger up the velvet.

Slippery.

I closed my eyes in disappointment. Took a breath. Opened them back up and smiled. I had to appeal to this woman's ego—her desire to see me beg. "I don't see how I can gain access to the right places, people—gain this Dorian's trust without you. He must have adored you, and as smart as I think I am—honestly, without you, I'm lost."

"Oh, honey, he's not going to want to see me ever again. You see," she said, picking her hands off her lap and lighting another cigarette, "the last time he saw me, I had a knife at his throat. I was trying to murder him."

## Chapter Twenty-One

The combination to my safe was, predictably, my sister's birthday. I punched it in, feeling the exhaustion, the sheer, miserable disappointment of the day flood into me. I had the name of the club—predictably, the Church—where Dorian and other members of the Sacred 36 spent their time, but it would take me eons to get somewhere without Cat's presence. I'd tried to push her on that whole tried-to-murder-Dorian business, but she'd refused to budge. Kept telling me that maybe she'd tell me the full story someday, when I was ready, whatever *that* meant, but there was nothing I could say, or do, to get her physically involved.

I'd texted her a day after we'd met, told her that if she really wanted to help me, she'd come with me to the Church. She'd responded with an eye roll emoji around midnight. I'd sighed heavily and rolled over in bed, frustrated, combing my brain to come up with something that would motivate her.

I punched the last number in the combination and opened the safe. Every night, I made sure the gun was unloaded, spinning the chamber of the weapon. I touched it for reassurance before I slid it inside the box, the cold, glossy metal simultaneously comforting and terrifying. Alejandro hated it. I couldn't blame him. But the gun was staying.

Yesterday, I'd tried Cat again, really laying on the guilt. She'd responded at 3:00 A.M. *Really? You think that kind of thing works with me? No way darling, not even when it comes to a girl as adorable as you. I despise the 36.*

I'd gotten up for a middle-of-the-night vodka tonic then.

I sighed, closing the tiny door of the safe. At least Cat had had a picture of Dorian. It was years old, but I felt sure I'd recognize him. I pulled my favorite pink silky pajamas on and folded myself into bed. I was half asleep, my mind moving over thoughts of my mother, when my mind flashed with a realization, and I sat bolt upright.

I pulled the phone off the side table, yanking the cord out hard enough to break it, and clicked airplane mode off.

*Don't you want revenge? On Dorian?* I texted, my heart thumping in my chest.

For a while there, I thought she might not be up. Or that she'd had enough of me. Or perhaps that I'd gone too far. But then I saw the three dots, and my heart pumped harder, so hard I felt like I could hear blood rushing in my ears.

The dots disappeared.

"Goddamnit!" I yelled, and then clapped my hand over my mouth. I didn't want to wake Alejo up. The dots reappeared, and I clutched the phone. They disappeared. Then they reappeared again.

"Come on, Cat," I said. "Work with me."

Finally, she texted back. *How would I get that?*

"Yes!" I yelled, and I could hear Alejo groaning loudly from his room. "Sorry!" I yelled.

"It's okay," he said, sleep lining his voice. "Just shut up, okay?"

I turned back to the phone. *If I can prove he had something to do with Naiche's death, he could go to jail. And I know I'd have a better chance of proving that if you were along for the ride,* I texted.

Silence.

"Fuuuck," I whispered.

Then dots. Then they disappeared.

"This bitch," I said, shaking my head.

The dots reappeared. Then, *Baby, you drive a hard bargain.*

I could feel my skin go electric. If she'd really tried to murder him, she hated this guy. There was no way she didn't want revenge. And I could serve it up on a platter.

*So?* I texted.

The Church was bustling that time of night, the lights dim, the inside of the church-turned-nightclub dark—but the neon strobes were floating, strange little angels, above our heads.

Cat had me by the hand. She'd insisted I come alone.

I wondered if Dorian would even be there. Cat had reassured me, patting her gigantic forties-style coif—her aesthetic for the evening, complete with 1940s-era clothing—that he was there almost every night. I had no idea what that meant. If he didn't own the place—and he didn't—how could he be there every night? Cat told me he had business there. An office.

An office?

Corpse's "POLTERGEIST!" was pounding out through the speakers, a dark, erotic reverberation beating its way into the most secret parts of my body. The pull on my hand became urgent, and I tried to gently push dancers out of the way without causing their drinks to spill, and I was caught, temporarily, in between a couple—two women with shaved heads—who did not see me trying to get around them, my hand breaking from Cat's grasp. Cat had slipped through them, her form tall and imposing yet almost seeming to become part of their dancing for a moment, effortlessly—but I had been unable to complete the act, move with her, and she had to turn around, place her slim hand on one of their shoulders, slide them away from each other, and lead me through.

"This way," she mouthed, her red lips curving into a lovely little smile.

At the back of the Church, there was a short, pretty woman with facial piercings identical to Cat's. Cat leaned in, the woman frowning as she grew closer, but after listening to whatever Cat whispered in her ear, she looked around furtively and then pushed at an ornate outcropping, which slid left in the near darkness, revealing a black tunnel.

Cat smiled and walked in. It was clear I was expected to follow.

The darkness swallowed me.

Inside, I could see that the floors were lit up on the sides along the bottom, just enough to see the way forward. I'd half expected torches flickering on either side.

"He's always here. In his office."

I followed Cat, and shortly, we came to a door. She knocked.

"Come in." It was a deep voice, made dim by the thick wood.

She twisted the knob, the heavy metal-and-wood door opening with a dusty *whoosh*. Inside was a large red velvet couch against the wall on the right, two matching chairs in front of a large black desk, an ornate black candelabra on one end. The walls were painted black, burnished metal sconces flickered with artificial candlelight, photographs of various sizes of men and women hung in opulent gold frames, and a filigreed golden fireplace anchored the room, the mantel covered in black objects: crows, a cloche holding mushrooms, another mirror, a smaller cloche. There was a chair shaped like half a birdcage with a black cat asleep on the seat, a series of dark metal birdcages at the foot. Where fake candlelight didn't light the way, Edison bulbs did. These folks were nothing but consistent when it came to their aesthetic.

The cat lifted its head briefly, then curled back into itself and closed its eyes.

A man—clearly Dorian—sat behind the desk. His face expressed shock, but quickly he tamped it down and smiled, pulling two fingers over a very Edgar Allan–esque black mustache, then down to stroke the goatee beneath, his gaze sparkling with intelligence and mischievousness. I had to admit, goth boys had never been my thing, even during my brief goth phase. But there was something about him—his pale skin contrasted with his black hair and eyes, his chiseled features, his perhaps overkill wardrobe, complete with cravat and smoking jacket in silver and dark blue—that appealed. There was a kind of gentle animal magnetism. I could see what my sister had seen in him.

"Bring any knives this time, Cat?" he asked, turning a ring with an elaborate symbol I couldn't quite make out around on his finger. I couldn't tell if his eyes were sparkling with fear, humor, or anticipation.

She laughed. "I'm fresh out, I'm afraid."

It was interesting. Their dynamic was all witty banter, but that had been genuine shock on his face when she'd come in. But he'd put it away quickly.

There were piles—upon piles—of what looked to be cocaine on the desk, neatly packaged, much of it. Some of it lay in the shallow metal cups of small scales.

Now I understood. His office.

"Please, have a seat," he said, gesturing to the two ornately carved wooden chairs placed neatly in front of the desk. As I settled in, I wondered if that was a bloodstain I spotted on one of them. This time, I'd brought my gun. I was sure he knew, as his eye went to exactly where my holster was hidden beneath my jacket as I tipped back into my seat, but he was playing it cool.

"Drink?"

"Sure. Olivia?" Cat asked.

"Sure," I echoed.

Dorian uncorked a bottle of red that he'd plucked from the built-in shelf behind the desk and poured all three of us a glass.

I watched him sip before I did.

"You look familiar," Dorian said. "Don't tell me . . . I love to guess. I love guessing games. I always win."

I smiled uneasily. I bet he did.

He stared at me for a time, stroking his mustache, his black eyes piercing. "I'll get there. I've seen a face . . . like yours. Not your face. Well. No, wait. I have seen your face. Online—in the *Denver Post*. You're that—" He paused to snap his fingers. "How lovely! You're that American Indian lady who tries to detect paranormal activity in hotels and other old buildings. I've thought about hiring you myself. I have an old house, you see, and I swear, it's full of ghosts." There was something so old-fashioned about his manner, not just his dress, his overall gothic aesthetic, but even the way he spoke.

"I—" I started, but he interrupted me.

"Wait. Don't tell me. I can see there's more. I know your face from more than the internet."

I sat back, and he continued to study me, his fingers moving over his facial hair in a rhythmic fashion. His hand stopped.

"Of course," he said, his hands erupting from his goatee and floating into the air. "Naiche—you must be her sister. Of course," he repeated softly. "I'm sorry. I adored her, truly, as I'm sure Cat has told you."

Cat snorted.

"I never . . ." he said, trailing off, his glance moving furtively to Cat and back again to me. Genuine sorrow flashed across his face, and just as quickly, was put away. "Why don't you tell me why you're here? What you want from me?" He sat back, his eyes narrowing. I could see one sensuous, long-fingered hand separate from the other to rest on his muscular leg.

"Sure. Thank you for seeing me," I said, wondering just how responsible for my sister's "suicide" this person was. I told him what I'd told Cat, what I'd witnessed at the Brown—including what I feared for my mother. I was hoping, no matter what his agenda was, he'd feel sorry for me.

"I see," he said, standing up, pacing, stroking his jet-black mustache. "I want you to understand something. When we, the Sacred 36—and we are a people who have been compelled by what we believe the Brown stands on for generations—did our *ceremony*, in, ah, the language of your people . . . we never intended for your sister to replace Mrs. Stillwell. In fact, we didn't know that she'd appeared in room 904 at all. Though we performed the ceremony around her for both dates, we'd kept her away from it on purpose—to protect her. We thought your sister could create a link to the other world. Maybe she could help Mrs. Stillwell move on, break the curse. We—I am very curious about that mirror. That room. About how Mrs. Stillwell was able to make that connection to the other world at the end of her life and commute, it seems permanently, to that mirror. We have our records, but they're incomplete. The thing is, Olivia," he said, my name curling around his tongue, "she isn't just haunting the Brown. She was able to make the mirror into some kind of portal."

"Cat tells me that Mrs. Stillwell was the originator of the Sacred 36," I said, my eyes narrowing thoughtfully, wondering what he would say next.

"She was the founding member—my great-great-grandmother," he said. "And she had a book called the *Handbook of Ceremonies* that she created with every powerful ritual you could imagine, including the relevant one in regard to your sister and the Brown. Only problem is, I can't find it." He finished with a twirl of his black mustache.

I leaned forward, hands on my knees. This was exactly as I'd thought. I had him.

"Tell me more about the book," I said.

He opened his mouth, then closed it.

"I want you to know I felt more for Naiche than just about anyone. I swear," he said, abruptly coming up to me, and, kneeling down at my feet, he looked up at me with a pleading, almost erotic expression. "She loved her mother. And you, even if you didn't believe her."

A spike of guilt struck me, and I leaned back.

"I want to help," he repeated, placing his hand over my fingers and curling it around them. A current of hot electricity passed from his skin to mine, and though I wanted to remove my hand from underneath his, I knew that if he thought he could manipulate me, I could learn more.

I could feel Cat's eyes on us, hatred radiating out of her in waves. "Good," she said venomously. "You owe her. You owe me too."

"I do owe Naiche," he said, keeping his eyes on me. "You, not so much."

She scoffed.

He massaged my hand ever so gently with one thumb, and I could feel the hot charge of sex in it. He stopped. He stood up, stared down at me. "We were only trying to break the spell, I hope you know that," he said, smiling softly, regretfully.

"Could I attend the next gathering of the Sacred 36?" I asked, my tone sweet, dulcet.

"I don't think so . . ." he said, his head cocked, his eyes holding either lust or suspicion, or both. "The people who attend are very private. And they count on me to keep that promise of privacy."

Cat stomped her foot, her eyes flashing. "Can't you let her play at your stupid little goth club? Jesus Christ, Dorian—you're responsible for her sister's death, and now you're not going to work with her so her mother doesn't die too?"

He flinched. "You know as well as I do that it's more than a club. It's dangerous. There would be consequences—for me—if I brought this delightful young lady in," he said. "As you yourself stated, look what happened when I brought Naiche."

"You really are an unadulterated cad," Cat said, her eyes narrowing with disgust. And with that, she turned tail and left, the door slamming resoundingly behind her.

"I understand," I said, standing up, purring with each syllable, circling him, one hand trailing his shoulder ever so slightly. "But don't you think you'd have a much easier time breaking this thing with me alongside?"

"Of course," he said, his eyes following my touch. "But I'm afraid . . ."

I interrupted him, sat back down on the chair in front of him. I looked up, anticipating the shock on his face when I revealed my wild card. I wasn't disappointed. "I know you're going to want to work with me. I'm pretty sure I have your *Handbook of Ceremonies*."

## Chapter Twenty-Two

I met Dorian in the lobby of the Brown, and he led me to the elevator, one hand casually reaching back, his fingers beckoning. I only hesitated a moment before I took it, and though he didn't turn around to see if I would or not, I could feel him smiling.

"Where we going?" I asked, letting go of his hand, the door closing with a kind of strange finality as it did.

He smiled mischievously, one finger reaching up to curl around his black mustache. "You'll see."

Today he was wearing a red velvet blazer over a pair of gray houndstooth slacks, a watch and fob spilling from one pocket to the next. Black-and-red paisley loafers. A soft gray T-shirt, a slim chain flowing down into the depths of it. Though it was over-the-top, I couldn't deny his appeal.

"You look nice," I said, sitting back against the wall, letting him know that I was appraising him.

"Ditto," he said, his gaze moving down to my favorite gray boots and back up again with a Mephistophelian smile, and a shudder passed unbidden through my body. I'd worn a tight black tank tucked into a black satin miniskirt, an ornate pair of beaded earrings I'd bought from an Anishinaabe artist I loved online in my lobes.

He waited until we were alone in the elevator and came up close, one hand casually resting above my head, pressing into the wall above me, though he was only a few inches taller, his hips swinging slowly to almost meet mine.

"I—"

"Hold on," he said, hitting the emergency stop button.

I'd thought the alarm would sound, but there was nothing but silence. He leaned back a bit, and as I peered upward, he pulled a near invisible panel open where his hand had been resting moments before.

I scooted out from under him, allowing him room to work. "You could've warned me."

He shrugged. "I could've. But here's the thing," he said, sidling up to me and pushing one hand in his pocket. He pulled a silken red eye mask out and dangled it on one finger in front of my face. "You need to wear this if we're going to keep going."

"A bit early for that kind of request, isn't it?" I teased.

He laughed. "Humor me." He pulled it over my head and adjusted it tightly over my eyes. He took my hand.

"No peeking," he said, a finger stroking my palm.

"Never," I responded, but I could see through a tiny sliver on the left side.

The panel he'd been fooling with had three bright green buttons. He'd depressed the one in the middle, and the elevator had started up again, almost feeling like it wasn't going up or down but in an entirely different direction altogether, though I knew that couldn't be.

After a few minutes, it bounced to a stop, and the doors slid open to reveal a hallway in art deco designs of black and gold, two thick lines sliding up the walls and separating. A flash of early Lynch came to mind, his strange inner landscapes, his obsession with fifties noir.

Dorian pulled me gently but firmly after him.

At the end of the hallway was an ornate black door—reminding me of the one in the escape room that I'd gone to with Victoria and Sara. Though that had been days ago, it felt like eons.

He pulled the mask off my face, and I readjusted my hair.

Dorian walked in front of me and, pulling out an ornate silver key, unlocked the door. I felt as if I'd entered a fae underworld. It was a large, cavernous room, the size of a ballroom, with vaulted ceilings painted in golds, blacks, reds, and silvers—strange landscapes with wolves and what looked to be various cryptids, some with red eyes, looking like various incarnations of Bigfoot, some like Windigos. There were dark pools, mirrors, and, of course, the murals included Native Americans of all nations in traditional dress. There were plants everywhere, all of which seemed to be growing out of the walls: black mambas, petunias and violets, a blanket of black velvet alocasia, and black lilies.

There was a theater of sofas, black velvet. Tall ornate candelabras with immense black candles burning in them. And, in the middle, what looked to be an altar of some sort, though it appeared to double as a podium, and exactly thirty-five other people in attendance, some in masks (though these had eyeholes) themselves, all of them chatting quietly as the door opened, heads turning to look at me, an uneasy silence falling as we walked in, an awkward broken chatter quickly replacing it.

Dorian escorted me to a couch, gestured for me to sit, and sat down close beside me, one finger trailing softly down my left arm.

"You have to remember," he said, his expression turning earnest, "your sister was much beloved here. And you look so much like her."

I nodded, though I didn't really think I did. Perhaps to them.

"Did you bring it?" he asked.

I nodded again and reached for my satchel, pulled *Ghostland* out, and extended it to Dorian, who took it gingerly and turned it around a few times, sniffing as he opened it up. He began fingering through its pages.

He looked up at me abruptly. "I want you to know, we respect Native culture and history. We invite Native activists, historians, every year to speak on local issues we can help with. We give to the American Indian College Fund."

I took a deep, hitching breath and adjusted on my seat. "Perfect angels, huh?"

He laughed, his head tipping back. "Now, I wouldn't say that." He pulled his jacket off, revealing the pale, curved muscles underneath.

It was my turn to laugh. Uneasily.

"I'll be right back," he said, his fingertip stopping in its motion and tapping. I watched him go, the crowd parting for him, folks stopping him here and there, looking back at me. A few of them toasted me as they did, though as of yet I had nothing to toast back with. Dorian remedied that by returning with two drinks in hand. A glass of red wine for me, and for himself, an amber concoction in a crystal glass.

"As you can see," I said, clearing my throat, "the book appears to be a collection of stories."

"So you think this," he said, gesturing to the book, "is some sort of mirage?"

"I do."

"And what makes you think it's Luella Stillwell's *Handbook of Ceremonies*?"

"Well," I said carefully, thoughtfully, and then I told him about how I'd gotten the book at Regina's apartment, what had happened there. And then how the Ouija board had come to me. That his ancestor had spoken through it, telling me that I had the book.

"There's just one problem," I said.

"Oh?" he asked.

"My assistant and I threw some of the most powerful deglamourizing ceremonies imaginable at the thing—it's policy in our paranormal domicile."

"I see," he said, his head cocking thoughtfully.

"As I'm sure you know, quite a few objects turn out to be something other than what they appear. But not *Ghostland*. It stayed exactly as it came to us."

He sighed heavily.

"The book did belong to your ancestor, so perhaps one of your ceremonies would work. After all, that's a powerful connection. And Luella's father—your ancestor—participated in the Massacre, which seems to be at the center of all of this. I have to assume the book connects to it in some way."

He sighed again. I wasn't sure if he'd known that was something that *I* knew. "Yes, though the 36 don't understand the connection entirely. Just bits and pieces." He smiled at me sheepishly. "We'll work on this together, then?"

"We will."

"You hear from Cat, by the way?" he asked, looking down at the book, clearly trying to sound casual.

"Did you two . . . ?" I started.

"Once. Long ago. And though she broke up with me," he said with a gentle sigh, followed by a modest sip of his wine, "she's somehow never let me forget it."

"I get that," I said, rolling my eyes, thinking of Josh. His texting. Showing up where I was. I slipped my phone out of the pocket of my blazer, but there was nothing beyond a few junk emails popping up. I slid it back in and smiled uneasily.

Dorian was clearly curious but said nothing. He seemed to be graceful that way, polite, for all of his animallike secrecy.

He clapped his hands down on his knees in a dad-like gesture. "Well. Why don't I introduce you around?" He pulled me up with one hand and curved his arm around my back as we moved.

"This is Kathia. She knew your sister well," he said, pushing me gently over to a short, muscular woman in a cream-colored pair of slacks and a matching white button-down, her face wearing an expression that was sophisticated, guarded. She smiled, spoke of my sister's moods. Her phobias. Her brilliance.

"I came over to her apartment many a day, insisted she get out of bed, take a shower. Get to work," Kathia said.

I felt guilt burn in the pit of my stomach. I knew she hadn't left her depression behind entirely, but I guess I'd assumed that the last round of rehab and the Zoloft had mainly taken care of it. It was clear that she'd been too embarrassed to show me the truth. I'd been so ambitious then—I'd published paper after paper in *Psychology Today,* other journals. I tried to console myself, tell myself that depression not only hadn't been my specialty, but it was something, until my sister died anyway, I had simply not experienced in an extended or deep way. But as Kathia launched into a story about a particular moment of insight that my sister had had about, of all things, mortality, one that had really hit Kathia hard—I couldn't help but feel the guilt deepen. I shouldn't have been so cavalier. Maybe if I hadn't, she'd be here now. I'd thought I could control the situation. That I understood it.

Kathia could see the guilt in my eyes and squeezed my shoulder. "We—well, we should've been more careful with the ceremony." Here, she flicked her eyes over at Dorian, who I thought shook his head, nearly imperceptibly.

Was he hiding something? Or did he just want to spare my feelings?

"We didn't understand the profound effect it would have. And I think . . ." Dorian said, draining the rest of his wine, "since we didn't have the original ceremony, we were doomed to fail. I just wanted to allow Naiche a space to communicate with Luella. Tell us what lay beyond the portal, the mirror—how she'd gotten trapped. Why, beyond the little we know about it being an ancient ceremonial site, it had such power. And more than anything, I hoped we'd break the curse. But she was too vulnerable, and I too ambitious."

I felt my heart twist with sympathy. "I blame myself too."

"Another round?" he asked.

I nodded. But then something strange happened. Everyone in the room, except for Dorian and me, stilled completely.

"He's here," Dorian whispered, his eyes shutting briefly.

# Chapter Twenty-Three

A cruel blue wind began to blow through the chamber, turning everything to ice, both Dorian and I shivering violently. The rich, acrid smell of blood and sulfur turned the air foul, the sound of screams from children and women gathering in the corners of the room. The rest of the 36 remained immobile, as if they were carved out of marble.

"Who, Dorian? Who's here?" I asked, my teeth chattering.

The presence was strong, full of masculine rage. I could see it coalescing around Dorian, a black shadow.

*You*, it said venomously, the form becoming clearer, its fury so intense it knocked me back. I tried to peer into the shadow, but it was as if I was looking through milk glass.

"Who is it, Dorian?" I asked again. "I can't help you unless you tell me."

"Luella's father. John Chivington. My ancestor."

A violent shudder pulsed through my entire body. The leader of the Massacre.

*Indiannn,* it said with venom in its voice, and to my horror the form became clear. It moved through the void, a strange, dark heart moving in and out of Dorian's chest, blowing outward. A man in soldier's regalia, its face distorted, almost zombielike, its mouth cracked into a yawn of unnatural fury. *Indiannn,* it repeated, its mouth salivating as it did.

I locked my hand onto Dorian's shoulder. "Dorian," I said. "Stay calm."

"I can feel him on me," Dorian said, "his breath, when I'm half asleep, I—"

I pushed Dorian into one of the plush velvet chairs and sat down next to him.

*Mine,* it said, its mouth opening again, great gobs of ectoplasmic spittle falling down its chin. It put its ghostly hands onto Dorian's shoulders, trying to push mine off—or was it trying to get into me too?

*Savages,* Chivington said, *give power.*

"You found a way to cling to your descendants, didn't you?" I asked Chivington. "A way to haunt them, still hungry for power—even in the afterlife."

The thing's eyes grew black, and inky snakes looped out and around its spectral head.

*You are the source of power,* it said, hunger in its voice, its eyes flashing brightly, its mouth flooding with spectral saliva.

It was my turn to shudder.

I stood up, put my hands out, palms up. I began my prayers.

"Grandmother, protect me from this spirit," I said. "Give his great-great-great-grandson the power to push him away. The power to be forgiven."

*Forgiven!* Chivington screamed indignantly, its ghostly face inches from mine, an icy wind blowing from its spectral body, its eyes black and full of fire.

I began to shiver, and the wind grew so intense I had to work to keep standing. I planted my feet firmly, working my thigh muscles as hard as I could.

"Sever, separado, cut this line and free this man," I said, pulling a string from my coat and severing it as I did.

The ghost screamed and flew into Dorian, Dorian's body going rigid and then still. The room grew silent, warmer. I worried Dorian had lost control, his skin already beginning to grow bluer by the minute, his eyes opening with a kind of fury I felt sure wasn't emanating from Dorian but from his murderous ancestor. However, Dorian's arms began to shake, hard, and then his mouth opened, a shout of "No, leave me! I don't want what you want!" coming from his upturned lips. Dorian's body vibrated, and the wind stopped, giving ground to an almost ominous stillness, my body knocking forward violently. I recovered my balance just as the room went dark, the blue light of the dead illuminating Dorian's body like a candle seconds later, one that went out in a flash through the ceiling as with a whistle of fury, Chivington departed.

## Chapter Twenty-Four

Dorian was pushing a very full glass of red wine into my palm, and I was gratefully accepting it. Though Dorian was already vampire-pale, somehow, during the night's misadventures, he'd managed to move to a near-pearlescence, one hand around a glass of what looked like whiskey. It had been a lot, and I felt wrung out, raw. I needed to get home, curl into my bed and not exist, with the help of a little trazodone. I'd already had to answer Alejandro's multiple concerned calls and texts. I'd told him I was okay, there had been a thing with a nasty genocidal colonel, but that I'd handled it and was fine, and would be home soon. He'd answered, *Just don't fuck Dorian*. I'd responded with a resounding *LOL*. He'd texted again to make sure I'd be okay on my own and told me he'd found a hottie from Arvada to spend the night with, a guy he'd boned a few times.

"Gay-dad okay?" Dorian asked, a bemused expression on his face, one hand stroking his black goatee. The whiskey seemed to have helped him, added a little color to his face.

"How'd you know I call him that?" I asked, sitting up on the red velvet divan a little straighter.

He put one finger out a touch near me, just far enough away—

but just close enough to light a little charge, despite the evening's trauma. Cat had been right, there was something magnetic about him. "I just know," he said, laughing.

"You okay?" I asked. I wondered how Chivington had gotten his hooks into Dorian so effectively without Dorian letting him, inviting him in.

He looked down at his lap. Then back up. "I am. I've been dealing with it for a long time. It wants to fill me with hate. But I'm not like that," he said, a smile on his lips.

I decided to let it drop and moved toward him, just a bit, on the couch.

"So, when my sister . . . died, and you and Cat argued," I said, trying to put it as diplomatically as I could, "she just lit out? Or . . . ?"

Dorian had been stroking the velvet and paused, clearly relieved that I was changing the subject. "Slipped out like the kitty cat that she is. Typical of the wealthy. Everything intrigues them—at first. And then they get bored. And then they get mean, or in her case, they scratch," he said, raising his fingers into a claw and scratching at the air.

I chuckled, and Dorian smiled at me, cocking his head.

Despite what Dorian had just said, I'd recollected Cat saying something about inheriting her wealth from an ex—but of course, I didn't know her as well as he did. He was from generational wealth himself, so I considered his wry observation about the wealthy to be an unintentional warning about himself.

I sighed. Drained the rest of my cup. "I should probably go."

"Stay for a few minutes. I know we planned on working on the book, but I'm beat," he said, spreading one palm outward. "And I enjoy your company."

I smiled. "Okay." It was clear he didn't want to be alone.

"I can tell you're thinking of your sister," he said softly.

"All the time," I responded.

"She was so sensitive," he said, looking off and then back, resuming his stroking once more. "She was wonderful to be around. But hard too."

I felt a lump form in my throat. God, how he had known her.

"One time—" He stopped. "Is it okay that I tell you this?"

I nodded. It probably wasn't, but I was in control. Mainly.

"We'd been trying something, a new ceremony. Attempting to communicate with Luella, to prevent the next cycle. But though some people have seen her in between cycles, we never did. Naiche was exhausted. I was too. And she talked about the first time she saw something. She was five. She said she always tried to crawl into bed with you, but you didn't like her to."

A spike of guilt hit me.

"Sorry if I hit a nerve," he said gently, putting one hand on my shoulder and squeezing.

"It's okay, go on." I leaned into his hand, and he began to lightly stroke my hair.

"It was a shadow figure. By her bed."

"Hat man," I said, nodding slowly, and his caresses paused.

"Yes, that's what she called it. Turns out lots of people have seen him. Wild. Anyway, she said that you called her. Right when she was most afraid. Like you knew. And it dissipated. As if the sound of your voice struck fear into it. That stuck with me."

I remembered that. I'd woken up in the middle of the night. I'd been having a nightmare about Naiche. Something monstrous was trying to eat her. And not just eat her, disappear her very essence into its furry black maw. I had woken up, asked her if she was okay. After a few minutes, she'd responded. Said she was okay now that I was awake.

I closed my eyes. "I should've listened."

"Hey," Dorian said, scooting closer to me. "We all have those regrets. God knows I do. We share that, about her."

"Still," I said, pushing tears down. I hated crying in front of others. However, despite my efforts, a few droplets escaped my lids.

"Now, now," he said, pushing his thumb gently onto my cheeks, the hard muscles in his arms going round, working to artfully pull me onto his lap. "Don't do this to yourself."

I wasn't sure I trusted him. In fact, I was pretty sure I shouldn't, but I also figured at the least if I led him on, maybe he'd lead *me* to something having to do with my sister's death and, hopefully, to saving my mother. Plus, he was hot, and I was strong. I could handle it. I melted into him. He held me. And when I pulled back, he kept my gaze. It was like a pulsing, intense thing was in between us, and when he went to kiss me, I let him.

An hour later, I was cracking open the door to my apartment, smiling. Dorian and I had kissed, then he'd petted me until I purred like a cat. But then he'd held my hand, and I'd curled into him for a while. And like a gentleman, he'd told me good night.

The minute I walked into the living room, I knew something was off.

"Olivia?" It was Josh's voice.

I reached for my holster, forgetting I'd left my gun at home. In my safe.

# Chapter Twenty-Five

The hair on the back of my neck spiked, and I worked to gain control, stay silent. I'd been taking martial arts for years. In fact, I was a black belt. However, though I had a nice proportion of fat to muscle, I was also much smaller than Josh and had no idea if he was armed. Or how he'd gotten into my apartment. Maybe I could just slip back out the way I came, before—

He came around the corner fast, tucking something into the back of his pants as he did, his blue button-down half undone, a large hank of hair over one eye. He was red-faced, his expression goofy. But his hands were clutching, spasming really, at his sides.

I grounded myself, keeping my tone natural. "What're you doing here, Josh?"

"We need to talk," he said, swinging one arm around me and pushing my hair back. "And I knew that Alejandro," he said, his tone turning venomous, "wouldn't let me in."

He was skipping over the part where I wouldn't have let him in either, and the part where he must've watched our place until he saw Alejo leave. My heart was knocking against my chest, but I kept calm, let him keep his arm around me. Much as I hated his fucking guts, I had to keep it chill. I was simultaneously glad Alejandro had found a hookup for the night (at least he'd be safe) and wished desperately that he hadn't.

"Let's sit down," Josh said, taking my hand.

I tried to hide the wave of revulsion I felt with his clammy fingers around mine and let him lead me into the living room, settle us on the couch.

"Sorry about just coming in here like this," he said, running one slim-fingered hand through his hair, pulling the lank piece back up into his well-coiffed blond cut.

He wasn't sorry.

He began gently massaging the back of my neck, and I fantasized, briefly, about what it would be like if I were holding a knife and I were able to bring it down sharply into the meat of his hand. "I know why you pushed me away," he said, "well, beyond your clear commitment-phobia." He chuckled affably.

I stopped myself from rolling my eyes. "Oh?" I asked, sitting back, relaxing one arm across the edge of the couch to put him off his guard and, hopefully, to gently offset his massaging.

"Good, you're listening," he said.

I stood up rapidly, squared my shoulders, planted both feet firmly on the ground, and brought one hand swiftly toward his neck. I thought, for a second, I might have him, but he was quick—he caught my hand, stood up, and twisted my arm behind my back.

I tried not to make a sound, though it hurt like hell.

"You don't want to do that, Olivia," he said, growling, his lips on my neck. "I know the combination to your gun safe."

I went cold.

The chuckle came back, but this time there was an animal edge to it. "Your sister's birthday."

"How did you know that?" I squeaked out, my blood running cold.

I could feel the gun then, my own gun, the hard metal poking into my kidney. He threw me down onto the couch. I looked up at him, his face red, sweaty, his blue eyes like blackened clouds. He plucked the gun out from the back of his pants.

"You know how," he said, shaking his head, his words punctuated by his tapping the gun in his left hand. I winced. If he didn't have the safety on, he could blow a hole right into one of my vital areas. I liked my vital areas. I wanted to keep them.

He rolled his eyes. "Really. Don't play coy, Olivia. It's not a good look."

"You ass," I said, regretting the words as soon as they left my lips.

He lifted the gun, pointed it at my chest.

"I'm the ass? I am?"

"Look," I said, resisting the urge to raise my hands in a defensive gesture, "I genuinely don't know how you know my sister's birthday." And yet, even as I said this, it slowly dawned on me, what he was implying. "You knew her?"

He let out a wet, exasperated sigh. "I *know* you know, Olivia. And I know now that Alejandro must have told you we went out. And that's why you broke it off with me," he said, brushing his hair back again. "I should've told you, but I didn't want it to be weird."

"No, I didn't know," I said, my expression apparently sincere enough to convince Josh that I was telling the truth.

"You really didn't?" Josh asked.

"No," I responded.

He lowered the gun, just a touch.

"She . . . showed me pictures of you. Told me about how smart and ambitious you were," he said, his mouth trembling into a small smile. "I knew you were my type. What I deserved. And I like women your . . . coloring," he said.

I stopped myself from rolling my eyes.

"But don't you get it?"

"Get what?" I asked.

"Alejandro."

"What about Alejandro?" I asked, my brow furrowing.

"He's the one who murdered your sister."

## Chapter Twenty-Six

My mind reeled. I felt, for a moment, that I might pass out. I bit the side of my mouth, regained control. Then, "Why would Alejandro kill Naiche? He loved her."

"That weird group she belonged to, the 36? He belonged to them first. He brought her in. I know all about their stupid obsession. She talked about it endlessly—God, she was boring. It was Alejandro who convinced her to die in that room. Think about it. Who else could've gotten her to go along with it?"

"Bullshit," I whispered.

"Ask him about it then," he said, his gaze piercing. "He was trying to get her out of the way and what the 36 had planned for her was a perfect excuse—I have that on good authority. You and Naiche were too close. No one could get in between you two." His expression went black then.

I took a deep breath. "We were."

He sighed, a long, windy sigh full of desire and resignation, and piled next to me, his blue eyes staring into my black. "Finally, you're listening—"

I formed both hands into a thick fist and brought it sideways, hard, into his windpipe.

He made a sharp choking noise and tried to sit up, and I slammed my doubled-up fist into the hand that held the gun, the metal skittering hard and fast into a corner. I stood up, his body clattering to the floor like an oversize toy, and I ran for the gun.

His hand clapped on my ankle, his breath staccato, and I fell hard onto the left side of my face, my nose exploding with pain, adrenaline the only thing keeping me from curling into a ball. I could feel blood rushing down my cheeks as I whipped around to face him, his grasp still tight around my ankle. With my other leg, I kicked him square in the cheekbone, my shoe connecting with the sharp, handsome planes of his face with a satisfyingly crisp noise, blood now streaming down his face, his hands wrapping protectively over it.

I laughed, blood falling into my mouth. With my ankle free, I scrambled up as quick as I could.

I ran for the gun.

He was still unable to speak, though I thought I heard an attempt at "bitch" juttering out of his lips as he tried to climb up onto his feet behind me, his legs, thankfully, collapsing out from under him.

I knew I better hurry.

The gun had slid under our drink cart, and I had to get down on my knees, a position I knew Josh favored, to reach for it. One finger hit the metal, but I only managed to knock it farther under the cart.

"Fuck," I said, pushing forward, Josh's hand clapping right around my ankle once more, his breath already hot against the back of my neck.

I lunged forward with one last spurt of effort, hitting my head on the top of the cart as I did. My hands wrapped around the gun, and I kicked again, this time hitting his shoulder. He squealed, and I was able to scoot out from under the cart and stand up.

I stood over him, panting, blood running down my face, both hands on the gun, and pointed it right at his face. "You're right, I am a bitch."

He glared at me, a combination of rage and hurt on his bloodied face. He made a move to get up, and I shook my head.

"I will shoot you," I said, cocking the hammer back. He stilled.

My left hand released the piece to slip into my pocket, my eyes on Josh as it did. I dialed 911.

"And my sister wasn't boring, you unbearable narcissistic shit," I said, jetting forward and clocking him in the head before he could figure out what I was doing. He passed out, and I tried not to, the sound of sirens gaining ground, the flash of blue and red leaking into the lurid orange glare of the city lights.

# Chapter Twenty-Seven

"I'm going to chip you like a cat," Alejandro said. He'd just finished mopping Josh's—and my—blood off the floor and was standing above me, one hand holding the rag he'd used to clean in his clenched palm. I'd offered, but he'd told me to sit, ice my face.

"Really, Dad?" I responded, one hand around a glass of wine, the other over the rest of my face.

Alejandro paused in walking to the laundry room, his hands on his hips. "I should be your dad," he said, his voice breaking.

My face fell, and I felt my lower lip tremble.

He closed his eyes, his whole body wilting. "I'm sorry," he said, opening his eyes. "I didn't mean that." He'd known my dad and knew how hard his death had been on me. "I'm just . . . frustrated. Josh is scary. And I *told* you that gun would be turned on you. Statistically speaking—"

"I know the stats, Alejo—"

He rolled his eyes and stomped into the laundry room.

My nose was swollen, but Alejandro had taken a good look at it and pronounced it not broken—and I figured since I wasn't in a ton of pain, he was probably right (that, and his sister was a nurse). The police had come and carted Josh off. He'd tried telling them that I'd held him at gunpoint—that this was a couple's argument in which I'd gone savage. Though I had a healthy distrust of the cops, luckily for my brown ass, they'd seen right through him. It'd helped that one of the cops was a Black woman, who couldn't help but produce a subtle look of disgust Josh's way the minute I'd opened the door.

"I think I did pretty well for myself," I said, Alejandro returning from the laundry room. I pulled my left hand off my face just long enough so that I could gulp wine—and painkillers. It was about 1:00 A.M., and though I knew I should sleep, there was no way that was happening for a while. This was especially not good because I'd convinced Victoria that we should take the Ouija board to room 904 tomorrow and hold a very guided séance in front of the mirror—with my mother. We were running out of time, and I was growing desperate.

"Put that back on your damn face, would you?" Alejandro said, pushing the ice pack into my hands. I did as I was told. Alejandro had just wrapped his date up when he got my call. "Almost getting shot in the neck by your ex is now defined as 'doing well'?"

"It's not my fault some guy my sister dated liked a picture of me a little too much," I said. I shook my head, wincing as I did.

"Your sister dated?" he asked, his expression going strange.

"That's what he said."

Alejandro was silent.

"Look," I said, shifting the ice, "at least this time, the cops have a clear record of Josh violating that restraining order. And for the record, I *did* call them the last time he showed. Dude just is great at jumping ship right in time. And I think he was fined—which clearly wasn't much of a deterrent . . ." I said, pausing to look at the mirror in front of the divan. I turned my head to the left, then to the right, tenderly touching the spot I'd hit when my face connected with the floor.

"That's the thing about restraining orders, they don't do shit," Alejandro said. "My sister—"

"Got one and was still almost killed by her ex," I said, interrupting. "But she had to try. And luckily, I guess, he ended up in the ol' slammer anyway. But armed robbery isn't really Josh's thing. He's white-collar crime at best—and you know how tolerant they are of men like that. So, though I should've had a smarter combo for the safe, and though I hate guns, I really do, you can't be here all the time, Alejo, you just can't."

"I can try," he said, his voice taking on a desperate squeak.

I sighed. "Alejandro, you have to fuck sometime."

He laughed, just a little.

"Or go to the store. Or to the range."

He twisted his lips in a frustrated grimace and threw himself down on the couch beside me. "You need to start making smarter decisions," he said, pouring first for me and then for himself. He'd pulled the bottle out of the refrigerator the moment the cops had left, right after he'd retrieved the ice pack from the freezer.

"Calling me a slut?" I asked playfully, elbowing him gently in the side.

He rolled his eyes, patting me softly on the arm. "If so, join the club," he said. He ran his hands over his thick, curly hair and sighed heavily.

We were silent for a while, and I held the ice pack to my face.

"Josh said something that made me think," I said, breaking the silence, "that maybe he had something to do with my sister's death."

Alejandro blinked rapidly.

"He said that Naiche and I were too close." I paused to think.

"So?" Alejandro said, a little too quick.

"Maybe he wanted to get rid of her—maybe he was part of the 36. If they were dating, maybe he was able to get her to sacrifice herself in the room."

Alejandro was quiet for a good, long time, his pupils shifting right to left rapidly. Then, "I don't know, Olivia. That's pretty complicated. And Dorian's already admitted it was his cult behind the whole thing."

I sat back, pushing the ice pack to my face. "Yeah, but Dorian said that they made sure not to put her in the room the night it happened. So maybe Josh was behind getting her there."

It was Alejandro's time to sit back contemplatively. "But don't they just reappear?"

"Yeah," I said, feeling uneasy. I closed my eyes. "Let's get some sleep."

Alejandro sat up fast. "Girl, yes. I'm beyond exhausted. Don't hesitate to get me up if you need me, okay?" He leaned down and squeezed my shoulder.

I smiled, but that feeling of unease crept further and further into my heart. Why would Alejo not tell me that he knew my sister and Josh had dated? Was Josh lying? Was he behind the whole thing? And if so, was Dorian lying then? A darker thought, then: Was Alejo lying? If so, why?

I watched Alejo as he retreated to the bathroom to start his rococo nightly facial routine, my entire body buzzing with the need to sleep, that feeling of unease taking hold so sharply, it was like a knife at my throat.

# Chapter Twenty-Eight

*www.ghostequipmentforreal.com*
*Spike EMF Energy Sensor FOR SALE*

*This bite-sized sensor uses new, micro-detecting technology via an on-board magnetometer to alert you IMMEDIATELY when the dead have entered the room. Whenever an EMF spike occurs, light and sound via an electromagnetic energy pod let you know the deceased are ready to communicate. $75 per pod.*

I'd checked the rest of my equipment when we'd first entered the room, and it was silent, the room temperature at a comfy preset sixty-eight degrees. My mind floated back to the last time I was in here. It had only been a few days ago, but it felt like a lifetime. I'd bought a plethora of EMF pods because I'd read on a paranormal blog that sometimes the little guys were more sensitive to smaller emissions, especially when garnered through the refracted energy of a portal, like a mirror.

"You hear back from the cops?" Victoria asked. She was lounging on the dark blue velvet chair, her long brown arms casually draped on the armrests on either side of her. She pulled her phone out and sighed, slipped it back into her little Gucci clutch. I could tell she missed Sara, but Sara hadn't responded when I'd texted earlier, asking if she wanted to join.

I was pacing, occasionally stopping to glance at the mirror, which was already heavy with ghostly vibes. Things were intensifying in my life in ways that I wasn't sure I could keep pace with. "Yes. Josh did incur a *minor* fine the first time he violated the order. Luckily, that lawyer recorded the whole thing. Unfortunately," I said, smoothing my hands over my knees, "Josh has a very good lawyer on retainer. And though it's still in process, I'm sure he'll just get off again with another minor fine. You know how it works, the law bends over backwards when it comes to men with money."

"I never liked that man," my mother said, sighing.

"I know, Monique," Victoria said. "Me either."

"I'm so sorry," Dorian said, leaning forward, his elbows on his knees. He shook his head, his wavy, glossy black hair shining in the light, the strands tied back with a rich, bloodred tie.

I walked over and squeezed his shoulder appreciatively before I resumed my pacing. I'd invited him for the express purpose of letting him think he was growing close to me, though honestly, I enjoyed his company a little too much. I was hoping Victoria could get something out of him. She was a strong personality, off-puttingly direct, and sometimes it caused people to blurt things out that they hadn't meant to.

I'd also invited Sasha. He'd muttered unhappily under his breath when he'd seen me squeezing Dorian's shoulder. I'd told him about what I was up to, and as usual, he'd told me that what I was doing was dangerous. I'd asked him if he was jealous, and he'd told me quite frankly that he was.

"Did the cops tell you anything else? I think Josh had something to do with your sister's death," Victoria said, her lips pursing. Just like my mother, she'd hated when I'd broken it off with Sasha.

"They're saying that a woman has an alibi for him the night of my sister's death," I said. "He was at a sex club." It was plausible. He'd even gotten me to go to one when we were together, the blue-and-pink lights pulsing, the location underground, shady.

"Figures," Victoria said.

"Gross," Sasha said, shifting uncomfortably.

Dorian laughed, and Sasha looked away.

I glanced over at Alejandro, but his head was buried in his phone.

I sat down with a frustrated plop next to Dorian.

"I'm guessing a lot of women are willing to give a lot of alibis for that douche," Victoria said.

Alejo laughed hollowly.

"I think he did it, I really do," Victoria said, sitting up straight. "I think he used your little club as an excuse to get her somewhere he knew she'd die, with the idea that—"

"To be fair," Dorian said, interrupting politely, "much of this is on us. We were overconfident. We thought we could beat the curse, and talk to my great-great-grandmother, and gain access to the world she'd created a portal to. We wanted to stop women from dying, and your sister wanted to help us. All I know," he said, "is that one minute she was with the Sacred 36. And the next? In this room. Maybe, though . . ." he mused, his fingers massaging his goatee, his eyes half-lidded, "he knew something we didn't? She did bring him to a meeting, before we got together. I mean . . . what if he checked her in at the right time? She didn't tell me that she'd checked in at all. So either she was up to something I didn't know about or someone was pushing her to check in three weeks before the date the women reappear." He shook his head. "Honestly, that time in my life was so intense, parts of it are a bit of a blur. And there are things my ancestors set into motion that I don't have the power alone to stop."

Sasha nodded thoughtfully, but I could see Alejandro's shoulders rock up into tense knots. "Wait. I thought you and the 36 checked Naiche in on the night three weeks before they reappear?"

I'd already told Alejo that Dorian claimed that wasn't the case.

"No, as I told Olivia, we kept her away from that room. Not to mention that just because she checked in at the right time doesn't mean that she'd be the person the Brown would choose. We just wrapped the ceremony around her."

"Reckless," Sasha said, shaking his head. "She was a good girl."

"I know it was," Dorian responded. "I know she was."

Sasha let out a small, disapproving puff of air.

"But what *if* Josh checked her in?" Victoria said. "He's an evil, sociopathic dickhead."

"But why?" I asked. "What was his end goal?"

"I was thinking the same thing," Alejo said. "Yeah, he's totally obsessed with Olivia, but isn't that needlessly complicated?" He put one hand out, palm up.

"Something was obviously different though," Victoria said. "You wanted to break that curse, and instead she replaced Luella Still-well. Why? What was different? I think that Josh's *end goal* was to eliminate Naiche, so that he could grow close to Olivia. And I think he knew more than all of you give him credit for."

"Hmmm . . ." Dorian said, sitting back, and as he did, his unique scent floated my way—he smelled like sandalwood and musk and something deep, earthy, woodsy.

I wasn't sure about that. He could've just broken up with my sister after rifling through her things and finding my phone number. She never left her screen on lock, and he could've looked at it while she was in the shower. Or if he was really that violent, he could have just killed her, if he genuinely thought she was a deterrent to being with me. Why the big production? I shook my head in frustration.

"We did try a brand-new ceremony, though," Dorian said. "And by the way, Mrs. Becente, I want to extend my deepest sympathies. What we did was wrong, and your daughter paid the price. I thought . . . I thought I was strong enough to change things," he said, his voice wavering.

I could see Sasha watching Dorian, assessing him.

After a moment or two, my mother spoke. "She was her own person. You couldn't have made her do anything she didn't want to do."

"I appreciate that," he said, his voice softening, his full, dark pink lips parting.

"And you can just call me Monique."

Sasha narrowed his eyes.

"But wait, a new ceremony?" Victoria asked, her eyes moving to slits. She was razor-sharp. She'd been bored at MENSA meetings.

"We didn't have the *Handbook of Ceremonies,* so I wrote a new ceremony, one I was sure at the time was going to break the curse. I'm actually pretty good at that, generally," he said, rubbing one elbow and then the other, his expression sheepish.

"Wait a minute," I said, remembering he'd said as much at the meeting of the 36 I'd attended. "Come to think of it, if you have the ceremony we need, all we need to do is perform it the night the women reappear. What do we even need the *Handbook* for?"

"I don't know about that, Olivia," Mom said. "Let's not play fast and loose with my life."

"Of course not, Mom," I said.

"And Olivia, remember: my ceremony, as far as I know, didn't work. I suspect that if we can throw the glamour off *Ghostland,* we could break the curse for real this time."

"Well, but what if Josh did get in the middle of your ceremony? Your ceremony might've worked if he hadn't," Victoria said, and Alejo shook his head.

I began to fervently hope that *Ghostland* was the *Handbook of Ceremonies.*

But beyond that, something was bothering me, flickering at the edge of consciousness. "She called me that night," I said.

"Oh?" Dorian asked, his gaze turning my way with a studied casualness.

"Yes. She told me she was going to die. To come there—here," I said. "And, though the footage goes blurry at times, I was able to clean some of it up. There's someone talking to her off-screen at one point."

"I *knew* it!" Victoria said, slapping her palms down on the thighs of her pale blue jeans. "Someone was here. Someone knew she was going to reappear here. And was in the room when she did. Maybe she *was* about to break the curse, and they—Josh, in my opinion—wanted to make sure she didn't for whatever reasons."

"I don't know . . ." Alejandro said.

"Let's just get this show on the road, but look—I'm a pretty good hacker. Honestly, hacking into systems is so easy that it bores me." Victoria rolled her eyes and readjusted in the chair. "But I'm going to see what I can find out about Josh."

"I still have to go back to *why*. Josh isn't exactly Mr. Occult," I said.

"And let me at least look at this ceremony," Sasha said. "I can tell you if I think it's strong."

"I'll think about that," Dorian said.

Sasha narrowed his eyes again.

"I suppose . . ." my mother said, "if he wanted to kill Naiche, this whole thing would stand as a really good cover-up."

"Right?" Victoria said. "Naiche might have shown him the altered ceremony, and he might've bunged it up by checking her in, all while pretending to be on her side."

I was silent. Or it could've been Alejandro who'd pushed her to do the same.

"In any case, let's do this. This is tough enough as it is," Alejandro said, his chest fluttering slightly with a deep sigh.

"I know, I know. Maybe we'll learn more," Victoria said. Her eyes widened then, her mouth curling into a smile of curiosity.

"You, ma'am, have no nerve endings," Sasha said, laughing uneasily.

She threw her hands up. No matter how risky, or emotionally difficult, Victoria loved an adventure.

I took a deep breath, and we all gathered around the board. I was sandwiched in between Sasha and Dorian on the couch; my mother, Alejo, and Victoria in the chairs on the other side.

I glanced up at the mirror, which was set above the bed, and then at my mother. I hadn't wanted her to do this with me for lots of reasons, but Victoria had sat me down and told me that if I wanted shit to get done in the few weeks we had left, I had to invite her. I hadn't liked it, I'd fought her like hell, but in the end, I'd agreed.

"You sure about this?" I asked my mom, one eyebrow shooting up.

She nodded, tugging at the cuffs of her white T-shirt.

I turned the pods on, one by one, the red lights circling with a flourish and then going steady. I'd scattered them around the room, though primarily they surrounded the mirror. I stood up and walked over to the mirror, looked into it, and closed my eyes, running my fingers along the black-and-gold filigreed frame. It was harder to focus on communicating with the dead when the dead was a family member. One you knew you'd wronged by thinking you had everything under control. The mirror in and of itself was not only ornate, beautiful—but fascinating. The concierge had told me that it came from the Stillwell Mansion—that it was one of the items Luella Stillwell had brought with her when she came to live here, and the Brown had been allowed to keep it after her death. There was a story surrounding it, though I had trouble verifying its validity—Dorian had told me that even he had no idea if it was true or not.

The story was that Mrs. Stillwell and the Sacred 36 used it in their séances, and that one night, with the help of a medium, they'd been able to conjure the spirit of an "Indian maiden," a phrase that nauseated me. The "maiden" had stayed on this earth because she was heartbroken, and the Sacred 36 had tried to channel her energy, but instead had trapped her.

I opened my eyes and worked to still my mind. To remember how much I loved my sister, how she, of course, didn't mean me harm. I thought of her face, her long, downturned black eyelashes—I'd told her how much I envied them, how they made her look shy.

"I am shy," she'd always said in her small, breathy whisper of a voice.

I sat down and asked for everyone to hold hands.

"I don't know if I want to hold his hand," Victoria said, pointing at Dorian with her lips. "He's kind of an unrepentant flirt."

Instead of being offended, or protesting, Dorian threw back his head and laughed. Then pushed his hand into hers and wiggled his eyebrows.

"Just don't *bore* me," she said, with a flip of her hair. But I could see the hint of a smile quirked at the corner of her lips.

"Never," he responded. There was something about his voice that was always a touch smoky.

Sasha rolled his eyes.

I closed my eyes, pictured a lush green forest with chipmunks, jet-black crows, and elk. It was raining, the drops falling in between the branches of the pines, the aspens—the water filtering through the light. It was one of the images I used to center myself. "Dorian, Mom," I said, focusing on the sound of the rain in my mind, "put your hands on the planchette."

They did as they were told, Dorian's long, milky-pale hands next to my mother's slender-but-short dark brown.

"Naiche," I said, trying to stay in the space of that filtered forest light. "Please. Help us. Forgive me . . ." I said, and had to stop, my voice breaking, the image coming apart with my feelings of regret, of sheer, unadulterated pain. With simply *missing* her. Mom's hand left the planchette, and she leaned forward across the table. She placed her hand firmly on my shoulder and squeezed reassuringly. I took a deep breath and continued. "For not coming to the Brown when you asked me to. I didn't take you seriously, and I know it cost you your life." I hung my head, the image gone, images of my sister replacing them. Her heart-shaped face. Her freckles. Her eyes clenched tightly, mirroring her body, after my father died.

Dorian's hand also broke contact with the planchette, and joined my mother's briefly on my other shoulder. I felt my shoulders give, just a little, and I let myself breathe.

"Thanks," I whispered. Her ghost was weighting the room like a mist, like a drug I'd taken that was just coming on, and as frightening as that was, the sheer delight in seeing her again, no matter how angry she was, no matter how terrible the circumstance, was overwhelming. I could feel joy lighting up the parts of me that I thought had blackened, shriveled completely to dust when I'd come to understand that she was gone. I could feel parts of me expanding, breaking into her. My stomach dropped, and my body seized, my back arcing into a curve, my mother gasping in fear. She was here.

One of the pods blinked, my body relaxing enough to pull out of the rictus it had struck, and I could feel my skin frost as the temperature in the room moved down, just a few degrees, then more—and more, though I didn't want to get up to check the instruments for fear of disrupting the process. I blinked, trying to regain control.

"Naiche—"

I was interrupted by a sharp, animal scraping noise. It was the planchette moving across the board, slowly at first, then with increasing speed—it grew wild. It began to buck, and even after my mother's and Dorian's hands left the wood, it spun, around and around.

"Naiche," I repeated, her name like an incantation.

I shook my head slowly, savoring the new air, reaching out, my skin prickling like there were a million tiny cuts across each pore.

My body felt like it had been struck with electricity, my arms going straight in front of me like they weren't my own, my back folding backward so hard I thought it would break, my eyes fluttering sharply into the back of my head, moving me to another world. I sat in that liminal space, in a state that felt not quite human, my new mind turning to something from perhaps the corner of the room, maybe a small moan, I wasn't sure. I tried moving further into my gift, to work with the pain, further into what I could feel was gathering, and this time the moan was loud, charged with the supernatural. I felt my body trying to hitch a ride into the unknown, swaying into the fairy world and then back, as the air in the room thickened with anticipation, with pain. *Her* pain.

My mind reeled, like I'd been flipped upside down. I went to scream, but my voice was gone—I had no voice. And then I was lost, suddenly, in one of her memories. She was here, in this room. A man's voice spilled out into the echo chamber that was her memory and I worked to focus, to understand what was going on, who was talking to her, but it was almost as if I was looking at the room underwater. I blinked to clear my eyes, but what was in front of me remained hazy. I could hear the man's voice, but whose voice, exactly, was unclear, though the tenor was definitively masculine. My sister's voice was weak, sad. She sounded like she'd been crying, and her pain was oceanic, overwhelming. The man's voice was calm, insistent—but the words were nothing but dissonance.

In a flash, I was back in the room, my eyes ripping open. I stood, my friends looking up at me with worry in their eyes.

"Your eyes . . . were white," Mom whispered.

The planchette began to move again, not chaotic this time, directed. Specific. No one's hands were on it.

Victoria, of course, took control. She swallowed, visibly, then began spelling out the message. "V-E-S-S-E-L!" Victoria said, clapping.

"Vessel?" I asked, mystified.

The planchette moved to *Yes*, and hovered, the sound of moaning like an ever-present low-vibe song.

"Does Olivia have the *Handbook of Ceremonies*?" Dorian asked, his voice keen, tense with excitement.

"Naiche, please, be careful," Sasha said. "Remember that these are people you love."

The planchette began to move, but suddenly it bounced off the board, hitting the mirror, ricocheting and slamming into the floor, narrowly missing Dorian's head, who'd ducked out of the way just in time.

The pods were going wild, blinking and blinking, the temperature so icy I could see my breath. The EVP meter was beeping so loudly it was like the call of an ambulance. That was when I could feel it, my body going cruelly taut this time, the curve so sharp I screamed—my whole being moving so quickly into the other world I felt that all that would be left of me would be ash. My sister was there, her eyes blazing white, her mouth opening . . .

My eyes flashed open. I was standing in front of the mirror.

She was there.

My mother was behind me, holding me, her eyes on the mirror, her terror and excitement clearly too strong for her to speak, to do anything but keep me upright. I could feel her trying.

"Naiche—" she finally managed.

Naiche interrupted her, her face wide and white and furious. "Olivia," she hissed, black mist coiling around her. She looked down at me, her eyes turning red, dangerous. My mind flashed, briefly, to a time when she was so angry at me that she'd almost struck me, one hand poised in front of my face, her lip trembling.

The mist began to leave the mirror, curl into the room, envelop the velvet and wood, and where it touched me, I felt cold so icy it was like pain.

"Shit," Victoria said in a low whisper.

"Tell me what I need to do!" I said, desperation lacing my voice.

She pointed to the Ouija board, her eyes blood now, fury. She opened her mouth, her lips vibrating with a scream so otherworldly I worried my ears would bleed. Everyone clapped their hands over their ears, and the mist moved into the room so completely it was as if we were at sea.

Just as suddenly as the scream began, it stopped. And she was gone.

## Chapter Twenty-Nine

I'd spent the night at my mother's house. She was strong. You had to be, to survive losing both your husband and your daughter. She'd always been strong; she'd had no choice. A dark-skinned, unenrolled Native woman trying to make it as a journalist, with bigotry on all sides. She couldn't be white, and though clearly Native, she wasn't Native enough for many Natives on this side of the border, and though technically Latinx, she wasn't Mexican enough either—my family had kept close to their roots—and our ancestors had come across sometime in the mid to late 1800s, marrying into an Irish family and then into one with Cherokee roots, another Chickasaw. My mother had chosen the last name Becente, and my father had taken it. She'd grown a résumé via pure grit. She'd never given up, and she'd had a great career—found a darling, kind, caring husband whose family had supported their union immediately. They'd built a life together. They'd been everything I'd aspired to be: smart, determined, easygoing when they could be, and tough when the moment required it. And more than anything, they were deeply good people. But so much had worked to break my mother anyway, and though she'd wanted to communicate with my sister for years, seeing her ghost, full of preternatural fury, had pushed her to the edge.

Not to mention that none of us were sure what was going to happen to her in less than two weeks now.

Alejandro and I were headed to the sex club.

"Are you sure she's okay?" Alejandro asked. We were descending the gray concrete stairs that led to the club. There were condoms and gum wrappers beat into the corners into a mix that almost appeared black, tar-like. I shuddered. I had nothing against sex. But I had everything against filth.

I sighed. "I think so. And we're running out of time."

Alejandro nodded.

At the door, we knocked. Alejo knew the password. Though I'd only been here once with Josh, he'd been here several times, but he frequented the strictly gay sex club in the Highlands much more.

We'd thought about calling ahead, seeing if the owner would meet us during the day, but both of us eventually figured that they'd be more willing to give information about Josh—who was certainly a consistent customer, and therefore money in their pockets—if we came in on the sly, asked questions as if we were maybe interested in doing business there, versus interrogating the owner to see if Josh had had something to do with the murder of my sister.

The door was painted with a thick, viscous-looking layer of black paint, and there wasn't a sign, either on the street or on the wood, to give any kind of identity to the location. Kind of like a speakeasy but horny.

A little panel slid open, and I smiled, despite myself.

"Digable deuterogamy."

The panel slid shut, and I felt a moment of panic, worried that the password had changed and we wouldn't be let in, but moments later I heard a large, metallic latch coming loose from its moors, and the door swung open.

The large, shirtless, hypermasculine man in tiny blue shorts looked down at us with a mix of derision and interest, though I don't know how he managed that, as we entered, and though it was relatively early for the likes of any respectable club, it was still throbbing with the sounds of "XXX" so loudly it felt as if it were trying to make its way under your clothes. It was so loud I worried about getting anything out of the bartenders that I could understand, even if they were willing to talk to me.

I knew that there were countless well-maintained rooms that people could pay for past the sparkling silver-and-sepia bar at the front, but since that wasn't either of our agendas, we made our way to the stools, found a couple empty, and sat. This part of the club was filled with rich brown leather couches with large pieces of gears or clocks, maps, above each, in a kind of steamy, steampunk aesthetic.

"I think I'm in the mood for a cosmo," I said. "You?"

"That sounds great," Alejandro responded, settling into the chair next to me.

I waited for the bartender—a woman with dyed black hair in classic pinup style, complete with large, curled bangs—to have time for us, and ordered. She looked like she might be Josh's type, or at least know something about him that might be helpful.

When she came back with the drinks, I asked to start a tab and whipped out my business credit card, which just happened to be glowing platinum. She looked down at it and back up at me and smiled, a small sparkle appearing in her eyes.

"Hey," I said, before she turned away. I scooted closer, hoping she could hear me. "Super quick question, if that's okay?" I smiled disarmingly, hoping it'd have an effect.

"Sure," she said, shrugging, the straps of her black leather harness, plastered over a tight buffalo-check tank, moving up, then down. "I've got a minute or two."

"Great," I said, pulling my phone up and out of the pocket of my jeans. "You know anything about this guy?"

She stared at the phone in front of her, her eyes narrowing in concentration. "I'm not supposed to," she said finally, archly.

My heart skipped a beat. I knew I'd have to go hard and quick. And I'd have to lie, which I hated.

"Got my sister pregnant, then disappeared," I deadpanned.

Her mouth turned up. "Liar," she said.

I could hear Alejo chuckle, and I elbowed him.

She was good. "Okay, okay, you got me. But what he did was worse, it's just . . . hard to explain, or believe, for that matter," I said, sitting back.

"Don't worry," she said, leaning forward, her elbows at her side, her light brown eyes lined in black liner, cat-eyed like mine. "I fucking hate the guy. And I have zero loyalties to this place, as long as you're not going to let anyone know what I know—which isn't much." She ran her tongue over her top lip, and I could see the silver gage clack against her teeth as she pulled it back in.

"One hundred percent," I said. "I'll even give you my card so if shit goes down, you know who to blame." I pulled it out, gave it to her, and watched as her eyebrows arched up, then down.

"Paranormal investigator, huh?" she said, her eyes sparkling with delight.

I nodded. "I think that Josh might—*might*—have had something to do with my sister's death." It made me nervous to nearly shout this in a semicrowded sex club, but when it came down to it, what choice did I have? She knew something.

"Now I can tell you're telling me the truth," she said, pulling a bottle of high-quality scotch out for herself, looking around covertly, pouring, and taking a small swig. "Dude's a creep. I'm into ladies, okay? Never touched a dude in my life. Not a point of pride," she said, looking Alejandro's way. "Just a fact."

He raised both hands in a no-offense-taken gesture and sipped at his cosmo.

"And even if I was into dudes, first of all, I'm not obligated to bone anyone I don't want to, and more to the point, this joint has a strict no-fucking-the-customers policy. We do that? And this place starts to look like it's a different kind of establishment than it is, and it is absolutely not that kind of establishment," she said, though I had to lean in close and really concentrate to hear every word. "No shit towards sex work either," she finished. "Totally respect the oldest profession in the world, it's just, that ain't what we do here, and it ain't my thing.

"But this guy," she said, shaking her head, flicking her eyes down again at the photo of Josh on my phone, "would not take no for an answer. Came in almost every day, with the same girl. They'd case the room, looking for someone to play with, I assumed—though come to think of it," she said, her eyes going distant for a moment, "they never touched each other. Anyway, when that would fail, he'd come swaggering his ass over to the bar. Told the manager I wanted him banned after the third time he kept me from serving customers with his pushing me, but I always got the runaround. Fucker even wrapped his meaty hand around my arm to stop me from walking away once," she said, her eyes narrowing. "Turns out, he's invested money here. So my manager felt that he couldn't tell the guy to split, barring something illegal."

I nodded. Josh was a pushy, entitled asshole, but I already knew that.

"Luckily, that was a few years ago. He stopped coming, and I hoped he'd moved on to another sex club with looser rules."

I nodded again. "How long ago?"

"What?" she asked. It was so loud in there.

"How long ago?" I asked, increasing the volume of my voice and leaning in farther. I had a low voice, like my mother, so though it carried in terms of volume, distinguishing exactly *what* I was saying in a crowded, hot room was hard.

"Oh . . . shit." She squeezed her eyes almost shut. "Four . . . no, almost five years ago." She shook her head. "Can't believe I've been here this long. They pay well. Customers tip big."

My heart squeezed again. "You have any info about her? The

woman he was always with? I promise, just need it to contact her, ask a few questions."

She looked at me piercingly, assessing me, the veracity of my statement. The Deftones' "Change" came on over the speakers, and my heart convulsed. It had been one of my sister's favorite songs, one of my sister's favorite bands.

Apparently, I passed muster. "I know a girl who used to work here. She does. She *did* hook up with him and got fired for it, though I can't say that made me sad. Still have her number on account of the fact that she was always text-begging me to take her shift."

I breathed in relief.

"Don't know if it's still her number, but have no reason to think it's not."

I nodded, and Alejo handed me the small iPad I kept strictly for business. I opened the document where I was keeping the information for my sister's situation and turned it over to her. She tapped for a moment or two and handed it back complete with a name and number. It was local. Marie was the name.

"Don't have her last name," she said. "Sorry."

"Pictures?" I asked.

She thought for a moment, then, "No."

"Thank you," I said.

"Good luck," she said, placing her hand on my wrist briefly and squeezing. She went off then to get a customer a drink, one who'd clearly been waiting a while.

"We lucked *out*," Alejo said, shaking his head. "I did not think we'd get that much right off the bat."

"Yeah. But who knows if this is still her number, or if this woman knows anything."

He screwed his lips up in a gesture of frustrated acquiescence.

I looked at my watch, the cream-colored face gleaming faintly in the dim bar light. It had been my father's, and though it was a painful reminder of the fact that he wasn't with us anymore, I also wore it because I still loved him and wanted that reminder despite the heart sting. "Gotta go," I said.

"Trying to get more out of Dorian?" he asked.

I nodded. "We're going through his library, see if he has any ceremonies that might work on glamours, though I still don't know if *Ghostland* is the *Handbook*. If not, maybe he has something that can lead us to the real one."

He cocked his head, narrowed his large, dark eyes. "Get it."

I laughed.

Alejo sucked the last of his cosmo down, and I did the same, feeling an anticipatory shiver move through me at the thought of being next to Dorian, of breathing in his earthy green smell. I felt guilty for being attracted to someone who was, at minimum, at least in part responsible for my sister's death. But however guilty he was, I knew working with him might save my mother.

# Chapter Thirty

Dorian and I were sitting around a large dark-wood table in the offices of the Sacred 36 underneath the Brown. There were loosely around forty tomes from the office's libraries piled on top, from slim to weighty. They were books that contained ceremonies for pulling the glamour off an object, and we'd tried every one—and every time we tried, the evil presence I'd encountered in Regina's house would begin to surface, and we had to shut it down. There were candles, flowers, herbs, crows' feet, other dried animal parts, and broken glass strewn everywhere. The books were mainly ones that had been in Mrs. Stillwell's personal library, though some were ones Dorian or other members of the 36 had acquired or pulled from their families' collections. He even claimed that one was a translated version of the Voynich manuscript. Primarily, they were books on the occult, the paranormal, séances, and what Mrs. Stillwell and others of her time deemed "exotic" spiritualities. He told me that he'd combed through every one, searched room 904 countless times, this space, and even before the big renovation, in between sales, Mrs. Stillwell's former residence, and he'd found nothing that would concretely lead him to the location of the *Handbook of Ceremonies* that would tell us without a shadow of a doubt that we weren't wasting our deglamouring efforts on the wrong book.

Either way, the thing had a hell of a defense system.

His feelings of guilt seemed sincere. I knew exactly where he was coming from, in terms of being too confident to think you could be wrong. I'd believed with every fiber of my being when Naiche called me the night she died that she was being melodramatic.

"So," I said, placing my finger to hold my place in the crease of the book I'd been examining, "there's really *nothing* in Luella's diary that indicates where the book is? And how *did* it get out of the hands of the Sacred 36? And if this is the book, who threw the glamour on it? And more importantly, how to break into the damn thing without setting off its defense system."

Dorian sighed in the way someone sighs when they've been dealing with an issue for years and years, when it has weighed heavily on their minds for as long as they can remember, when they've exhausted every possibility, and despite every reason to stop, they keep going. In that small moment, I admired him.

"Her diary is—at least in parts . . . how do I put this?" He crooked one finger around his lip, his thumb resting on his chin. "Almost coded."

"Coded?" I asked, sitting up straight.

"Yeah, I mean, mostly it's complaints about her husband, her lover—or about a party or a séance that went well. But there are parts where it feels heavy with meaning that isn't on the surface, if you know what I'm saying. But though I have a master's in English," he said with a small laugh, "and she's my ancestor, I can't decode what she's trying to say. Or who she was trying to say it to."

"Is the master's in English why you have an, let's just say, alternative profession?" I asked, thinking of the coke I'd seen in his other "office" at the Church.

He laughed. "That's some of it, yes, though most of my peers who didn't go on into academia have decent cube jobs. Mainly, however, it seemed, alongside bribes for the local law enforcement, a smart way to invest what remained of the family money and keep my gentlemanly lifestyle."

"Would you mind if I took a look at her diary?" I asked.

"Not at all," he said, standing up and going to a small podium. He plucked the book from the stand and delivered it. He stood over me as I turned the pages, his smell wafting down and into me, the warmth of his skin a living thing.

I nodded and he set one hand on my shoulder lightly and leaned in.

"I've marked the two pages I *think* have some meaning behind the meaning," he said, pointing to two small cloth bookmarks. I turned to the first. "And sorry I didn't mention it earlier, it's just, like I said, I've spent years upon years trying to figure out where that damn book is, and I've pored over every word, countless times. So has the Sacred 36."

I squeezed his hand. He squeezed back, one finger running along the edge of my hand for a moment before I withdrew.

I thumbed through the old, thinning paper—the smell emanating from the diary a dusty vanilla. "See," he said, pointing and leaning farther down, his breath thick, sweet. "This line in this particular passage, about her lover. It's . . . weird."

I read it out loud. "'Bulkeley has the key to my heart. But he keeps it with Keli, where no one can find it.'" I thought for a moment. "So this is something. Remember Nese, the two-spirit?"

He cocked his head inquisitively, his eyes bright.

"They told me that they were giving me 'the key.' I still have yet to understand what they meant by that, but the fact that Luella's mentioning a key seems more than just a coincidence. And I've been dreaming of them, of the Massacre. They're trying to show me something."

He nodded. "Not to mention that the *Handbook* has a keyhole."

I felt a wave of profound self-annoyance. "That's right!" I rubbed at my knees. "Jesus, there must be an *actual* key. Is there any reference to a Keli anywhere? A love triangle, possibly? Maybe this Keli has the key?"

"No," he said, straightening up. He began pacing. "That's what I thought too." He paused at the bookshelf, placed one hand on a ledge, and leaned. "After her husband died, her lover married a younger woman. But her name wasn't Keli. No Keli in the original 36, either. No friend of hers named Keli. I've never understood this reference to a person named Keli."

I shifted in my seat, stretched. "What's the other passage?" I asked, moving my hands back to the book, and he returned to his position above me, one hand on the chair, his breath again on my neck, my response electric.

"The last one—this line, here," he said, leaning down again, his hair whispering against my neck, causing an involuntary shiver to pass through me—one, I was sure, that didn't go unnoticed. "She stopped journaling, I guess, after he left her." He flipped to it, and I peered at the print in front of me. It was messier, much harder to read, but I could make it out. "'The ghost of my heart disappears and reappears in a land of unmaking. The only thing I can do to protect that weak muscle is to tell the world stories. Different stories, and new stories, a storm of tales, new formations every year . . .'"

I blinked, deep in thought. "That one's harder to parse apart. But it also has a weight to it." I sighed. "You know . . . *Ghostland* is a collection, at least on the surface, of short stories."

Dorian straightened up, echoing my deep sigh. "That's true."

I closed the book up and turned around. Dorian smiled at me, and in that moment, he looked almost like an exhausted father, rather than a risky sexual choice. A gothy father to be sure, but one who emanated comfort, security.

"Can I borrow—" I started but was interrupted by the sound of an incoming text. I glanced down. It was Victoria.

*Jenny's gone too far this time.*

"What now?" I asked, rolling my eyes.

"What's happening?" Dorian asked, straightening.

I cleared my throat. "There's this overanxious newspaper reporter who wants to make her career by shitting on me—"

"Jenny Kunza," he said, closing his eyes briefly and shaking his head.

"You know her?"

He cradled his head in his hands. "Everyone in the paranormal community knows her. For some reason, our interests, if you will, really seem to piss her off. I've seen her takedowns—or attempted takedowns—of you. They're, if I'm being kind, frivolous. But also dangerous. And you may not remember, but not long after your sister's death, she wrote a big article about me. It was her usual line," he said, half sitting on the table. "I'd given her the wrong outlet for her mental health issues, so her death had to be my fault." He sighed. "Which, I felt guilty enough as it was. Is. It was hard. Not to mention the pile of hate mail I got. I had to change my number. And my locks." He crossed his arms over his chest. "Watch out for her. I've also heard she's a covert racist, and I'm sure a successful woman of color gets to her even more than your run-of-the-mill white guy."

"Yeah, she says that I'm Mexican in every article, even if she's just slipping it in. Which is a half-truth at best. I might be some Spanish. In fact, I'm sure I am—the unibrow I have to pluck every other day makes that clear."

He chuckled.

"But traditionally, parts of my family went up and down from Mexico to this country. Then, for political reasons, ended up in Texas, married some Irish, some southeastern Natives who also ended up in Texas, then they ended up here. But I'm Indigenous. She knows that. But she likes to stir up—in my opinion anyway"—I said, pointing to my chest—"anti-immigration sentiment, because she knows that'll rile her readers up against me."

Dorian cocked his head. "Do you consider yourself Latinx?"

I slumped. "I don't know. People have used that word to describe me, but I'm not sure it's a fit. In academic circles this stuff is a cluster. So many fights over so few resources," I said, thinking of Sara.

"Tell me about it," Dorian said, uncrossing and crossing his arms. "That's another reason I decided not to pursue my doctorate, try to get a job as a professor. During my master's, if I had *one* more white guy sidle up to me and say, 'Well. There's no way *we're* going to get a job in *this* climate.' Meaning because we were white. And male. When, honestly, the majority of who I saw get jobs were white."

"Right," I said. "And in my case, on top of it, I'm not entirely sure where my Apache family was originally from, just that they were in the mountains in Northern Mexico before they were pushed into Texas, where they were recorded as either Black or white—and I don't think my Cherokee or Chickasaw family is on the rolls. I guess that used to be US census policy—marking folks as Black or white—when it came to most urban Natives," I said, shrugging. "And in Texas, let's just say the recordkeeping in the mid-1800s was spotty at best."

He nodded.

"Anyway. Victoria's just sent me her latest. Sorry, she seems more upset than usual, so let me make sure this isn't an emergency."

I read, and my stomach fell sharply down to the floor and kept going.

Dorian put his hand on my shoulder. "Whoa. You just got several shades paler. What's going on?"

I opened my mouth but couldn't speak. I emitted a frog-like croak. I gathered myself. "She's . . . she's saying that she thinks Alejandro murdered Naiche."

# Chapter Thirty-One

### The Uncovering of a Murder: The Untold Story of Fauxvestigator's Sister

In true telenovela style, the story of local paranormal "investigator" Olivia Becente is long-winded, complex, and full of falsehoods. When first looking into Mexican-American Becente's claimed paranormal abilities, I assumed there would be numerous exaggerations, as family lore in regard to these kinds of "gifts" was to be expected and is incredibly common. However, what I couldn't have anticipated were the outright lies—and countless victims. But nothing could've prepared me for what I learned: Becente's assistant, Alejandro Garcia, murdered her sister (allegedly).

Though it's still unclear how strongly Olivia Becente played a part in the alleged murder of Naiche Becente almost five years ago in room 904 of the famed Brown Palace, my anonymous source tells me that the dagger used to kill Naiche Becente is in Mr. Garcia's possession, hidden in the home he shares with Mrs. Becente.

I would ask the people of Denver to demand that Mr. Garcia and Mrs. Olivia Becente be taken in for questioning under the weight of this new evidence. Call, tweet, email, and protest if you must for justice. This devious duo have made tens of thousands of dollars off the backs of people who have lost friends, spouses, and children, desperate for some false connection to them, to the financial detriment of real scientists, mental health professionals, and grief counselors who not only could've helped the victims, but whose livelihoods were diminished. I ask the people of Denver to hold these alleged murderers accountable.

I looked up. Dorian was holding the phone loosely at his hip, his mouth open, his face as pale as mine now. I felt sick. This was perhaps the most evil, manipulative thing I'd ever read. I'd brushed her articles off because I'd found Jenny Kunza to be silly. Prone to exaggerations. Small-time. Even desperate. But I'd underestimated her desperation.

Dorian blinked, rapidly. "I . . . wait. Is the dagger in your apartment?"

I shook my head, feeling a spike of deep unease root itself in my stomach. "No. And there's no way he murdered my sister." I felt doubt sink into my heart, thinking about what Josh had said to me the night he'd broken in. What, exactly, was going on?

He took a deep breath and sat down next to me. "I'm not saying that," he said, putting one hand on my shoulder. "But are you *sure* that dagger isn't at your place?"

"Wait. I need to call Alejandro, like, right now."

"Yes, sorry, of course. Let me give you some privacy." He left the library. I picked my phone off the table where Dorian had left it and went to click on Alejandro's name, but Alejo was already calling me.

"Olivia! Have you seen—"

"I have. I'm so sorry. Look, were you with her that night?"

Silence.

I felt sick. "Alejo? Are you there? Alejandro, please, tell me . . ."

"I was. But it's not what you think."

My stomach plummeted for the second time that day. "What's going on? I don't understand."

"Listen to me, okay? So, the night—wait, someone's knocking."

I could hear his footsteps against the hardwood floor, the door opening. A muted conversation. Then, "Olivia, you have to get here right away. And call our lawyer. It's the cops. They have a warrant to search our apartment." The phone went dead, and that's when I saw the texts and messages that had started pouring in.

*You faker!*

*Fraud!*

*You and your little gay boyfriend are going to jail, you fake ass bitch!*

*MexiCAN bIITCH! GO BACK TO WHERE YOU BELONG!@!!!*

And, worst of all:

*MURDERER.*

## The Massacre, Part III: Interlude

Soldiers opened fire from the southwest on the lodges of the people, the thunder of their cannons filling the air. People began flooding out of their tipis, the red running down their leathers, their knees buckling, their hands going to their hearts, theirs and their children's. Like lightning, their bodies became blood and smoke and, finally, ghosts, as the white flag Mo'ohtavetoo'o had raised was shot down, the white flag they had been told would keep the blood safely in the bodies of the people.

Nese felt a great winding movement in their heart, their hand moving to cover their eyes in slow motion, a feeling of unreality they had never felt the likes of—not during ceremony, not when the diseases hit, not when they had marched and marched without hope—entering their mind.

This cruelty. This evil.

Now Nese knew what they meant when their medicine men preached of the devil.

Most of the people died from rifle fire, their screams reverberating on the snowy plains, but some of the Heévâhetaneo'o began running up the bank of the river as the soldiers came flooding into the people's camp, their guns pulled up, aiming, shooting, laughing, the wool of their uniforms exuding the smell of madness, of animal fury.

Many of the Heévâhetaneo'o ran up the embankment, their legs working like the pistons of the trains that brought the Vehoc to their lands in numbers that were unthinkable, that brought death and death and death. The people's arms were full of their babies.

A few made it to safety by moving quickly, by burying themselves in the sand in the embankments north of the camp. A few cut horses from the camp's herd and rode toward another camp, the soldiers after them like rabid dogs, their mouths foaming.

When the children ran, the soldiers chased. They cut, they shot, they took women's parts and made sport with them, laughing at the desecration of their bodies after they were broken apart, the chasing down of children after they thought they had escaped, the mocking words that Nese knew the shape of spewing forth from their decaying mouths like fecal matter. This is when Vő'kaáe Ohvő'komaestse began to sing a journey song, thinking this would stop the soldiers. But he too was shot, in the middle of his song.

It happened, this sickness, in such a short time that Nese's mind reeled with the surreality of it, the pure, unadulterated butchery. As Nese was cut down with a dagger Chivington pulled from his belt loop, they saw the soldiers walking on the massacred bodies, the dirt the color of rust, the snow falling on the filthy hats of the soldiers who continued to laugh and laugh and laugh.

The bodies of the people began to freeze, the site now humming with a kind of terrible power Nese knew would last a thousand lifetimes, would warp the nature around it, would almost destroy the spirits of the ones who would come after. The trees would keep watch, would lean darkly into the ones who came, the owls would always circle, the grass always carry the color of the people's blood.

Nese watched as the spirits of their nation moved toward the Seameo, the band of light that led the way to Ma'heo'o, and refused. Nese would stay. Nese would haunt.

# Chapter Thirty-Two

Alejandro's face wore an expression of barely disguised terror, his arms crossed over his chest, his face wan, pale. The living room had already been violently turned over, and there were upended drawers on the floor, with string, expired credit cards, and old photos pouring out of them like tiny oceans. My phone was flooded with hate messages from randos, though there were even more messages of support from those in the paranormal and Indigenous communities, telling me to hang on, offering help and words of wisdom, and mainly just making statements of support in my name on social media. Of course, there were a number of self-righteous "Who claims her?" posts from a handful of right-wing Natives retweeted by white nationalists and those clueless on the left, but my mother and I were used to that eye-rolling rhetoric by now.

Dorian and I tried not to step on anything as I closed the door, but despite my best efforts, my sneakers cracked a mysterious square of plastic open. "Shit," I said. Alejandro, who was leaning against a bookshelf, just shook his head.

"Olivia," he said, his voice hitching to a stop.

I went to him and held him while he cried, his arms covering me like an old, familiar blanket. I told him I loved him, and that our lawyer was on her way.

"You don't believe her, right?" Alejandro asked, pulling back abruptly and looking me so hard in the eyes that it felt as if he were peering into parts of me that I'd kept hidden even to myself.

"Believe Jenny? Good God, of course not," I said, shaking him gently. "And have you forgotten that she's accused me too? In fact, I'm sure creating this bullshit story is all about getting to me, though of course, attention at any cost is her real agenda."

"Aren't there fines or, I don't know, guardrails for publishing material like that?" Dorian asked. He'd parked himself on the couch and had taken my phone from me. He was busy locking my accounts down and then deleting them for the time being.

I could hear the cops in my room now, the sounds of their footsteps everywhere, and then a small crash. A chorus of laughter.

Alejandro took a deep breath. "You'd think, but no. I took a class on this in college, cultural literacy. It's Reagan's fault."

I laughed hollowly.

"No really, Reagan eliminated the Fairness in . . ." He snapped his fingers a few times, narrowed his eyes. "Broadcasting Act."

Dorian furrowed his brow. "I think I remember something about this. The eighties?"

"Yeah, that sounds right," Alejandro said. "Basically, it means you can publish what you want, and even if it's full of made-up bullshit, it's all under the umbrella of an op-ed. An opinion. And anyone can have an opinion." He paused here to shake his head tiredly. "Though notice she did shove 'allegedly' in there to try to protect herself from litigation," he said, sweat breaking out on his brow.

I pushed him gently down on the couch beside Dorian and got him a glass of water.

He took it and gulped gratefully, went to place it on the end table, but finding it was full of the collected odds and ends of our years together and beyond, sighed and held it in his lap. Dorian carefully brushed the detritus aside, took the glass from him, and set it down in the newly unoccupied spot.

Alejandro smiled gratefully.

I took a deep breath. I had to ask. "There is one thing I need to understand. Why were you with her that night?" I whispered, my eyes flicking over to my room, where the cops were busy flipping things over, shoving things off my nightstand, and in general creating a mess it would take hours to correct.

He hesitated a moment, his mouth going into a thin, pursed line, and then relaxing, like he was carefully considering what he was about to say to me. "She needed me."

"Jesus Christ, Alejo, why didn't you tell me?" I hissed. "Do you know the night that Josh broke in, he told me that you murdered her?"

Alejandro's face broke into a riot of confusion, his mouth open. He shook his head. "That man is crazy. Look. It's because she swore me to secrecy, because she didn't want to make you feel bad for not coming to her rescue. And then she died, and that seemed like," he said, dissolving into tears, "the last, the *least* I could do for her."

Dorian rubbed his shoulder briefly and then looked up at me, his eyes crinkled in an expression of sadness and empathy. "I'd say hear him out. Also," he said, pointing in the direction of the cops, "should we migrate to the hallway?"

I nodded in agreement, but I felt like my skin had been turned inside out. Like everything I'd known was unraveling. Even when Naiche had died, I'd had my mother and Alejandro. Now I might lose my mother, and I was learning things about Alejandro that had me worried, doubting.

"We should tell them what we're doing, so they don't think I'm running," Alejo said, the shadows under his eyes deep, black.

"Good idea," I said, and Alejandro ducked into my room briefly.

I closed the door, and we moved in silence to the end of the hallway. Luckily, the building had a small set of chairs and couches positioned there. We settled in.

"Go on," I said, my arms crossed over my chest.

Alejandro took another shuddering breath. "She'd called you. You'd . . . laughed at her."

I felt my chest seize in a spasm of guilt, and I closed my eyes momentarily.

"And she was desperate. She told me that she and the Sacred 36 had performed a ceremony—she didn't tell me the details," he said, pausing, his gaze moving briefly over to Dorian.

Dorian nodded.

"And in all honesty, though I always had some kind of faith in the supernatural, if she'd told me you all were performing a ceremony to try to break the curse of women dying in room 904 in one of the oldest hotels in Denver every five years, no, I would not have believed her. All I knew," he said, "was that she was very, very shaken up."

Behind the door to our apartment, I could dimly hear the cops moving presumably from my room, where I'd seen them last, and into Alejandro's. I'd glanced at them briefly when I'd first come in, two white men in uniform, their haircuts eerily identical. I unclenched my arms from around my chest and ran my hands over my knees anxiously. It seemed to me they hadn't found anything—yet, anyway. Perhaps they would tear the place up, we'd throw away what they'd destroyed, clean, put away the rest, and we could move on with our lives.

"She told me where she was, and I rushed over," Alejo continued. "She was hysterical, and as we both know, she'd tried to kill herself before, when she was like, really using."

I felt that squeeze of guilt again. Why hadn't I listened to her? God, I was so stupid.

He continued after rubbing at his eyes, then narrowing them in a state of recollection. He issued a gust of breath. "You know, she swung the door open so violently I jumped back, I remember that. And she was wearing this antique dress." His eyes narrowed even further, into an expression of confusion. "Black. Beaded."

"It was something of my ancestor's," Dorian said, sitting up. "I figured that it would help break the ritual to wear something of the one who began the curse. Of course, that just helped to solidify her as a replacement," he finished, his voice thick with the same guilt circling my own chest.

Alejandro continued. "I could barely understand her, honestly. I assumed she was using again. And as to Josh? I don't know why he told you that I knew that they had dated. I didn't. Or at least, I didn't remember him."

Dorian's face screwed up then, as if he was remembering something important, and he opened his mouth to speak when the sound of someone coming up the steps stopped him. A moment later, our lawyer, Darcie MacLaine, appeared at the top of the steps.

"Could I see the warrant?" she asked.

I retrieved it from the apartment, confirming that the cops were indeed in Alejandro's room, and came back. She plucked the warrant from my outstretched fingers and read rapidly, nodding. She looked up. "Mr. Garcia, I need to understand if there's anything I should know that the cops might know, or find out, that would affect how I could represent you," she said, her eyes keen. "And I also need to know if you're comfortable talking to me in front of Mr. Stillwell and Dr. Becente." She glanced first at me, then at Dorian.

"I did not kill her. I didn't even know she was dead until I found out through Olivia," he said, nodding in my direction.

I heaved a sigh of relief. I knew that was true. But it felt good hearing it.

"And yes, I'm fine with these two being present," he said, gesturing first to me, then to Dorian. He went through everything he'd said to us moments before, answering the lawyer's questions when she politely and diplomatically interrupted him. Then he continued where he'd left off. "Eventually I got it out of her—Naiche, I mean, even though it was hard—why she'd called me. She was convinced that she would die in that room . . ." he said, his eyes going distant. "I do remember something about a woman and a mirror, but it was so broken and weird—and like I said, I thought she was using again—that I just didn't take it seriously, though I didn't argue with her, because I knew that when she'd convinced herself of something, there was no persuading her otherwise."

The lawyer remained attentively silent.

"And then . . . God forgive me, but after I'd gotten her settled in the bed, she was sleeping so soundly, I . . ." His voice broke up. "I left her." He placed his hands over his face, his body arching forward and down in an expression of pain, his elbows hitting his knees. "She insisted on staying in the hotel, no matter how many times I tried to convince her to let me take her home with me."

The lawyer let him cry, which I was grateful for. Dorian rubbed his back as he did. When Alejandro finished, he wiped his tears and took his head out of his hands.

"I know this is hard, but what did you do after?" Mrs. MacLaine asked, her tone neutral.

He wiped once more at his face and shook his head slowly. "It was so long ago. Five years. Let me think. I think I hooked up with a guy." He blinked, rapidly, then squinted. "I can almost recall his name." He shook his head. "I just don't remember right now, but—"

I heard someone clearing their throat a few paces from where we were sitting. It was the cops. Something in their expressions, sober, focused, made my stomach hit the floor. "I'm sorry, Mr. Garcia, but you need to come down to the station with us right now. If you come willingly, we won't need cuffs. But you should know, we've found what looks to be the murder weapon. In your room."

The other cop held a labeled plastic bag up for us to see. It was a long dagger. The dagger that I'd seen Naiche cut herself with, in the video. It was identical. And covered in old blood.

## Chapter Thirty-Three

We opened the door to the complex and were confronted with a wall of noise. Someone had leaked the business of the search, and there were cameras, suits, microphones, and countless faces crowding us as we made our way to the cop car.

"Did you murder Naiche Becente?"

"Were you in love with her?"

"Where were you on the night Naiche was murdered?"

And this one for me, "Did you conspire to murder her?"

Our only response was silence, and though that should've been difficult, it wasn't. Social media's degeneration into a garbage tidal wave of false accusations, pure unadulterated lies, hypervigilance, and bad-faith arguments regarding so many issues, and the way in which the hordes trotted en masse from one person to trash to the next, and rarely for good reason anymore, had desensitized the lot of us, online and off. There was nothing left, and on top of it, all three of us were exhausted, burned-out, and done. But the battle had just begun.

A cop tucked Alejandro's head as he bent into the cruiser, and Dorian, our lawyer, and I watched as the car circled the drive and disappeared, the reporters still swarming us with questions, the mics bumping into our arms, waists, faces predatorily as they shouted the same questions, over and over, in vaguely different, punchier, and more aggressive variations, hoping to get a response.

"I'll see you down at the station," Mrs. MacLaine yelled over the din, and Dorian nodded.

"Come with me," Dorian said.

"What?"

"This way," he said, pulling at my hand. We walked as quickly as we could, considering the human flood following us, and made it back to his vehicle—a vintage '67 black Jaguar. At one point, two reporters had gotten so close to me, I'd almost face-planted. Thank goodness Dorian was there to catch me, or I would've ended up with a face full of blood and a chipped tooth.

On the drive to the station, we were silent for the first five minutes. I was overwhelmed, spiritually, physically, and mentally, and I was sure Dorian wasn't far behind.

Finally, he sighed and reached over for a gentle, quick squeeze of my thigh. "You okay?" he asked, his slim fingers returning to the wheel.

"No," I said petulantly.

We both laughed, just a little. I knew I had to steel myself. This had already been such a difficult time, and I was under terrible pressure. And this was more, which just seemed so goddamn unfair. I rubbed my hands over my knees. I hesitated to call my mother, but she'd called numerous times, and I'd been unable to answer. She picked up halfway through the first ring. I explained what was happening, where we were headed. She cried. I cried again. Told her not to answer the phone or the door. That I'd keep her updated. And then I called Victoria.

"That bitch is insane," she said, her breath shallow, focused. "What are you going to do?"

I explained, and Victoria listened patiently. "Just know I have a lawyer too," she said, "and I'd be happy to send him your way if this one doesn't work out."

"Gotcha," I responded, my eyes wandering to the highway ahead of us, the crush of construction, traffic, and buildings streaming by in an endless sea of cityscape.

"And I'm still working on finding out any info related to Josh. Alejo didn't do it."

"I know," I answered.

"If I can just find some connection between Josh and Naiche beyond that he dated her, if I could prove that he was there the night she died—"

I didn't mean to, but I stopped her. "I don't know, Victoria."

"I don't mean to interrupt," Dorian said, avoiding a Honda that had careened into the lane in front of him and honking, "but like I said, though I have no idea what it could be, he might've known something we didn't. If I think about it, I'm sure he knew that the women reappear in 904, at the least. It's not public knowledge in the sense that it's something the Brown admits, but it's all over internet forums. I guess he could've sweet-talked his way into that room, somehow."

Interesting that Dorian thought of this detail now.

"Or hell, maybe he got his mitts on the *Handbook of Ceremonies*?" Dorian said, a note of exasperation in his voice.

That was a terrifying thought. As if Josh didn't have enough power without the aid of something supernatural. I tapped my newly painted, sharp red fingernails on the armrest. The thing was, I didn't remember him ever expressing interest in anything like that. In fact, in my apartment, he'd called Naiche's discussion of the 36 boring. His priority did seem to be his romantic and sexual interest in me. I shuddered.

Dorian took a sharp right, and I glanced down at the GPS. We were only a few minutes away.

"I did find out that the cops dropped the charges, by the way," Victoria said. "He was just given another shitty little fine."

I rolled my eyes. My God.

"So, he has some play," she said. "There's something there, something we don't know, I'm sure of it."

I nodded, then realized that Victoria couldn't see that and said, "Yeah." I wanted to believe her; I really did—but it just didn't quite add up. Why would someone like Josh need the *Handbook of Ceremonies* when he had so much power already?

"Hold on, Victoria." I turned to Dorian. "What does the portal do?" I asked, wondering why I'd not thought to ask that before. It was such a vital question, really.

His dark eyes narrowed in thought. "Well . . . we're not entirely sure. Supposedly, it not only grants you access to other worlds, but"—and here he hesitated—"it is rumored to give you all the power you'd want. Power over other people. Institutions. Governments. You name it, though that seems perhaps exaggerated. And"—he stopped, laughing a little—"eternal life."

Okay. Now we were getting somewhere. "Josh would absolutely be interested in those things. He's terrified of aging, first of all, and secondly, he's power hungry. In the extreme."

"See, I knew it!" Victoria said, the timbre of her voice vibrating over the phone.

The station was now on our left. Dorian pulled in and parked, the streetlights snapping on as he did.

"We're here. You do your thing, and I'll keep you updated, okay?" I said.

"Sure."

I was about to hit the end button when Victoria said, "Oh, one weird thing? Sara won't answer my calls or texts. I'm *pissed*."

"Me either. But . . . look, this stuff scares her. And, on top of it, I'm kind of a controversial figure, and you know how academia works. They say they're iconoclasts, that they're the intellectual and political leaders of the country, but mainly they're forced to be cowards. The few tenure-track jobs that are out there are hell to get, and you know they'd relish any reason to not give her tenure."

"That's *bullshit.* She's always tweeting this pseudo-radical shit on fucking Twitter," Victoria said, and I could practically hear her rolling her eyes.

"I know. I know. That's how you make your career now."

"God," Victoria said. "Anyway, I'll let you go. I'm going to do my own screaming on your behalf on Twitter because fuck that noise."

I went to tell her not to, but she'd already hung up.

Dorian was smiling. "I really like her," he said.

I laughed again, despite myself.

"What?" he asked, his eyes crinkling.

"Nothing," I said, patting him on the arm.

"No," he said, as I withdrew my arm. He grabbed it firmly but gently and pulled me in for a kiss, with just the right amount of roughness, then it was all soft.

"Shall we?" he asked, and I nodded, feeling disoriented.

He opened the door for me, and I got out. Dorian stopped. "Wait. I remembered something important about Jenny," he said, snapping his fingers.

I was about to respond when I came face-to-face with Cat.

"Cat?"

I'd stopped so abruptly Dorian had run into me. "Cat?" he echoed. "What the hell are you doing here?"

She opened her purse, a vintage sixties clutch, sparkling with orange-and-pink flowers that matched her dress, and took a cigarette case out. She pulled a slim smoke from the case and lit up, looking around to see if anyone was going to stop her. They weren't.

"There's something you should be aware of," she said, her voice a bored monotone. "I've told the police everything I know. I've told them that you pushed Naiche into doing that ceremony."

"Jesus Christ, Catherine, you know I didn't mean for her to die," Dorian said. "I thought we were close, before the knife incident, anyway."

"As you know, I don't get close to anyone. And I didn't like what you were up to with Naiche. It was dangerous. I was right. She died. I *told* you, you wouldn't be able to control that room or Mrs. Stillwell's spirit. God, you're arrogant."

He was silent for a moment, his mouth opening and closing. Then, "I had to try, Cat. My God, what would you have me do, nothing? Just watch these women die, every five years? When it was my family's fault in the first place?"

"She would've done anything for you, you fucking asshole," she said, stubbing the cigarette out on the bench, "and you led her like a lamb to slaughter. You deserved that knife at your throat. You deserved to die."

# Chapter Thirty-Four

I was lying in Dorian's arms, in his house, in his bed, my back against his chest, the rhythm of his breath a kind of silent, steady music. I'd asked him if it was okay if I came over. My eyes were closed against the most excruciating headache I'd ever experienced. I'd never seen his house, and it turned out it wasn't far from mine, and shared the aesthetic of his office—dark woods, Edison bulbs, ornate black chandeliers, and mirrors. I opened my eyes, hoping the Imitrex he'd given me would work some kind of magic on my head, and stared at the mirror in front of me, opposite to the bed, candles at the foot of it set on the antique chest of drawers, the light flickering in an invisible wind. He stroked my hair.

I didn't know what to think. After Cat had gone in, we'd gotten the news that they were charging Alejandro with Naiche's murder, though I knew the footage I'd seen in the Brown showed her cutting her own arms. But the murder weapon had been found in his room. Doubt niggled into my heart. I thought about what Josh had told me. Honestly, Alejandro's explanation for not telling me that he hadn't remembered Josh wasn't very convincing. And then there was the fact that Alejo hadn't told me, in five years, that he'd been there the night she died. I knew that the cops would never believe that the room had power, that it was the room that ultimately pushed women to kill themselves, but I also couldn't help but wonder if Alejandro knew more about the Sacred 36 than he'd let on. If he'd known about the power of the room. If he'd been the one to check her into 904 three weeks before she reappeared. He'd been close to her before she died. And he'd said it himself, he'd always had more faith in the supernatural than I had. But that was insane. I'd known him all my life. He was a good person. He protected me. Or maybe he'd been waiting for five years to get me into the same position he'd gotten my sister into.

"This is killing me," I said, my headache starting to turn downward into a dull roar.

Dorian shushed me. "Don't try to solve this right now. Look," he said, "Cat would do anything to hurt me."

I turned to him, looked him in the eyes. "Why?"

"Well," he said, stretching languidly, "though Cat always *said* her objection was that she didn't think it was right, what we were doing, what we were risking, I've always thought that it had more to do with the fact that she'd always been my right-hand woman. And that was changing. She hates loss of power. Or attention.

"I've been thinking about what Cat said. Your sister and I were so determined. And though it sounds wrong, I suppose that, yes, I would've rather a stranger died than your sister. I would. And if I had to do it again—"

This time, it was me shushing him, my finger on his lips. "You can't do that. You can't go back."

He kissed the tip of my finger gently, and then, his expression turning erotic, he opened his mouth, and I pushed my finger between his lips, my skin on fire, and he began to suck. I moaned hard. And then I turned to him, my clothes coming off, then his. And it was intense, and wonderful, and more than anything, it made me forget.

I slept. And began to dream.

Naiche was in room 904, the knife in her hands, Mrs. Stillwell in the mirror behind her. My father was a few feet away, and he was begging her to leave; he was pleading with all he was worth. He was telling her there was something she didn't know. She was screaming at him that she had no choice, that it was her or someone else, that she had the chance to stop the curse. To let her grow up—that we all needed to let her grow up. Mrs. Stillwell's smile became large, then larger, nearly eating her head, and I screamed and screamed and she laughed a nightmarish laugh and I closed my eyes in fear, and when I opened them again, I was the one with the knife in my hands, I was the one in front of the mirror. I began turning the blade toward my arms.

I woke up sharply, my hand to my chest.

Dorian was still asleep. I heaved a sigh of relief, glad I hadn't woken him. He looked peaceful, sweet; his dark, wavy hair spread out on the pillow.

My phone buzzed. I sat up, trying not to disturb Dorian as I did. My heart rate shot up. It was the app Alejandro and I had connected to our equipment. It was flashing. There was activity in room 904.

## Chapter Thirty-Five

I'd put my clothes on as quietly as possible and called a cab. There was a row of bright green bushes lining the sidewalk, birds proliferating in its branches. I pulled my hoodie on. Mornings were still cool. It was spring, and the air smelled of asphalt and rain and of lavender and garbage trucks. The cacophony of birdsong tilted the morning into something sweet, comforting. There were two birds whose heads were so close together, their little beaks moving so quickly, it was like they were having a conversation. I'd always loved spring, its freshness, renewal, its wild fertility. Naiche had loved fall: the pumpkins and pumpkin scones and pumpkin lattes. The costume parties, the trick-or-treaters walking around in the dusk, the apple cider, wearing yellow and orange sweaters and forest-green flannels. The cooling air, the multicolored leaves falling, the rhythm of life into death that it signaled. She'd always been melancholy.

The cab pulled up.

As soon as I entered room 904, I could feel it. My arms feathered into goose bumps, my breath a frosty stream. The other world was moving into this one, and I felt my head swirl with disorientation and with the whisper of mystery. I sat on the couch and waited. I stared in the mirror and tried to focus on my recent memories of Naiche. I had countless images, all piling into one: of her drinking an apple cider, her face broken out into an uncharacteristic smile, her hands clasped around the cup for warmth, the steam rising to meet her face.

I closed my eyes, let my gift float out and into the room, a prayer in Spanish coming to my lips, and the feeling of her began to hum, to vibrate into me.

I opened my eyes.

She was there.

She looked down at me from the mirror, her pale, heart-shaped face wearing an expression of grief, of years alone in this room, of untold memories and experiences that spoke of her access to another dimension.

"What am I missing, Naiche?" I finally managed.

She parted her lips, a mist spreading through the room, the temperature moving into an arctic chill. I pulled my hood over my head and worked like mad to push away the dream image of Mrs. Stillwell opening her mouth to Pennywise-the-clown proportions and focus on the world in front of me. The room now had an even dreamier quality, and though visually things were unclear, there was something happening here, something I knew with every part of me, my heart racing hard, that would bring me closer to the truth, to saving my mother.

In front of me the mist formed into a kind of landscape, with rolling silver hills, stars. A moon above. And an object I couldn't quite make out, a doll of some sort? I closed my eyes. It was so familiar, but I couldn't place it. I breathed the mist in, and it was cloying, thick. I began coughing. I was choking. I rolled off the couch, clutching my throat, and tried to see through the clouds of ghostly air. I clawed my way across the carpet, trying to get to the door, my brain fluttering in and out of consciousness, my lips, I was sure, turning blue, my need to breathe painfully desperate. I kept going, but halfway there I lost the battle, and I could feel the life leaving me, my eyes quivering, my throat closing with finality. I went underwater and then, just as quickly, came back up. The mist was gone.

I breathed, hard, until I'd caught my breath again.

It was as if the mist had never been there. Naiche was gone. There was nothing left of her in the room.

I felt frustrated, angry. "It's just like when you were alive. You do nothing but hurt me!" My throat was on fire. Almost immediately, I could feel guilt closing in.

I took a deep breath. And another. And finally, I was able to stand up. I had to get my shit together. She'd been trying to tell me something, and I needed to get over myself, my grief, my anger, my guilt—and focus.

My phone rang. I looked down. It was Dorian.

"I woke up and you were gone," he said, clearing his throat. I could hear a coffee grinder.

"I'm sorry. I had a dream. Well, a nightmare, actually. But I think it was Naiche calling to me, because when I woke up, I could see on my phone . . . Wait," I said, shaking my head. I was still so disoriented. "Let me start over. We have an app that connects to our equipment. At home, or wherever we're on the job," I said, trying to not distract myself with worry over Alejandro.

"I'm listening," he said, and I could hear him shifting the phone.

"And when I woke up from that nightmare," I said, beginning to pace, "the app was showing activity in the room." He kept silent as I recounted what I'd just experienced.

"Naiche's clearly trying to show you something," he said, the sound of a teakettle whistling in the background. It ceased, and then there was the sound of water pouring into what was almost certainly a French press.

"I know."

"Not to change the subject, but I have something to tell you."

My heart sped up, and I had to sit down. "Is it about Alejandro?"

"Yes. No. I mean, it's relevant. It's the something I recollected about Jenny Kunza, right before we ran into Cat."

"Go on," I said, maneuvering the phone around a bit.

"Olivia, I think Jenny had something to do with your sister's death. I think she likes to set things up, regardless of who gets hurt, so that she can have some kind of story. When Cat and I were still entangled, I remember her phone going off once when she was in the bathroom. And guess who was calling? Jenny Kunza."

My mind began racing.

Dorian knew what I was thinking. "It's too convenient. Jenny writes the article accusing Alejandro of murdering your sister. Then Cat, who hates me, tattles to the cops, trying to connect me to the murder. One way or another, both have something to do with this."

# Chapter Thirty-Six

I was sitting with Victoria in her sparkling white-tile kitchen, complete with copper accents, every possible variation of technical gadgetry available, and, of course, white wine. The cops were set to question me early that evening. I knew they thought that Alejandro and I had conspired to kill Naiche together. The lawyer had coached me and told me that they would try to catch me in something, and that because it would be an easy fix, and since it would match up with Jenny's shitty article, they almost certainly "liked" me as a coconspirator to the crime that they'd already charged Alejandro with. She also warned me that they would probably play the footage Cat had provided them with, and no matter what I saw, I had to keep my cool and not reveal anything.

I drank the silvery-yellow liquid down and tried to keep my wits about me. Victoria had called me an hour ago, telling me she'd just sold a house, that her husband was packing for a business trip, and that she'd found something about this whole situation at the Brown she had to show me, in that order.

"Okay," she said, pacing in front of the island. "I was doing what I do, looking at the Wayback Machine, and putting every possible variation of everyone's names involved in. And finally," she said, coming to a halt in front of me, her eyes sparkling, "I found something you're going to be very, very interested in." She sipped at her wine and asked me if I wanted a snack.

"Sure, Mom," I said, and she laughed, and pulled some cheese and crackers out from the cabinets and refrigerator and set them down on top of a fancy wood-plate-and-knife combination. We had a few bites, she drank again, and sat down in front of me with her iPad.

"Ready?" she asked, like she had some kind of wonderful surprise for me. Like it was my birthday.

"Ready," I echoed.

"Okay, so like—" she started, but was interrupted by her husband, Brett, stomping heavily down the stairs and yelling for her.

"Honey," he said.

"Oh my God, what? You ever notice that billyganna men always sound like they've just come in from a massage?"

"I—no," I said.

"I *did* just come in from a massage," Brett said, his handsome face turning down into a frown, his dark hair contrasting nicely with his blue polo. He was wearing a pair of freshly pressed khakis. He was always wearing a pair of freshly pressed khakis. I wondered if he slept in them.

"I know," she said, hopping up to give him a kiss. "That's why it's funny." She shook her head as if this were the most obvious thing in the world, and her husband's face lifted into a confused smile.

"You're so mean," he said, a note of excitement in his voice, the left side of his pink lips lifting in a small quirk.

These two.

"That's why you love me," she said, slapping his butt lightly.

He blushed then, just a little.

"Okay, honey, what's wrong?" she asked.

"I can't find my loafers. You know, the brown ones. My fav—"

"Remember, they're in the back of the car. You took them off when we went to the reservoir."

He nodded in recognition. "That's right. Thanks, sweetie," he bent down to give her a kiss and left.

"Thanks, Mom," I said, when he was out of earshot.

She cocked her head at me, her eyes going slant. "Very funny. Just you wait until you end up with the goth man of your dreams. You'll mommy him. He'll daddy you. It's a whole thing."

"Gross," I said, sounding like a petulant teenager.

"Grossss," she echoed in a mocking voice, and we both laughed.

She looked at me slyly, then.

"What?" I said, knowing exactly what.

"You bone Dorian yet? You ready to blend goth lives?"

"I'm not goth," I said, a defensive tone in my voice. I wasn't. I was also wearing all black today, and it was seventy-eight degrees.

"You're a freaking paranormal detective, and he's a cult leader."

"No, he's not," I said, thinking that actually, yes, he was.

"What's he do for a living, anyway? Sell his blood in tiny vials for people to put around their necks?"

"Very funny, and no, and let's see what you got, okay?"

She looked at me suspiciously, but I was hoping she'd let that go for now. I wasn't exactly keen on telling her that he made his living by investing the leftovers of his family money in the sale of illegal substances.

Before I could respond, Brett came back in from finding his loafers, topped Victoria and me off, and stared at the both of us expectantly.

"When you leaving?" she asked, her left foot tapping.

"Can't wait to get rid of me?" he said, a playful tone in his voice.

I could see Victoria consider a sarcastic retort and then decide against it. "You know I'll miss you."

He leaned down and they kissed.

"I'll call you when I get in," he said, and left.

"Go on," I said, readjusting in my seat.

"Okay, so this is from a blog. Woman's Cheyenne, a master's student at DU. Lots of, you know, the typical rage-tweets on Twitter designed to infuriate but also titillate white people," she said, snorting. "But I have to admit, bitch is smart. Read this entry."

She turned the iPad my way.

### Is the Famous Ghost Carlenna a Survivor of the Massacre?

There are those of us who know of the disastrous, disgusting events of the Massacre, which happened not far from where I'm sitting now, not far from where I grew up (Denver). The violence enacted that day is something I don't relish repeating, and in fact there are those who want to forget, to never utter the words again, but if you're not familiar with one of the most grotesque examples of colonial violence against primarily women, two-spirits, and children of the Cheyenne people, you need to see the resource linked here.

However, today, I want to address a disturbing rumor. Like many, I'd heard of the haunted house turned colonial entertainment palace, or "escape room," the ghost of a Native woman named Carlenna supposedly haunts. Some are saying that she wasn't "half-Indian" (a narrative generated long ago and perpetuated by the owners of the escape room designed around this story) but a surviving Cheyenne from the Massacre. I have my doubts. Unlike Wounded Knee, where it's well documented that two soldiers who massacred Lakota people took on surviving babies, there is no such documentation, not that I could trace, for the Massacre. In looking into it, I was able to find records of a woman named

Carlenna who was adopted by a man who participated in the Massacre. Does anyone in the paranormal, or better yet Indigenous, community have any corroborating evidence? This scholar, for one, would like to know if the rumors are true. If so, the idea that Carlenna's spirit haunts one of Denver's historic houses genuinely upsets me. If true, I feel that her relatives should be traced and allowed to give her peace.

I was stunned. When I'd gone to help the men who ran the haunted house, the escape room, they'd never mentioned it. I thought they were just college bros capitalizing on something that had turned a little too real for their tastes. Perhaps they didn't know. Or care.

I put my head in my hands. "Wow," I said through my fingers.

"Right?" Victoria said, prying my fingers off my face. "Shit. I wish Sara was here. I'm great at finding stuff, but she's good at analyzing it, is the thing."

It seemed excessive for Sara to cut Victoria off, even though it was me she was worried about. I still had to wonder if her feelings for Victoria weren't the real reason.

"You know how you guys hooked up that one time in college?" I said, temporarily shifting tacks, hoping my tone was friendly, nonconfrontational.

"Yeah? Well, it was a few. I was crazy then," she said, laughing.

"There are times when I've wondered if Sara wasn't entirely over you," I answered, worried she'd push back, get angry.

"No, I don't think so," Victoria shot back quickly. But her face reflected otherwise. I could tell she'd be processing that one tonight. Which was good, because if I was right, Sara would never say anything, she'd just suffer in silence, secretly resenting Victoria while still in love with her.

"What time is it?" I asked.

"Time for you to get in an Uber and get down to the police

station," she answered, and I felt a swell of nervousness hit first my stomach, then migrate to every part of my body. I needed to still that feeling, remember that Alejandro was my friend, that he was not guilty. That I wasn't guilty. But thing was, I felt guilty all the time.

# Chapter Thirty-Seven

The room was four gray concrete walls and a metallic folding table. I was sitting on an unsteady scratched-up chair, facing what was clearly two-way glass.

"Ms. Becente," the cop said, his breath hot.

"It's Doctor," I responded, interrupting him.

"Doctor, Ms., it really doesn't matter."

I sighed, and crossed and recrossed my arms over my chest. I'd changed into one of my power suits. A three-piece cream-colored dream from Ralph Lauren. I narrowed my eyes. "Matters to me when you're talking about almost three hundred thousand dollars of debt."

The cop seemed momentarily flustered, but recovered quickly and stood back. "Here's the thing. We've been able to clean the footage up of the room on the night in question. Alejandro Garcia is in the room with her. We know he's not only your best friend but your assistant. We have"—he paused to push a piece of paper in front of me—"records of your sister's calls to you that night. You might as well admit to us that you and Mr. Garcia planned this. And that he executed it for you. That he coerced her into suicide. For you."

I was silent. I felt sick.

"Multiple stints in rehab, all paid for by you and your mother."

"So?" my lawyer asked. She was standing behind me, in her own power suit. "Naiche had a problem. The family rallied. To indicate that this is any motive for murder is patently absurd. Are you going to charge my client? And if so, what's the basis of your charge for Dr. Becente or for Mr. Garcia for that matter, besides a dagger that might be something my clients acquired during the process of their everyday business? Have you tested the blood on the knife? Is there any proof that it's the knife that Naiche Becente used to suicide? And why *wouldn't* Mr. Garcia's DNA be on Naiche Becente's person, considering the two spent considerable time together? You might as well dismiss the charges now, save us both time."

He glanced at her. Then back at me. "Just so you know, we have your mother coming in after you," he said, his smile wide, toothy.

It was true my mother was my weak spot. But she had nothing to say that would be anything different. I sat back, silent.

Someone knocked at the door, and the cop turned.

"George," the cop at the door said, jerking his head.

"I'll be right back," George the cop said.

Once he shut the door, my lawyer came forward. She nodded toward the glass, noting silently that it was more than possible that someone was listening, watching.

"Just keep doing what you're doing. They've only got what they've got. If they had more, they'd show you," she said.

The door opened. George the cop was back. He had the baggie with the dagger in his hands, and I felt my heart seize with anxiety. My lawyer squeezed my shoulder and stepped back.

"Labs are back. This dagger? Your sister's blood is all over it. And you know where we found it."

# Chapter Thirty-Eight

*www.ghostequipmentforreal.com*
*APF-D Processor FOR SALE*

*Cut that white noise from your ghost hunting with this newly restructured APF-D processor. A one-of-a-kind technology that when used in conjunction with our spirit box (also for sale, $150) can eliminate static, and create crisp, clean audio. $279.60*

I'd watched my mother go in the little room, the same room I'd been in thirty minutes ago. I'd tried scrolling ghostequipmentforreal to take my mind off what was happening, but it hadn't worked. Mrs. MacLaine had talked to Mom before she'd gone in, coached her briefly. My mother was tough, smart; she wasn't prone to gaslighting or coercion, and I knew that the lawyer had helped reinforce the skill set my mother already had in place. Still, I was nervous. My sister was a raw spot, a place of incalculable pain. And all this was ripping up old scar tissue, tissue that had barely been allowed to heal in the first place. And it wasn't good that they had Alejandro on tape. Or that the cops had found that dagger, with Naiche's blood all over it, in Alejandro's room.

Mom had smiled at me before she went in, squeezed my hand. Told me not to worry.

I sat outside on a beat-up orange plastic chair, one that reminded me of my days in high school, my bag in my lap, feeling as if my skin was turned inside out. The worst part about moments like these for me was that when I was weak, vulnerable, my power clicked on like a light at low ebb, and nothing I did shut it off.

The memories of men and women, sex workers and criminals, heroin addicts and pimps walked through the hallways, their bodies shadowy and bright, their mouths cranked open in sorrow, rage, an endless loop of memories that had been so intense at the time that even if some of these people were still living, or dead and gone, their memories had stuck to these walls like a kind of psychic glue, and they were providing an echo playing out in front of me. One woman, though, wasn't an echo—she was here, if only in spirit, and she stood in front of me, weeping in a short red dress, telling me to please find her daughter, to tell her that the money was under the tile with the yellow stain in the kitchen. I told her I would, and the woman cocked her head, put her translucent arm out, her fingers glancing on my skin, her sadness like a fever. My cheek still hot, she lit out.

My mother came out of the room, and I stood up.

She smiled. It was a tired smile, but I was glad to see it.

"You did well, Monique," the lawyer said to my mom.

I handed them lattes I'd gotten from the coffee shop across the street.

"They're processing Alejandro, but don't lose hope. I'd love to talk to you," the lawyer said, nodding, "outside."

We settled into a couple of weathered green benches.

"I gave them nothing," my mother said. "I don't think their case is as airtight as they're making it out to be. I think," she said, her eyes moving sideways in that gesture I knew all too well, the one that said *I'm onto this shit,* "they just want to wrap this whole thing up neatly, because it's in the papers, and it makes them look bad."

"That was my feeling too," Mrs. MacLaine said, finishing her latte and standing up to toss it. She sat back down. "I'll be honest with you, it's not good that the dagger has Naiche's DNA. Or that the cops found it in his bedroom. Or that the footage places Alejandro in the room the night in question," she said, sighing. "But if you'll forgive me for putting it this bluntly—the footage also clearly shows Naiche cutting herself."

I took a breath.

"I think we may just have to wait them out. Not give them anything. Hope that something more comes up to counter the narrative. I know it stinks," she said, standing up, "but go home. Try to get some rest. His bail hearing is tomorrow, and I'm going to try to get him out for as little as possible. You see, I know the judge." She smiled mischievously, one dark red nail tapping her leg.

"Okay," I said. I hated the idea of Alejo in jail overnight again, but since we didn't have a choice, I figured I'd at least try to take her advice.

We said our goodbyes, and Mom and I made our way to her car, the door, as usual, sticking as I tried to open it.

"There's a trick to it," she said, coming around and performing a series of bangs with her hand until it opened.

"Thanks, Mom," I said, and slid in.

She turned onto Alameda, her breaks squealing just a little.

"Mom. When was the last time you took this car in?"

"It wasn't that long ago."

I sighed. She just didn't want to tell me that it wasn't in the budget. "I'll make the appointment. I'll pay. Your brakes are making noises. That's scary."

"It just does that after it rains."

"It hasn't rained for a week."

"It rained yesterday," she said, contentious.

"I'll make the appointment, and I'll pay—" I knew I was repeating myself, but I couldn't help it.

"No, Olivia."

"Mom, I have the money—"

"You might not after all of this, Olivia. Lawyers are expensive."

I was quiet.

"And considering what was in the newspaper, all this controversy, who knows if you'll have business. I don't know why that woman's after you, but she's good. Not smart, that's for sure—I've read her middling articles, if you can even call them that, but she's canny. Smart enough to get the cops after you, smart enough to get Alejandro arrested. So let me handle my car. You handle, well, God. Everything you have to handle right now."

I was quiet again. Then, "Mom, it's okay that you need a little help, I can afford—"

"This is just like you," she said, her voice raising.

That stung. I felt like she'd pierced my heart, quick and hard. And I didn't even know what she meant.

"What? What does that mean?"

She sighed, and I could tell she was trying to gain control of herself. I glanced over at her. Her brown skin, her wide face, her beautiful, slanted brown eyes, so like my own. I was tall like my father, longer-faced, lighter-skinned. But in so many ways, I was nearly her twin. I'd always thought of myself that way.

"You, just . . . and I did too . . ." She trailed off, her voice breaking. "We did things for Naiche."

I was incredulous. "Yeah, so? We had to. We had to send her to rehab, make her eat when she was rotting away in that bed after Dad died. She was fucked up. And now I know why. Now I know what it's like to see things you don't want to see. To tell them, no—to *beg* them to go away. And, finally, to realize that they won't, that resisting only makes it worse."

"But you took over for me, I mean, as a parent. When you should've let her find herself."

I closed my eyes at the unfairness. "Mom? What was I supposed to do? You survived when Dad died, but you two were so close. So damn close," I said, swallowing hard. "So that Naiche and I had to become close. And when he died, you were there physically, but for a long time, you weren't mentally, spiritually."

It was her turn to grow silent. I thought she'd fire back. But no.

"I'm sorry."

"It's okay, Mom, but that's when she got hard into drugs. Then when we thought rehab worked, hard into the Sacred 36. Which killed her."

Mom flinched. Then, "You need to keep your wits about you."

"Oh my *God*, Mom," I said, slamming my palm down on the armrest, "of course I am!"

"Stop hitting things!"

I took a breath. "I'm sorry. But Jesus, Mom, it's not my fault that she . . ." I couldn't finish. I could feel my eyes well up, and though I swallowed hard, I couldn't stop them.

"I'm not saying that," she said, taking one hand briefly off the wheel and patting my arm.

"Then what are you saying?" I said, wiping a tear from my face.

"I don't know. Maybe I'm saying that you're right, your dad and I were too close. That it screwed you two up. She was codependent, and you . . ."

"Go on," I said, feeling moody, petulant.

"I think when your father died, your sister decided to give up and die. Everything she did after that was a way of putting herself in the line of danger. And if you think I'm blaming you for that, you're wrong. If anything, I'm blaming myself, for putting whatever made that happen into motion. Or for not stopping whatever caused it." She paused. "And when it comes down to it, I know damn well there was nothing anyone could've done to stop her. But you . . .

You're like him. Pragmatic. Which is a good thing. But your way of surviving was to cut your emotional life down to the quick. You've never been serious about a man."

"I'm happy living with Alejandro. And I date," I said, my tone defensive.

"But you even cut your academic life off, Olivia. And you'd spent so much time, gotten into so much debt. I knew your father would've been proud of you if you'd gone on to get a professorship."

"Mom. First of all? I couldn't be a professor if dead people were coming in and out of my life. All day. I mean, I have to work to shut it down. And I'm often unsuccessful. And secondly, maybe I did do too much for Naiche. Maybe that *did* contribute to what happened to her. But also I had to take care of you. And by the time you were better, and I'm not trying to guilt-trip you, it would've taken years to build my career back up and get a tenure-track job. You know how it is. If you're an adjunct, or even if you do something else, and don't publish, they hold it against you."

"I'm sorry, Olivia," she said, finally. "I just wish you'd give Sasha another chance. He's a kind, good person. And he still likes you."

"Look," I said, putting my hand on her shoulder. "Sasha's great. But I think we figured out that we weren't a match. And my love for psychology died a natural death." I laughed morbidly. "And who's to say it wouldn't have anyway. Frankly? Considering how strong my abilities have turned out, any traumatic event might've triggered them. And for the record, I'd rather be with you than fucking off in front of some class in like, Michigan or somewhere I was able to get a job. Publishing articles only two other people would read. I've spent years processing all of this. And you're right, my instinct is to fix everything for everyone, and I shouldn't have tried to fix Naiche so hard that she couldn't fix herself. I'm happy, though sometimes I worry I'm holding Alejo back from a long-term relationship. But, in any case, this is who I am—who I was always meant to be. And this is the right path for me," I said, realizing it was true as I said it.

"I would've been an exceptional professor. But what I do now? Not to sound self-aggrandizing, but I save lives."

"That's good, that's really good, Olivia." She focused on the road ahead of her, and though we were silent for a while, I could tell she was thinking all this through. As hard as losing my father and my sister had been for me, I couldn't imagine what it had been like for my mother. And when I thought about it, I realized that I needed to make more time for that. Not just fixing things for her, or offering to pay for things, but asking her how she was. If she was okay. I was always so buried in my work, my friends and their dramas—mine—that I hadn't made time to ask my mother, who had done so much for me, how she was. If she was lonely.

"Are you lonely, Mom?" I asked.

I thought she would laugh me off. But instead her answer was steady, cool. Honest. "Sometimes," she said.

"How come you never dated after he died?"

She turned right, then left, and we passed an elementary school. I thought about when Naiche and I were that age. How hard my parents had worked not only to keep us safe, but to give us every opportunity in the world. I couldn't imagine being a parent. Pouring all that love, that time, into someone so vulnerable—all to have them perhaps die. Or just wildly disappoint you.

It was clear she'd thought about this and come to a conclusion long ago. "I guess I just got done with that part of me, you know?"

I glanced over at my mother, still so beautiful, intelligent. Her thick dark hair, dark skin, and slanted black eyes. Her barely wrinkled skin. She looked more like my sister than my mother.

"You're a catch though, Mom."

This time she did laugh. Then she sighed. "Losing him felt like losing a part of myself. And that hurt so much. And then, after your sister . . . I just wasn't sure I could risk feeling that deep, dark part of myself ever again."

"That's how I feel."

Her brows furrowed. “But you’re young.”

“So are you.”

“Fair enough,” she said, sighing deeply. But it was a sigh of relief rather than stress. “Let’s talk about this more.”

“I’d like that,” I said, patting her hand.

She smiled. And for the first time in a long time, I felt good. Maybe even hopeful.

“Cool if I make that appointment for your car now?”

She laughed again, that rich, musical laugh of hers. “Fine.”

I turned to the window and watched the traffic go by, the shapes coalescing into the shape of Naiche’s eyes, watching me. My sister had been a good person. She’d wanted to help people. In fact, my feeling had always been that it was part of why she used. She felt too much. And it wasn’t that I felt too little. It was that I knew there was a price to pay for letting yourself, arms wide, eyes closed, fall right into something. But it was becoming clearer to me every day that whether you wanted to or not, you eventually fell anyway.

## Chapter Thirty-Nine

In my dream, Naiche's alive. We're in the Buckingham Broker, my parents' favorite restaurant, the red carpet so red—rich bloodred—the lights of the brass chandeliers reflecting in the floor-to-ceiling mirrors, my father laughing at something audacious my mother's just said. My parents' friends surround us: the artists, the scientists; Ted, I remember, was my first crush. Half Pakistani, half white, and all wit, he lit the table up, pulling my father's pocket protector out of his pocket and leaning back in the red leather booth, slamming it down to make a point. My father saying *hey* softly and putting it in its place; my sister's soft, tiny hand in his under the table. She was quieter than I was; she was gentle and strange. Her seashell ears tune to something we can't hear, something in the distance that is making its way up, and as it does and no one sees it except for little her, she curls into my father and shivers.

*What's wrong?* he asks.

She doesn't answer. She just curls further into him.

Just like that, the warm atmosphere shifts and I can feel the first sliver of fear inch into my belly like a knife, the rich vermillion carpet and wood tables turning black, the color draining downward as if it's being exsanguinated. I look down at my hands. I can see they've become adult hands, and I feel terror slither through me. My sister is across from me, and she is as she was just before she died: beautiful, sad, her rich dark hair slightly wavy. In fact, it's moving as if in a wind, or as if it's underwater, and the fear that started in my belly has moved up. It's everywhere now and my sister is crying, she's telling me to run.

Alejandro steps into the room and I feel better. He is comfort. He is home. He is standing above the table in a beautiful caramel suit, but they don't see him, they continue talking and laughing, my mother downing her favorite, a glass of cab. But when I look again, the wine is too red, and it runs down her chin, and her eyes light up—they are a predator's. Her teeth are long. They are sharp. I shake my head and I move to stand up, but my limbs are numb. The cacophony of the room growing cruel, I can't hear myself think, they're so loud and I'm numb. I can't tell them to stop, and I can feel the sharpness in my ears, the blood runs down.

Alejandro smiles and not only do the people at the table see him now, they grow instantly silent, their quiet like a thunderclap, and they turn to him. They pray in a language I can't understand, and he closes his eyes, taking in their adulation, his arms out. Josh appears as if out of nowhere, his mouth pulled into a cruel, crafty smile. Alejo turns to me, his expression full of frustration. I want to know more about why he's upset, why Josh is there at all, but Alejo pulls out a knife and Naiche begins to wail, an unnatural plaintive sound, and I want to comfort her but when I look down, the knife is in my hands. I hold the knife. The blood on the knife is mine.

I jolted upward out of sleep, gasping, the terror of the dream still on me. I closed my eyes, trying to comfort myself.

"Shit," I said, rubbing at my eyes, then blinking rapidly, trying to get up to speed with this reality. This *shitty* reality, I thought, though it was better than the one in my nightmare. When I finally felt my heart return to its regular speed, I got up and moved into the kitchen. It was so empty without Alejandro.

"What the hell is my head doing?" I said to myself. I ground some coffee and put the teakettle on the stove, leaning against the counter, still trying to wake up. I popped some bread into the toaster, pulled butter and raspberry jam out of the fridge, and when the kettle whistled, I poured the water into the French press Alejo had gotten for me five birthdays ago. I stirred with a big wooden spoon and sat down and ate my toast and drank my coffee.

My phone dinged. I groaned.

*Ready for more crazy?* It was Victoria.

*No,* I texted back.

*I'm sorry Olivia, but you need to see this.*

I clicked.

**Police Doing Nothing to Hold Murderer Accountable**

As the Denver Police Department move forward with their investigation of Mexican-American Alejandro Garcia's alleged murder of Naiche Becente, my source tells me that the alleged murder weapon has indeed been found in the home of Mr. Garcia, also the home of his alleged accomplice, Olivia Becente.

Our community has dealt with so much: crime, the pressures of illegal immigration, and economic instability. However, it is my observation that the good people of Denver are a generous group but one that has to have limits with those from demographics that have proved to be deleterious to our delicate mountain home. If the people of Denver have any doubt as to the violent nature of Mr. Garcia, doubt that he could commit a crime as heinous as murder, let me eliminate that doubt now. Mr. Garcia has a history of violence. His prior is for assault and battery at a local bar. He was taken in, charged, and fined for punching an innocent man in the face.

Are the people of Denver not going to protest? Not going to demand justice?

I was interrupted in my reading by a sound that I realized I'd heard minutes before. A dull thud. This time, it was harder, louder.

"What the—?" I stood up, putting the phone down. I went to the window. We had a second-floor apartment, and I could easily see what was going on below me. There were about ten people wearing an expression of fury on their faces. Two of them had signs. One read, JUSTICE FOR NAICHE! The other, PUT IMMIGRANTS IN JAIL WHERE THEY BELONG!

"How did they get my address?" I wondered out loud, but another *thunk* interrupted my thoughts. It was a rock. They were throwing rocks at my window.

I'd had it.

I threw jeans and shoes on, got what I needed, grabbed my keys, and shoved them in my pocket. On the way down, I thought about how shitty it was to mention Alejandro's prior without context. A man had come up to me in a bar. He'd hit on me unrelentingly. I wasn't into it. Which I told the guy, multiple times. When Alejo realized what was going on, he told the man—nicely—to stop, to move along. The guy, who was so drunk his eyes had more red than white in them, looked Alejo up and down and then pulled his arm back for a sloppy punch. Alejo ducked, I jumped up, and the guy's hand bashed straight into the wall. Infuriated, he came right after Alejandro, and this time, Alejo couldn't avoid it. The only thing he could do was sock the guy right in the head. As soon as the man was hit, he swirled cartoonishly and went down. Alejo called the police. Alejo stuck around until they came. But when they took his account, they still charged Alejandro with assault and battery.

Downstairs, I slammed the door open so hard, it hit the wall.

The protesters stopped yelling; their anxious mouths paused. There was a short bearded guy who'd obviously been the one throwing the rocks at my window in front, as one was in his hand, his arm lifted halfway. He was so stunned by my actual presence his mouth was still open. There were mainly women otherwise, most middle-aged and white, but one was Native. She was the one holding the JUSTICE FOR NAICHE sign. I looked at her dead in the eyes. She looked down right after. God, Natives like this embarrassed me.

"You all think you're doing justice?" I asked, shaking my head.

The small crowd went silent for a while, a couple of them blinking in response, as if I'd asked a really tough math question. Finally, one of them yelled, "Yeah!" She was a middle-aged white woman in skinny jeans and a button-down. She looked like she'd just dropped her kids off at middle school. Others echoed her sentiment, quietly at first, but then with some force.

"You don't know shit!" I said. "Go home."

"We don't have to do what you say! Free country," a tall man in a pale blue suit said.

I laughed. "That's true. And in the country you all want? I have the right to bear arms."

A few of them narrowed their eyes in confusion, looked at one another as if I'd spoken in a language other than English.

I was done arguing. Done engaging with people who had no interest in equity, in justice, in anything approaching a conversation. At best, most of them had nothing better to do. At worst, they simply enjoyed hurting people. I pulled my gun out of the back of my pants.

The crowd startled.

"Leave! Now!" I said, and though they muttered, their arms wilted, one by one they got in their cars and left.

I shook my head. I knew one of them could've been carrying too. I knew that hadn't been the smartest move. But what was I supposed to do? Call the cops?

I sighed heavily and closed the door, locking it firmly behind me.

As I lay against the door, something began swimming up and into the foreground of my mind. If Alejo hadn't done it—and in my heart of hearts, I knew he hadn't—how *had* that dagger gotten in our apartment?

I had grown too reliant on my paranormal abilities. I had to think. Think like I was a regular detective. Who had the most to gain from Alejandro's being put away for Naiche's death, just on the surface of things? And who had access to our apartment?

My eyes flashed open. "Oh my God, I'm so *stupid*."

# Chapter Forty

"In a wild turn of events, suspect Alejandro Garcia has been cleared of all charges in regards to the murder of Naiche Becente. Mr. Garcia was released this morning on his own recognizance after it came to light via an anonymous tip that the evidence against him had been planted by PETRO CEO Josh Bateman."

"Turn it up!" Victoria said, clapping like a kid, and I complied.

"Mr. Bateman has been charged with planting evidence and tampering with a murder investigation."

Victoria, her husband, and I were watching Channel 4, and cheering from my couch. Victoria had called her husband and told him to bring the wine. I had plenty of red, but Victoria insisted on white. We were waiting for Alejandro—his mom was picking him up, and though he wanted to spend some time with her first, he'd called and said he'd come over as soon as he could. I'd nearly cried listening to him on the phone. He'd sounded exhausted but there was a clear overtone of relief and joy.

"Is this not the craziest thing you've ever heard?" the male newscaster was telling the female, a polished smile on his innocuously handsome face.

"Pretty crazy!" she responded, the film rolling over to footage of the police station where Josh, his head ineffectively ducked down to avoid identification, was being led into the building.

"Any information about why he planted the murder weapon?" the male newscaster was asking, and the female one shook her head no.

I turned the volume down as they moved on to other news. Thank God while all this was happening, Alejo's alibi had come in. He'd finally remembered the name of the guy he'd hooked up with that night—his info was still in his phone. At the time of Naiche's death, Alejandro wasn't at the Brown. There were texts from his hookup to back it up.

"Stupid. Fucker. Had it coming!" Victoria sang. "Cheers!" she said, and all three of us clinked glasses.

"Just call me 'anonymous source,'" Victoria said, standing up and turning the TV off and the stereo on. It was linked to my Spotify, and she switched it to "dancing music," finding Kelis's "Bossy." She pulled me off the couch and hip-bumped me until we were both dancing.

We were interrupted by a knock. I turned the music down. For some reason, even though Alejo wouldn't have knocked, I thought I'd be flinging the door open to his face. But it was Sara, wearing a sheepish expression.

Victoria was in the middle of a full-on turn-around-in-a-circle dance move when she finally spun in the direction of Sara. Her eyes narrowed. "Oh, hey," she said, refilling her glass.

"Can I come in?" she asked, her eyes wide, hopeful. She was wearing one of her Kmart suits, a beige number. It seemed to me that, more than likely, she'd just gotten off work, and instead of going home to her cat, Mija, she'd come straight here.

"Don't you have a book to write that four people are going to read? Or like, something revolutionary on Twitter to tweet?"

"Come on, Victoria," I said. "Cut her a break." I took a sip of my drink. "And isn't it X now?"

“Whatever,” Victoria said.

Sara’s face fell, and I could see that she was holding back tears. “Just. First of all,” she said, wiping at a tear that had fallen down her face. “I’m sorry. I’m scared, okay? You’re right, both of you. You’re always making fun of academics, and I’m always super defensive about it, but like, we are cowards. I admit it. But a Native in my department started after me. And I don’t have tenure.”

“Oh, boo-hoo, tenure,” Victoria said. “God, you guys act like it’s the freaking holy grail. Just quit. I can get you into real estate like th—” Victoria had started to snap her fingers when Sara interrupted her, sharply.

“Jesus, Victoria, it’s not just about the money, okay? I fucking like what I do!”

I yanked Sara in and shut the door.

She started weeping in earnest now, and I pulled her in for a hug.

Sara cried for a moment and then stopped, stood back. “And I’m sorry, I’m just . . . there are some things that *are* more important than tenure, and that’s standing up for your friends. And I didn’t. And that was wrong.”

I nodded. I got it. That used to be important to me too. Academia had been the core of my identity, much as I couldn’t imagine it now. In fact, there were times when I wondered if I hadn’t poured myself into my academic career so hard in order to avoid what I must have known instinctually was brewing beneath the surface.

“And I have to get two of my nieces through college. And also, Victoria, not everyone is as smart as you. You make money in your sleep, with your real estate and your investments. If you lost all your money tomorrow, you’d just build it back up.”

“I guess,” Victoria said, plopping moodily down on the couch.

Sara’s lip trembled. “And Victoria, I’ve been meaning to tell you for a long time that . . . and I know you know . . .”

Victoria’s head shot up then. “I know *what*?”

I knew what was coming.

"Hey," I said to Victoria's husband, "want to join me in the kitchen?"

"Where are you two going? Shit, don't leave me alone with her," Victoria said petulantly. "She's all emotional."

"Victoria," Brett said, "you know she's in love with you."

I blanched. I had no idea he'd known.

Victoria's mouth opened. Then closed. And then she blushed, just a little, and looked down at her feet.

I poured a scotch and handed it over to Brett.

"It's obvious," he said, drinking the scotch. "And honestly, Victoria's been unbearable without you, Sara. She misses you," he said. "I'm going to let you ladies talk. I'll be golfing," he said to Victoria, kissing her on the cheek.

I admired Brett. He could be jealous, mean. Or creepy. But instead, he was understanding. Human.

"Frankly," he continued, "if you'd been a little more aggressive in college, she probably would've married you instead of me." He laughed then and shrugged. "Though we both like money, I can't deny that. And we like to have fun. You're very serious, Sara. Anyway." He drank the rest of his scotch and left.

"I didn't know you were that into me," Victoria said, brushing her hair behind her neck.

"Should I go too?" I asked.

"NO!" they shouted in unison.

"Okay, then," I said, sitting down.

"How didn't you know? Jesus, Victoria, I practically worship the ground you walk on. I've never had a girlfriend or a boyfriend," Sara said, her lip trembling. I handed her a glass of wine and refilled Victoria's.

"Okay, okay, maybe I knew, but I didn't want to think about it. I mean, I moved on. I thought you would too. And that we could be friends. I do like you. I just. I really love Brett. I know I tease him like hell, but we're a good match. And I missed you, Sara. It really hurt when you wouldn't call me back."

"Could you blame me? I was trying to process my feelings."

"Process," Victoria said, rolling her eyes.

"Yes, process. I needed to figure out how to get over you."

Victoria sighed. "I'm sorry. You know me. I'm not the most sensitive person. But I care for you, and . . . I'm sorry."

"Thank you, Victoria," she said. She was silent for a moment and sipped at her wine. "I . . . think I might like someone."

I squealed. "What's her name?"

"Don't go making me jealous!" Victoria said, slapping at the couch.

We sat for a bit, drinking and talking, the music up, until the door opened. It was Alejandro. I shot up, ran over to him, and hugged him hard.

"Let me put my bag down before you get melodramatic," he said, but I could tell he was happy to see me. I let go of him so that he could put his stuff down, then attacked him with another hug.

"I'm going to go shower the stink of jail off me," he said, sniffing under one arm and then the other, his face screwing up.

"You smell fine," I said, shaking my head and smiling.

"You wouldn't say that if you were in a rational state of mind," he said. "Seriously, I'm probably going to throw this T-shirt away."

"Go shower," I said. "Then burn it."

He walked over to the bathroom door and paused. He turned around. Then, "I'd like you to meet Sam."

"Sam?"

"Yeah. He's . . ." He paused to shrug. "Pretty great."

I felt a short surge of jealousy and pushed it down. "Sure. I'd love that."

He smiled. I'd had a feeling there was someone special. As I looked around the room, I thought about my little community, how they were all finding their people. Was Dorian my person? Did I even want that? I honestly wasn't sure. As Alejo went into his room and then over to the bathroom, I tried to sit with myself, make peace with the idea that if he wanted to move out and in with his boyfriend, I had to be a big girl about it. I had to be Alejandro's friend and not hold him back. But first, I thought, pulling my wine glass to my lips, I had to make sure my mother survived. We had a week.

# Chapter Forty-One

*www.ghostequipmentforreal.com*
*Ghost Box FOR SALE*

*This sparkling-new, remade spirit box will allow you to speak to the other side—and for the other side to speak to you. Any potentially intelligent entity that exists in a space will be unable to resist the raw radio frequencies the box emits, and through our top-of-the-line software, will, in a ghostly environment, make themselves known. Warning: This rebuild is particularly strong and may draw unwanted entities. $367.98*

The door to the Stillwell Mansion creaked open. Troy greeted Dorian and me, his blue eyes creasing pleasantly around the corners as he smiled and gestured for us to follow him inside. I'd called him the night before and asked him if I could come by in the morning. He'd asked how my case was going, and this round, I told him I wasn't just a detective, I was a paranormal detective—and that my mother's life was in danger. He'd been silent for enough time that I thought he might hang up on me, but then he'd said that he'd seen things in that house, working late at night. That was good. That meant that there were memories I could tap into. That maybe, just maybe, we could find where the *Handbook of Ceremonies* was, or if *Ghostland* really was the *Handbook*, how to unlock the whole thing. Where the key was. Or perhaps something that could save my mother, even if we never ended up with the real book in our hands.

"Are we cutting into your work?" I asked Troy.

He shook his head. "No, I need a break. I've been buried in this case all morning, and there have been no breakthroughs. And the client keeps emailing, asking if there've been any breakthroughs," he said, cocking his head sheepishly.

"Oh, no," Dorian said, pulling one hand through his hair.

"Yeah. Occupational hazard, I suppose." Troy paused to laugh a short, breathy little laugh. "By the way, how did that situation with your ex turn out?" he asked, his face screwing up with concern. "That's not my field, restraining orders, assault, but I know enough about it, I've seen enough."

"He broke into my apartment. Again," I said, shaking my head.

"Wait a minute," Troy said, his eyes growing distant. "Didn't I see him on the news? Something about . . . planting a murder weapon?"

"In my apartment," I said. "The very one."

"That was your apartment?" He shook his head, incredulous. "I don't know why I didn't put two and two together. I'm so sorry."

"Thanks," I said.

Dorian put one hand reassuringly on my arm and squeezed. I patted it with mine.

"Really," Troy said, covering his mouth briefly. "Again, not my field—but if there's anything I can do to help, let me know. You okay?"

"I will. I carry a firearm. I'm not saying they're the solution." I held my hands up. "And to be clear, I'm one hundred percent against repeating rifles, but though he found my gun," I said, my eyes narrowing, my lips crooking into a smile, "let's just say I got it back."

Troy looked impressed, and I could feel just a touch of jealousy winnowing over my way from Dorian.

Troy sighed deeply. "Right now, my life is beginning to look even more boring than usual." He chuckled. "In any case, turning to the matter at hand, I hope this doesn't sound too perverse, but I have to admit, I'm intrigued."

I understood. If my mother's life weren't at stake, it would've struck me the same way. Much as I'd been pulled into my profession unwillingly, there were parts of my job that allowed me to peek behind the celestial curtain.

"This place is more than just old and spooky. That room upstairs? Remember I told you the first time you came that I thought I'd seen something?"

I nodded for him to continue.

"I'd heard the stories. That Mrs. Stillwell wandered the hallways. That the room carried her spirit. But I'd heard that about the Brown too. So I didn't take any of it too seriously. But I was working late one night, and I kept hearing scratching noises coming from upstairs. I was alone. There was a thunderstorm. I ignored it. But it kept going, so I went upstairs to investigate, thinking an animal had gotten trapped."

I took in a sharp breath. The same room I'd had that weird experience in. I'd nearly forgotten. I'd seen my sister in my visions, my dreams, and in the mirror—but that thing in the mirror had been something else altogether.

"And the scratching noise, it seemed . . ." he said, his eyes going distant, "to be coming from behind the mirror. It got louder and louder, and then I thought I heard whispering." He shuddered. "And the lights went out. And in the lightning strike? I thought I saw something in the mirror. Needless to say, I booked it out of here. I think I even forgot to lock the place." He laughed uneasily. "I'm just glad I didn't wet myself."

Dorian and I echoed his laughter.

"One question, though," he said, narrowing his eyes thoughtfully and placing one hand on his chin. "If you're looking for a book of ceremonies that Mrs. Stillwell wrote, that belonged to her, and she's trapped in the mirror at the Brown, why aren't you trying to get in contact with her there?"

I sighed. "I've tried. My assistant and I have gone over there and begged Mrs. Stillwell to appear, to tell us where the book is or how to break into *Ghostland*. But she's never shown up. Either my sister completely displaced her, or she's not coming out to play. Only my sister. And her messages about the book are frustratingly cryptic."

"Wow," Troy said. "That's really maddening."

"It is. But that's what we're here for," I said, trying to pull a note of determination into my voice. In all honesty, I mainly felt hopeless and lost, Alejandro's release notwithstanding. I still wondered if Mrs. Stillwell's diary wasn't hinting that the *Handbook* had been kept by her paramour and then mislaid when he married someone else. I shook my head to clear it. Either way, this was the place to start. This was where her primary adult memories had been made—where, beyond the Sacred 36's meeting place underneath the Brown, they'd done the majority of the ceremonies in that book, and almost certainly the one that had trapped her in the mirror. And if this didn't work, then maybe I'd take one more crack at trying to get Mrs. Stillwell to appear in the hotel mirror and tell me where that goddamn book was or if *Ghostland* was the *Handbook* after all.

"Where do you want to start? Or look? Or," Troy said, laughing awkwardly, one hand reaching behind his neck, "do what you do?"

I glanced over to Dorian in silent conferral. "I'm thinking the spooky room." I squinted my eyes thoughtfully.

He nodded, clearly thinking it through. "I mean, I suppose

you should sit in each room of the house, theoretically," he said, fingering the antique pocket watch spilling out of his trousers. "But that seems like a waste of time. And I'm guessing you'll know where to go once you get started. I guess," he said.

"Okay if I set up some equipment, as long as I don't disrupt anyone or anything?" I was hoping the answer was yes. I was strong, but the equipment helped to guide me. And things were coming down to the wire—and this was my best lead.

"I don't see why not," Troy responded.

"Great. Let's get to work," I said. Dorian and I went back over to his car, where we'd piled whatever wasn't in the Brown into two large blue duffel bags, and hauled the bags back over to the mansion.

I pulled my EVP recorder out, my EMF laser grid kit—that one was especially helpful in large spaces—my thermal motion camera, and, of course, my brand-new ghost box, which I kissed soundly as it exited my bag.

Dorian laughed and ran his hand down my arm, sparking a tiny fire beneath my skin. "I'm a little jealous."

"You should be. This baby is handsome," I answered, and he laughed again. He began setting the camera up in the hallway. I watched him for a moment before I set about my own work, appreciating the time he was taking to help me. Alejandro needed rest, and he wanted to reconnect with his boyfriend, and Victoria and Sara were having a long reunion lunch. They'd all expressed their willingness to help, but I'd told them that Dorian could get this one and that it was okay to tag team. But that I'd let them know if I needed them.

"Troy, you probably have to get back to work," I said. "Dorian and I should head up to that room."

Troy nodded his assent. Dorian put his hand on my arm again, and looked me in the eyes for a while before asking if I was okay, if this was something I felt that I could do. Or if I just needed a break before proceeding. I sighed deeply and told him that really,

I had no choice. That things were coming down to the wire. What I didn't tell him, mainly because I didn't want to jinx it, was that all this was starting to come together in my head. The things that I'd experienced, the historical events, all of it was coalescing for me. And I was sure there was something in that room that would push the final piece in place. Last time, it had caught me off guard. This time, I was prepared.

# Chapter Forty-Two

The equipment started beeping hard and fast before we even reached the room. The EVP recorder switched on as we ascended the first few steps, and I knew I'd catch anything I couldn't hear or see today, as unlikely as that was. I could feel it, not just Mrs. Still-well's memories, like an invisible fog rolling out and into me, but a living entity. Not human. Not of this world. A scent that smelled like fetid breath blew down, and I blinked at the stench of it.

"Am I smelling something . . . off?" Dorian asked, one hand on the banister for balance.

"You are. It's here," I said, feeling a black anxiety crawling into the space behind my heart. I kept climbing.

At the top of the steps, the EMF laser shot on, and long, bright red beams started to circulate in the hallway, doubling over themselves and coming back. I could see something in the beams, something long and tall and disjointed.

"Jesus," Dorian said.

"This thing doesn't just know we're here, it doesn't just want to stop us, it's fucking angry. It's known about me for a long time," I said, narrowing my eyes. I didn't even have to work to visualize, to move into this thing, its rage was so expansive. Like an ocean. And the tide was coming in, heading straight for me.

I put my arm out, held Dorian back. He looked at me, concern in his eyes.

"Actually, Dorian, I really appreciate you coming with me, looking out for me, and even asking me if I can handle this," I said, taking a deep breath, "but from what I can sense? I wouldn't feel right letting someone else come along with me. Whatever's in this house is strong. It's alien even. I think," I said, pausing to let my powers tendril out as much as I could stand, "it was in the room with me a few cases back."

I was thinking of the two women, the couple who'd invited me into their apartment not too long after all this had begun. The portal that had opened into another world. The entity that had been able to take on Alejandro's form. That was what was here. And that was profoundly disturbing. Because I thought I'd been seeking it out. When it had been seeking me out, and not just seeking me—hunting me.

"Are you kidding? I wouldn't miss this for the world," Dorian said with a tiny laugh. He looked excited, and I hoped that excitement wouldn't get both of us in trouble. It was true that what was here in this house was proof of another world. And his family had spent their lives trying to find that proof through séances, rituals, summonings. So many people spent their lives trying to break into the supernatural, whether they believed in aliens, demons, or an afterlife. I supposed my father, in his scientific way, had been no different. He'd built rocket ships. Rovers. Spacecrafts. All to come into contact with the unknown. And here it was. But the price of knowledge could be high.

"I can't guarantee your safety though, Dorian," I said, keeping my tone soft. "And, you know, I've become accustomed to your face."

He put one hand under my chin. "I feel for you too," he said, tenderness lacing his voice. "I want to continue to know you. You are so powerful, Olivia. More powerful than you understand."

I looked down, shy for once. He pulled my head gently back up, and leaned in, and kissed me, and though I could feel the entity pulsing around me, I was on fire. He was something I'd never anticipated, or even wanted. He was smart. Interesting. Irreverent.

"Okay," I said, after we broke apart, and he took my hand.

"What can I do?" he asked.

"Whatever I tell you to," I answered, smiling, one eyebrow arched.

"Hot," he responded.

"Just follow me," I said, pulling at his hand. I could feel something against me, that scalding, nasty breath more intense than ever. I gagged, and it pushed at me with a growl, hard, and I almost went down, Dorian catching me before I did. I had to focus.

I began to pray. "Grandmother, ancestors, hear me. Protect me from all unnatural things. Hold me in your heart. See to the core of this being and heal it so that it cannot harm me." I put my hands out and turned them upward and closed my eyes. I'd placed black crystals in my pockets before I'd left, and they were helping to amplify my prayers.

The growl was replaced with a squeal, and I could feel the thing struggle, the smell retreat like a foul wind. "We have to keep going while it's weakened," I said, moving toward the door. I could feel it gather its forces, and as I turned the knob, there was a weight against the bedroom door. I prayed again, this time in Apache, and I could feel the weight lift.

In the bedroom, it was ominously quiet. I sat on the old bed, the sheet covering it dusty, the smell of the being everywhere, its odor a pall. Dorian sat next to me, and we watched the mirror. It was cloudy.

I closed my eyes and asked for Mrs. Stillwell to speak. To come through if she could. I could feel Dorian tense beside me, his body like a live wire, vibrating, waiting.

I opened my eyes. I could feel her. I didn't know where she was, if the mirror in the Brown was a kind of portal that somehow connected to this mirror, if my sister was able to come through too, if the entity was holding both back, stopping them from moving on to the next world, whatever that world was. But there was something in the mirror in the distance. I worked harder, and it began to move forward, as if it were walking toward me over water. There was a shimmer as it came close, and it coalesced into memory. I wasn't sure if Dorian could see it, but I didn't want to interrupt to ask. It was of Mrs. Stillwell and her lover. They were laughing; it was late at night. They were walking down a moonlit path, her clothes slivery in the light. His hand on her back, her hand clasping a book. I felt my heart jump.

She walked up the stairs to what looked like a rounded redbrick building that felt vaguely familiar. There were a few buildings scattered in the distance, and I surmised that this must be early Denver. Inside, they stopped laughing, went completely silent. I could feel the entity try to push in, prevent me from seeing what I was about to see. My chest seized with anxiety as the windows slapped open and the stench grew, an unnatural wind moving all around the room, the sheets in the room flapping, then billowing, then blowing completely off their respective objects. One flew over the mirror, covering it.

"Take the sheet off," I said, almost blowing sideways myself.

Dorian leapt up, and though he had to cover his head with his arms as he went, his legs bracing hard with each step, he made his way up to the mirror and pulled at the sheet. At first, it flattened itself against the mirror, ripping in places that were stuck to the sharp golden angles of it, the sound of the entity growling deafening. He pulled, and fell back a few steps, and oriented. He braced himself, walking forward until he was able to put his hands on the sheet again, but the wind was too strong. He fell.

"Dorian!"

"I'm okay, I'm okay!" he said, getting up. He was able to pull the sheet off then by positioning his hands against the direction of the wind, and I watched as Mrs. Stillwell and, I assumed, her lover chanted and prayed around what looked to be a sizable telescope in a language I didn't recognize. It sounded, with the wind ricocheting around the room, like a recording being played backward. Mrs. Stillwell then carefully wrote something down on a piece of paper. Her lover pulled a plank of wood up and she placed the sheet under the plank and, with his help, pulled it back into place.

"I think I have what I need," I shouted. "Let's get out of here before the thing takes the whole building down, and us with it."

Dorian heard me, and we made our way out of the room, the entity swirling and growling all around us, my prayers loud and strong, keeping it at bay.

We made our way out the front door, the lawyers and their assistants outside milling in a state of fear and confusion, Troy up at the front of the group.

"The noises we heard," he said. "I honestly thought the building was collapsing."

"I'm so sorry," I said, "I had no idea it was this bad. It's not just Mrs. Stillwell in here, it's something else. I'm going to try to do a ceremony now to shut its access down, but I'll come back in case that doesn't work. There's something powerful in there."

"Clearly," he said.

"Stand back," I said, turning around to the group. "Whatever you believe, just keep your focus on me. Help me close this down."

I pulled a small mirror out of my pocket, and I began to chant a redirection ritual an Indigenous person from Peru had taught me. He was good. Probably the most powerful Roadman I'd ever encountered, and the ritual was tight, but you had to be outside and next to at least four trees for it to work. I prayed. I could feel the entity pulsing, pulling against me, snaking into my consciousness, telling me lies about my mother, my sister, myself. Anything to distract me, pull me apart. But it wasn't working. I knew who I was.

The squeal coming from the house sounded like a jet hitting the speed of sound, and then there was a noise like breaking glass. The crowd behind me gasped, and I could hear several of them step back, a small stampede. But after a time, I could feel it. The shadows were withdrawing. The smell receding. The house was, as the lady said, clean.

I took a deep breath. I turned to Dorian. "We need to get to the Chamberlin Observatory. Now."

# Chapter Forty-Three

"The Chamberlin Observatory was built in 1888 during the big craze around refractor telescopes after the moons of Mars had been observed for the first time through one," Dorian said, his hands gripping the wheel. "I know because my ancestor—one Mrs. Luella Stillwell—helped to fund it. Though it was mainly Humphrey Chamberlin's baby, obviously." He shrugged slightly.

"I'm guessing it had some significance for her at the time," I said, texting my crew with an update.

"Sure," he said. "That makes sense, considering her interests. Now they mainly host cultural events. I still get requests for donations." He chuckled softly, and I couldn't help but echo his laughter considering the illicit source of any donations, should he choose to contribute.

I was just grateful that she'd been able to show me where some sort of clue was. Perhaps if it was still there, and that was a pretty big *if*, it would lead us to the book or show us how to convert *Ghostland* to the *Handbook*. Or it would be the right ritual to free her and my sister and save my mother. I sighed. I was exhausted. I needed caffeine. I needed a nap. But this was too big, too urgent. I'd have to wait and try to find the reserves inside me somehow to make it through the rest of the day, though I was leaning back in the super comfy, buttery-soft leather of the passenger seat of Dorian's Jaguar and trying my best not to let my eyes close as he talked. I was just hoping we'd be able to pry up the board I'd seen in my vision and find out what was underneath it before security was called. Hopefully, no one would be around when we decided to depreciate historic, university-owned school property.

We parked in a nearby parking garage. It was a nice day, the calendar climbing toward the end of spring. The way there was verdant: the path lined with daffodils, their faces bouncing in the light wind, the shade from the trees making the walk pleasant. I thought I smelled lilac, a nice counterpoint to the foul stench I'd recently been forced to inhale, and sure enough, as we rounded the corner, there were several vibrant bushes, complete with birds lining the stems, their various melodies filling the air. I liked this campus. I'd considered pursuing my degree there, on account of the fact that it wasn't too far from where I'd grown up. But the University of Colorado had given me such an attractive financial package, I'd had to turn DU's offer down. Though the population of Denver had grown monstrous, the rents equally so, it was still a beautiful city. It was still home.

"Okay, so here's the plan," I said as we reached the stairs of the observatory. "If anyone's in there, we wait. Then we take this," I said, pulling the hammer up that we'd stopped at my place for, "and we work as fast as we can."

"Roger, roger," he said, making a captain's salute, and I whacked him on the arm playfully.

As we ascended the steps, I couldn't help but groan as the sound of someone giving a tour floated out, the acoustics resonating in the small, rounded building even with the door closed. We walked in, and sure enough, there was a bored-looking student giving a campus tour to about ten bored-looking high school students. Although one or two had that eager beaver look. I remembered that look. I'd been that student.

We floated to the back of the room, trying to look like unobtrusive tourists as the student droned on about when the observatory had been acquired by DU, how the students still used it, a bit about the history, ending with a monotone "Does anyone have any questions?"

The students milled in the way students always did, impatient to get whatever semi-adult obligation they were a part of over with, so they could go on to hanging with friends or staring at their phones. Which, to be fair, when I wasn't working on my semi-adult obligations, were some of my main life staples. I was surprised most of them weren't staring at their phones during the tour, but perhaps they'd been effectively admonished.

I prayed one of the eager beavers wouldn't ask a question and stall Dorian and me. Luckily, the group remained silent, and I whistled a silent breath of relief as they filed out, one by one, the tour group leader casting a curious glance at Dorian and me as she closed the door. I'd tried hard to play interested tourist, and Dorian had followed suit, staring out the windows and taking pictures of each other, but we'd clearly been waiting for the tour group to leave.

"Let's do this," I said, pulling the hammer from my satchel and walking briskly over to where I thought I remembered the proper plank was in the vision. I scanned the wood. They all looked the same. I was so tired, so tense. I was having trouble recollecting anything about details in regard to which one was the right one. I glanced up, squinted. I thought I remembered this ladder. But had it been on the left or the right of the bell-shaped bottom of the telescope?

"Shit," I said.

"Yeah," Dorian echoed. "I wish I could help you, but I was busy trying to yank demon-sheets off possessed mirrors when my ancestor appeared."

"Very funny," I said. "And you did great."

"Maybe look for any inconsistencies?" he asked. "Sorry, I know that's not helpful. Let's both look. There has to be something, some detail we're overlooking."

"Wait," I said. I looked up at the telescope, with its almost steampunk-ish aesthetic, the black metal, the brass gears at the top, the metallic ceiling with one sheet open to the skies. It was almost identical in terms of how it'd looked all those years ago. Thank goodness they hadn't put carpet over the wood floor. I closed my eyes. Used one of my visualization techniques. I was in a forest. It was calm, green. There was a meadow in front of me, a deer a few feet away. I was at the foot of a tree. There were mountains in the background, snowcapped. I was reading my favorite novel. I breathed. I moved, ever so gently, into the memory of the vision. It hadn't been but two hours ago. I focused on one detail. Mrs. Stillwell. Her arm. Her arm reaching down. I tried to replay, bit by bit, detail by detail, to the best of my ability, the vision.

My eyes flew open. "I know where it is."

I sat down by one of the planks and tried to find a loose nail. There. At one end. Just slightly, though you'd think it would've been punched all the way in, with so many feet pounding down over it, over so many, many years. Maybe it was that way on purpose? I took the hammer, turned it around to the claw, fit it over the nail, and pulled. It came out surprisingly easily, stopping at one point, and I realized that I could pull the plank up and sort of angle it sideways without disturbing anything else.

"Holy shit, do you see that?" Dorian asked, his voice brimming with excitement. He was over me, his breath hot.

"I do." It was a box. A very old box.

As I was reaching my hand inside to get the box, someone yelled at me from the doorway, startling me to the point where I almost hit my head against the telescope.

"What the hell are you doing?" she said.

I blinked and craned my neck so I could see who it was. It was the student who'd led the tour. I closed my eyes for a brief, anxiety-ridden second and then popped back into action.

She was keeping the door open, her body halfway in, her face holding an expression of quiet outrage. She walked all the way in, the door swinging shut, and put her hands on her hips.

I stood up. "I'm a professor here," I said, standing up straight. I *did* have a doctorate. I'd *almost* become a professor. And lastly, and clearly most importantly, I'd almost gone to school here.

"Who's that guy, then?" She narrowed her officious little eyes.

"He's . . ."

"I'm her graduate assistant," Dorian said. "We're looking at something that's reported to be here. And it's, well, incredibly important."

She was silent. Then, "Which department?"

"Obviously, astronomy," I answered, realizing my mistake as I did.

"Oh? Strange. Because it's a tiny department, and I'm a graduate student, and *I've* never seen either of you." She looked at me, then, her eyes going narrow once more. "Though you look familiar, and I don't know why, but in a bad way."

I had to do something to get her off my tail, if just for five minutes.

She snapped her fingers. "Someone did a TikTok on you. You're the girl who thinks she's some kind of psychic. I'm done here." She pulled her phone up and clicked something. "I'm calling security."

I made a decision. I reached down, pulled the box out, and looked at Dorian. He smiled. We ran for the door, and I pushed the grad student out of the way as I did, as gently as I could.

"You asshole," she said. "That's assault."

All I could think about was the fact that she'd dialed security, and we had to book it before they showed up. Her voice faded as we ran, my heart hammering hard in my chest, Dorian's irreverent and delighted laughter in my ears.

At the car, he clicked, we got in, and he drove us out of there as quickly as his antique engine would allow.

Once we were on the road, I could breathe. "Shit, that was close," I said. "I really hope she doesn't remember my name."

"I know. But even if she does and security follows up, we can tell them it's my property. I mean, technically, it is. Speaking of which, the suspense is killing me."

I'd almost forgotten about the box in my hands. Honestly, now that I had a second to process it, I couldn't help but think about how astonishing it was that it had survived all these years. I positioned it securely on my lap and pried it open, which took some doing. It had been under that plank for, what, a hundred years? Inside was a yellowed piece of paper with serrated edges. It was absolutely what I'd seen in the vision.

"Wait," I said, reading. My shoulders slumped. What the hell?

"Tell me," Dorian said, his voice filled with excitement. But I was about to disappoint him.

"It's a ceremony all right. But it has nothing do with mirrors, or portals, or other worlds—or about pulling people out of said worlds. It's essentially a love ceremony. Or at least I think so. In Hebrew. Which I only speak a few words of, but I'm definitely seeing the word for *love* and . . ." I squinted. "I think *flow*? Shefa. Yeah, *flow*. And of course, mitzvot, which is meant to, I think . . . open yourself to love. But usually God's love. But I think this is for human love. It's been perverted."

Dorian went silent. Then, "I'll take us to my place if that's okay. Let's just look at it again. Maybe we're missing something."

I snapped a picture of the page and texted it to Sasha.

"Who you sending that to?"

"Remember Sasha, the Hebrew scholar? I brought him in when

I first got the dybbuk box and the golem, but after the golem chased me around a little bit, and he got it to stop, we were both stumped."

"Sure he didn't chase *you* around?" Dorian asked.

I chuckled. "Believe me, that's over."

"If you say so," Dorian said, going silent.

My mind was wandering to all kinds of places, thinking about whether perhaps the ritual was in a code of some sort, or if this was a hundred-year joke, when my phone dinged. Victoria. *Call me* was all it said.

"So. Josh didn't kill Naiche," she said when she picked up.

My mind reeled.

"Remember when he said he had an alibi for the night Naiche was killed? His alibi checks out."

# Chapter Forty-Four

"Who's the alibi?" I asked. I'd nearly forgotten that Josh had claimed to have one.

When we pulled into Dorian's, I struggled to pick my purse up and open the car door, all while juggling the phone, but luckily Dorian swung quickly around and opened it for me.

"Thanks," I mouthed.

Dorian rounded the corner to the kitchen while I settled into a chair.

"Remember when you told me you and Alejo went to that sex club to find out if Josh's alibi was legit?" Victoria said.

"Yeah," I answered, readjusting the phone.

"Well," she said, "I followed up with the number you gave me of the woman who worked there."

I cocked my head, trying to remember the details.

"The one who he got fired? Remember, you said the bartender thought they were together and convinced her friend to hook up?"

"Ah, yes," I responded.

"I called her up. Guess who the woman who used to go in with him to the sex club was?"

"Shit."

"That's right. Jenny. And what do you want to bet Jenny's his alibi? Because it's all over the news. The cops had charged Josh with Naiche's murder, but the alibi he gave them when you asked them to look into him as a suspect checked out."

I shook my head to clear it. "Let me put this in order."

"Go ahead," Victoria said.

"So, Josh's alibi checked out, I assume, the first time. But now that they know he planted the dagger, they went in to double-check and they're sure he wasn't in 904?"

"Right," Victoria said. "At least that sounds right to me. And there's more. Jenny's been fired. Now she's a person of interest in the murder. So yeah, I think it's pretty clear she's his alibi. And she's started a blog. And you're not going to like what she's put in it, either."

"A blog," I said, blinking.

"And she's talking about a podcast on Twitter," Victoria said.

I rolled my eyes. Typical of narcissists who couldn't be held accountable for their actions. They just kept stepping down and down, yelling louder and louder, from ever-tinier platforms, gathering a small list of sycophants.

"Anyway, I'll keep you updated," Victoria said, hanging up.

Dorian came back around the corner and handed me a glass of wine. I sipped gratefully. "Jenny's been fired," I told him.

"She never should've had the job in the first place," he said, shrugging his tweed blazer off and setting it gently down on a chair.

"And she's started a blog."

He started laughing, one hand over his mouth. "Oh, God. I can only imagine. She wasn't much of a journ—"

My phone dinged again. And again. It was a notification from Twitter. I'd finally felt safe enough to redownload it.

*I knew it! Murderer!*

*Fake psychic vbitcvh!*

*I hope the cops arrest you and throw away the key!*

Sighing, I clicked on the link to the blog named after her book, *Fake, Faker, Fakest*, and sure enough, I was the first thing that came up.

**Fake Psychic Pulls Strings to Get Me Fired!**

I don't know what connections fake psychic and allegedly illegal alien Olivia Becente has, but she was able to pull strings at the obviously biased police force, one that has almost certainly been ruined by woke mobs, to get her Mexican boyfriend, Alejandro Garcia, pulled out of prison, and his charges dropped. And now she's somehow gotten me fired.

Innocent, hardworking everyday citizens like me are almost always the victims of today's woke politics. Whereas I've earned everything that I've gotten, people like Olivia Becente and Alejandro Garcia get what they want by bullying people with threats of racism, by cheating the system, and by taking your hard-earned money.

It should be obvious to anyone who cares about facts that Olivia Becente (allegedly) murdered her sister, Naiche. My team of concerned citizens gathered all the concrete, completely well-researched evidence the police would need.

Come on, citizens of Denver, we know the truth! She's proven to be a liar, a cheat, and let's not forget: a murder weapon was found in her home. That's a fact. The police know it's a fact. If you've been following my work, you know that I do real investigation, and only report back when I know something's the truth, with many corroborating witnesses and hardcore evidence. I was nominated for a Pulitzer! But they're covering it up in order to score points with the overeducated elite. I'm sure the only person who planted that weapon was Olivia, in order to make her boyfriend take the hit for her.

If you're asking why she did it, I have the facts. I was able to uncover incontrovertible evidence that Olivia hated her sister. That she'd had to pay for her sister's rehab one too many times, and she wanted to get rid of her so that she didn't have to deal with her anymore. But there's more. Her sister was mentally ill and believed herself to be some kind of paranormal psychic. According to witnesses, she had an elaborate story about how she could see and hear dead people and help people when their houses or hotels were haunted. Sound familiar? Olivia Becente mined her sister's sick brain in order to create the career that she has now and killed her off so that her sister couldn't accuse her of intellectual theft. And now she's getting RICH off people's sadness, and her sister's death.

Are you going to let this faker get away with (alleged) murder? You need to call, email, and, most of all, protest. Make this woman's life a living HELL. Find out where everyone she knows lives, works, and threaten to pull your business, threaten VIOLENT protests until the Denver police take this crime seriously!

# Chapter Forty-Five

I set the glass of wine down on the end table next to me, almost dropping it.

I sent Dorian the link and tried to ignore the steady stream of emails and calls that were pouring into my phone from former clients worried about me, concerned about what Jenny and her trolls were saying, while he read. The thing was, she had already halfway accused me of murdering my sister, so was I really surprised that she was fully accusing me at this point? The one bit of comic relief was the claim that she'd been nominated for a Pulitzer.

Dorian was pacing with the blog on his phone in front of him, reading. I could tell he was getting angrier and angrier with each word. "Bigoted asshole!" he said, sputtering and stopping. Then starting again. "The HELL?" Then, "Oh, are we projecting much?" And one last "Jesus H. Christ," before he stopped completely, the phone in his hand at his hip, his face a mask of stunned fury. Finally, he looked over at me. "I'm so sorry. I'm so, so sorry. Did you delete Twitter again?"

"Yeah," I answered. Trolling was one thing. But making shit up and encouraging people to destroy my real life? That was another.

"You know what," he said, pointing at me and shaking his finger,

"I've been meaning to tell you. I remembered something. And I think it might explain why you're the target of so much hate, though accusing someone of murder seems to be taking it all a step far," Dorian said.

"Go on," I responded.

"Remember how I told you that Jenny and Cat knew each other? I kept meaning to tell you. Jenny had wormed her way into a meeting, years ago. She was already, obviously, on her expose-all-paranormal-sensitives-as-fakes kick," he said, stroking his goatee, "and Naiche called her out. It infuriated her. Her face turned beet red, and she told us we'd all regret what we were doing."

"Yikes," I said.

"Right? You should've seen her. And then," he continued, grimacing, "Naiche laughed at Jenny. Told her that nothing her 'second-rate journalism'"—and here he paused to do air quotes, which my sister had loved doing—"would ever stop our work. That her mother was a real reporter with a degree in journalism, and that she and her sister sat around the table and laughed at Jenny's articles."

I giggled involuntarily. "We did."

"She lunged for Naiche."

My laughter died in my throat.

"Yeah. We had to tear her off, she was so rabid. We dragged her out, but she was kicking and screaming—and I don't mean that metaphorically—the entire way. Telling Naiche she better watch out. That she and her family were on her list now."

I took this in. Drank the rest of my wine. "You should have told me."

He sighed. "I'm sorry—I kept meaning to, but the last few weeks have been intense. Also, it seems stupid now, but Jesus, Olivia, you've seen her articles. They're laughable. She's the laughingstock of Denver. The only reason they didn't fire her earlier was because her daddy is rich as hell, and they feared the backlash. Now at least she doesn't have the platform she did."

I thought about this, rubbing my knees. "But in a way, it's worse. Because she now has zero limits, no job, no reputation to protect. In a way, being a loser, especially if someone else is financially supporting you, is the most powerful position of all. And she is good at spin, I'll give her that."

"If by *spin* you mean *lies*," he said, his mouth crumpling into a frown.

I laughed hollowly. "Do you think Jenny did it? She knew about the Brown. She knew about your plans. And she hated my sister. And me."

"But how would she have convinced Naiche to check in at the right time?"

I shook my head. "I don't know. But it's still weird that she and Cat were in contact."

My phone dinged, and I groaned. "Probably Victoria telling me about a mob gathering outside my apartment," I said, raising it.

"Oh," I said. It wasn't Victoria. It was Sasha with a translation of what we'd found in the box in the observatory.

*Hey, can you meet me at my place? You're not going to believe this.*

## Chapter Forty-Six

Dr. Sasha Teyf was sitting at his broad Bombay blackwood desk, one long finger pointing at a monstrous figure in an antique, yellowing book. His house was an old brick Victorian with a wraparound porch on Capitol Hill, not that far from the Stillwell Mansion. Inside was an academic's dream: dark wood bookcases lining the walls; small metal ladders attached so that one could hop on, climb, and find whatever book might be out of reach; circular staircases leading to different rooms; vaulted ceilings; old green velvet and leather armchairs and couches. The windows were large and stained-glass, with ornate green-and-bronze designs threaded throughout. And, of course, in the threshold of the front door, a mezuzah was fastened to the doorframe. His, I happened to know, was woven with all kinds of protective ceremonies. It was so strong that I could practically see the images of the rabbis who'd blessed it hanging about like ghosts. The walls of his office featured large black clocks, loads and loads of mirrors that had been blessed, all kinds of carefully encased Hebrew scripture that looked older than God, and a large picture of the Wailing Wall. He often went to the holy land to sit in front of the wall, sometimes for days, to pray for peace.

"This is Mammon."

"The demon of greed?" I asked, coming around to look. I'd left Dorian when I'd gotten the text, telling him I'd update him as soon as I had new information.

"Yes, though his origin is strange. He's biblical, but he's often attributed to Jews. Often takes the form of a wolf—"

"A wolf?" I asked, interrupting, thinking of Carlenna's story. That was strange. Too much to be a coincidence.

"Yes, that particular vision of him arose in the Middle Ages with the *Divine Comedy*. He's a recurring figure. Dante imagines him to be a fallen angel, ruling over the greed circle of hell. He's sometimes a charming but corrupt casino owner," Sasha said, laughing, "who invented hell's banking system."

I shook my head. "Not antisemitic at all," I said, rolling my eyes.

"Right? Like I said, a lot of people think Mammon has Jewish origins, but scholars of the Torah have found that maybe, and that's a big maybe, it comes from a Hebrew word for *money*. But it's more likely that it means 'that in which one trusts.'"

I nodded.

"But that's part of why what you sent me is so disturbing," Sasha said, lifting one hand to his yarmulke.

"Oh?"

"It's a perversion of the Mourner's Kaddish."

"Oh."

"Yeah," he said, turning to his computer where he had the sheet I'd sent him up, parts of it highlighted. "Traditionally, the Kaddish is meant to bring comfort to the living. To make us feel that we're not alone, even if we have lost someone we love. To bring about hope for Jewish people and desire for God's kingdom on Earth. See, but this"—he shuddered involuntarily—"takes the Kaddish and makes it into a prison. Or more like . . . a funnel."

"A funnel?"

Sasha squinched his face up into a knot, his green eyes crinkling. "A way to take a soul and trap it in a vessel, channel it. For power."

Like a portal.

"Could you do this with any object?"

"Yes," he said, "but what you've got here is kind of specific. Like it's"—he stopped to think, his cat leaping up onto his lap—"part of something else. Something bigger."

I nodded.

The cat purred under his hand, and Sasha continued to pet it. It was one of many throughout the mansion. Sasha loved cats.

"This particular ceremony involves a golem."

"Like the golem that came to life and tore after me?"

He nodded. "A golem whose sole purpose was to hold a key. It's like it's part of something so powerful, it had to be broken up into parts."

I drew breath. *Ghostland* had a keyhole.

"And when you read it out loud," he said, "watch."

*In the world he creates, he will awaken the dead.*
*He will deliver eternal life, boundless radiance through power,*
*Through him, and only him, you must pray.*

*Take the key trapped in the golem as the vessel,*
*The vessel for eternal life, for power*
*Awaken the ghost in the book, where all my secrets lay.*

As he recited the prayer, a darkness came over the room, a pall, and I felt a strange sensation, almost a constriction at my throat, and the mirrors in the room began to sigh, a strange white mist floating through them, though not anywhere else, nowhere but the mirrors.

"My mirrors have been blessed, or maybe *designed* is a better word, in a way that a lot of conservative members of the temple wouldn't approve of at all," Sasha whispered, watching.

I listened, rapt.

“There’s a lot of debate around mirrors in my faith in general,” Sasha said, tapping at the edges of his yarmulke, “but I have come to believe that because, historically, some priests used them to sanctify their hands, they can be utilized to view things from the other world safely.” He cleared his throat. “Technically.”

“Technically?” I asked.

“I mean, technically pretty safely,” he qualified.

“Great,” I said, watching as the mist in the mirrors took the form of a skeletal hand reaching for something. Out of the mist came a golem. When the hand reached it, it broke the clay figure open. Inside was a key. Sounds of screaming came then, almost unbearable, and my heart ached, realizing where I had heard those sounds before. In Cleo’s room, talking to Nese, the two-spirit. In the escape room, with Carlenna. It was the sounds of the Massacre.

As abruptly as it began, it stopped, sunlight flooding the room.

## Chapter Forty-Seven

Even though I'd witnessed her through the foggy lens of her articles and selfies, I'd never seen Jenny in person. Taking her in, I realized that the pictures she'd snapped for her profile had been highly manipulated. But it wasn't just her lack of physical beauty—because that kind of thing was relative and irrelevant when it came to someone's heart, their soul—it was the pure, unadulterated cruelty she radiated.

She was sitting alone in a booth, the seats covered in an amber velvet, the bar a few feet away a long marble masterpiece, the walls cherrywood, the entire vibe of the Cherry Hills Country Club radiating exclusivity, money. She had an iPad open in front of her, and she was clicking madly, pausing occasionally.

I stood over her, taking in the view from the windows: a rich green blanket of perfectly trimmed grass where men in khakis and women in skirts played golf, offset by a clear view of the snow-capped mountain.

Her brows furrowed as Dorian and I sat down across from her in the booth. She leaned back and folded her arms over her chest.

"I'll call security," she said, one eyebrow lifting, the tone of her voice feral.

"You could," Dorian said, and her brows refurrowed. "But the thing is, my father has been a member of this club a lot longer than yours has, and I've already talked to them. So that won't do you a lot of good." He smiled a pretty, sophisticated smile and adjusted his blue paisley tie. Smoothed his hands down his matching satin blazer.

Her furrow narrowed into a scowl, and she sat back. She turned to me. "What do you want? You got me fired. You got your little boyfriend out of jail."

"I didn't get you fired," I said. "And if anyone's been trying to destroy a career, it's been you trying to destroy mine."

"What career?" she said, lowering her voice immediately. "Psychic shrink to the world?"

A waiter came by and asked if we'd like something to drink. Dorian ordered two glasses of red.

"I'll have another," Jenny said, sloppily shoving an empty glass at him.

He frowned. "Perhaps something more refreshing?"

She frowned back at him, mirroring his expression. "Manhattans *are* refreshing. That's why I'm drinking them." She pushed the glass farther toward him, precariously close to the edge of the table. The waiter gracefully scooped it up.

"Your father . . ." he started, and Jenny interrupted.

"Screw what my father said. I *want* another Manhattan. What does he care, anyway? He's never around." With that, I could see a genuine look of hurt cross Jenny's face, though she quickly recovered herself.

"Yes, ma'am," he answered, scurrying away.

"Fucking men always think they know everything," she said, her tiny nose pulling up into wrinkled knot.

I was inclined to agree.

She looked at us, narrowing her bloodshot eyes. "Do you even know how ridiculous it is to do what you do? Or rather," she said with a sarcastic huff, "to *think* you do what you do."

I sighed. "At least my daddy didn't get me my job."

"Nouveau-riche nepo baby," Dorian said, echoing my sentiment.

Her lips turned up in a snarl as the waiter returned with our drinks. "Don't you talk about my daddy. He's a thousand times the man you are. Besides," she said to Dorian, yanking the drink out of the waiter's grasp before he'd placed it on the table. "You're one to talk."

Dorian shrugged.

I cocked my head. "I'm just wondering how far you've gone."

"How far with what? I'm just reporting facts, something you don't like," she said, swigging.

I sighed, took a sip of my wine, and listened to the backdrop of the conversations around us. Jenny was no genius, but she was shrewd, canny. I'd give her that. "You showed up to bag on the 36. My sister bagged *on you*. You didn't like that. You didn't like that she told you that my family sat around and laughed about your brimming-with-racism articles. So, you tracked Naiche. Found out about Josh. Somehow"—and here I threw my arms up—"convinced my sister to check into room 904 at the right time, got ahold of the dagger my sister used to kill herself, and gave it to Josh, who planted it at my place. And used the entire thing for attention by publishing a perverted timeline of the truth in your articles. All because we laughed at you? Lots of people laugh at you," I said, my voice dripping with satisfaction.

"No, they don't," she said, growling. "*Lots* of people respect me. Respect what I do. And I'm not a racist, I love *real* Indians, which you're not. You're a Mexican, and like Daddy always says, it's you people who're ruining the country," she said, taking a sip of her drink and wiping a trickle of brown liquor that had escaped with the back of her arm.

"What do you think? Natives just stopped at the border of Texas and said, 'Wow, we're not going down there! Too warm. Too much potential to create advanced civilizations'?"

"I—" she started, but I interrupted her.

"I kept thinking, *How did she get Josh, who generally likes a pretty face, to plant that dagger?*"

Dorian snorted. I knew it was petty, but I couldn't help myself.

"You're wily, I'll give you that."

She remained silent.

"See, that's the thing about you, Jenny. I think it started as revenge, but then it became a way to kickstart your garbage articles, and you stopped caring about how far you had to go to stage your version of the truth. You don't give a shit about the truth. You just care about making your career, which, by the way, is over."

She narrowed her eyes. "So is yours."

I sat back, took a sip. "You know, I don't think so. But," I said, pushing a strand of hair out of my face, "here's the thing. Right now? I don't care about your career or mine, though I can't help but wonder how you were able to lure Naiche into 904."

She shrugged.

"I have to wonder," I continued, "if you threatened her in some way that had to do with me. Or my mother."

"Naiche was super spicy on the surface," Jenny said, shrugging into the fabric of the booth and narrowing her eyes, "but in reality? God, she was weak. You notice that?"

I took a sharp breath.

"You're a real asshole," Dorian said, shaking his head. "And I've known a lot of assholes."

She laughed, leaned forward almost conspiratorially. "I tell the truth. If people want to hate me, maybe they shouldn't have lied in the first place. Tried to make their careers"—and here she stopped to roll her eyes—"through harmful behavior. I was just led to a great story. A great story that had the potential to save a lot of people from you preying upon their vulnerabilities. And their checkbooks." She sat back, an expression of smug satisfaction on her face.

"I'm not the one with a link to PayPal on my website and Twitter,

Jenny," I said. I felt sick. But I had to keep my cool. If she knew anything that could help my mother, I had to trick it out of her.

I took a deep breath. "The thing is, if you coerced my sister into 904 at the right time, you could end up being charged with manslaughter."

She sat up.

"I know you gave Josh that dagger, and somehow got him to plant it," I said, my eyes narrowing in thought. "I'm sure it was by telling Josh that if he just got rid of Alejandro, he'd have me to himself. In fact, you put that Alejo was my boyfriend in every shitty article."

"Gosh," she said, a heightened, girlish intonation to her voice, "isn't he?"

Though she was acting cool, it was clear I was getting to her. Maybe I'd try something more direct. "I'm just trying to save my mother."

She looked puzzled. Then her face broke into a broad, mocking smile. "Oh my God, you actually think that room works, you poor, stupid bitch," she said, laughing, one hand pounding the table.

Interesting response for someone who might be guilty of manslaughter.

"I'll play," Dorian said, his eyes flashing. "Then who kills the women, Jenny? And why did you check Naiche in if you don't believe it either? The 36 have been tracking that room, and the women who die in there for real, you spoiled brat, since my grandmother started this curse."

She sat back. "You people kill me, you really do." She adjusted her stained white T-shirt. "Look, I can't help you. I was with Josh the night Naiche checked *herself* in, and on the night she killed *herself*. Just like all of the other women obsessed with that room, and the whole ridiculous story surrounding it."

I closed my eyes briefly. I wasn't going to get anything useful out of her.

She waved at the waiter, who closed his eyes briefly, then opened them, plastered a smile on his face, and began making his way toward our table.

Jenny turned to us. "Good luck to you—or the cops—in proving I had anything to do with your sister's death," she said. "Sometimes"—she smiled up at the waiter—"a good story is simply delivered right to your door."

# Chapter Forty-Eight

"I don't want to touch it," Sasha said, his nose turning up at the golem.

"It's your culture!" I said, shoving the golem over to him like it was a creepy old baby doll.

"No, it's an artifact of someone who genocided Native people *exploiting* my culture," he said, shuddering.

"Sasha," I whined. "You deal with stuff like this all time. And you touched it before."

"It *is* fascinating," he said, gingerly pulling it up off his desk. "And I love the darker stuff, it's just," he said, "this thing radiates evil. And it came to life when I spoke Hebrew and chased you. Little . . . demon . . . *thing*." He turned it around and squinted at it, then looked up at me. "And you know I don't use that word—*evil*—lightly."

"You're just annoyed I interrupted you during your praying," I said, fingering a chalice on his desk.

"I am," he said, yanking it from my grip.

"You pray constantly," I said, now plucking a tallit from the back of his chair and examining it.

"I'm devout?" he said. "And don't knock prayer. It's how I'm going to help you with this thing." He pulled the shawl from my hands and impatiently reassembled it around the chair, turning, when he was finished, to gaze up at me, a look of almost parental impatience and tenderness in his eyes. "So. Dorian your new fling?"

"Maybe," I said, pulling *Ghostland* out of my satchel and setting it down on his desk. "Are you going to tell me what you found out or not?"

He sighed. "Of course."

I clapped my hands like a kid. "I knew you'd love a challenge."

"Only for my favorite goy," he said, taking my chin in his hands and winking.

"*Thanks*. Goys are white girls," I said, pulling my chin out of his grasp.

"No, they're non-Jews," he answered, pulling the prayer I'd found in the observatory up on his computer. "And you sure *like* non-Jews," he muttered, but I heard him.

"You're the best, you know that?" I said, smiling.

"I do. Anyway, let's just lay down every protective ceremony we know and then hope my house doesn't go up in flames," he said. "Starting with a cleansing of the hands."

I followed him to the bathroom, where he pulled what I knew to be his grandfather's cup off a large marble counter and washed first my and then his hands with it over the basin, reciting a prayer I only understood bits and pieces of, his fingers massaging mine tenderly.

"Your turn," he said. In the office, I pulled sage and a shell out of my satchel, set the shell down, lit the sage, and pulled my grandmother's eagle fan out. I waved the smoke over different parts of his body, then mine, praying for it to clear our eyes so that we could see clearly, our ears so that we could hear clearly, our mouths so that our prayers would have good intentions. Lastly, I asked my grandmother and the Creator for strength and protection. I had him wave the smoke over his head and then down over his body after I did the same.

I felt ready.

Sasha proceeded to recite the twisted, reworked prayer, my eyes on the book the entire time. I heard a strange, alien whining sound. I'd placed marigolds around the book and the golem, and Sasha had placed salt around the flowers. Despite these protections, I could feel it, the pure malevolence of the spirits around them both, the aching, arching blackness reaching around my heart. And squeezing.

I kept my intentions pure. I kept the image I had of my grandmother in my mind.

We watched as the mist we'd seen earlier came again, even thicker this time, but once again only in the mirrors. The whining sound turned into a groan. And then I thought I heard laughter, not unlike the laughter I'd heard when the thing that had been trapped in the book had taken Alejo's face and tried to pull me into the darkness of another world.

I began to sing, a small song my grandmother had taught me, one that spoke of having a good heart, a pure heart, and if one did, no harm could come to the one with that good, right heart.

The golem began to twist on the table, turn around and around, and then, most disturbing of all, wail, its small arms and legs flailing like a child's, its face contorting. Sasha kept chanting, and though my heart beat hard, I continued to sing, a counterpoint to whatever insanity we were invoking, allowing into Sasha's home.

The golem rose then, its arms splayed, a light coming from the figure, and, reaching its apex, its mouth split open, cracks appearing around its lips, then along the rest of its body. It screamed an earsplitting scream, Sasha and I clapping our hands around our ears. It began to laugh then, the sound maniacal. It flew apart, clay shards going every direction, one of them narrowly missing my eye.

I heard a metallic, clattering noise. A key had appeared and fallen to the ground. I went over to get it.

"Be careful," Sasha said, reprimanding me.

"I'll be fine," I said, plucking it from the floor, hoping it wouldn't burn me. It didn't.

"You're so reckless," Sasha said, his hand going to an edge of his curly, dark hair, his expression one of fear but also erotic heat.

"You love it," I said.

"No, I don't," he said all too quickly, a blush coming to his cheeks.

I turned to the book.

"Good God, look at it," Sasha said, his eyes wide.

The keyhole was expanding and contracting like a mouth.

"That's a first," I said. In my periphery, I could see the skeletal hand in the mist, but it was still. The mist was too, as if someone had put it on pause.

Sasha stopped me with his hand on my arm. "Are you sure? I think that thing . . . I think unlocking that book is precisely what the entities behind it want. In fact, I'm sure of it." He swallowed in an almost comic-book gesture of fear.

I stopped. I could hear that alien whining again, and my stomach turned. I knew my mother wouldn't want to be responsible for unleashing anything. But if I didn't move forward with this, she would almost certainly die, and the curse would remain unbroken.

"What choice do I have?"

Sasha sighed. "We always have a choice."

"Tell that to our ancestors," I said, frowning deeply.

"It's not that simple," he responded. "And you know it."

"I can fix this. I can control it," I said, pulling gently at my arm.

"If you say so," he said, relinquishing his grip and letting me resume my path.

At the book, I took a breath and plunged the key in the keyhole.

# Chapter Forty-Nine

I slid the key in and turned, the archaic sounds of the pins falling into place final, heavy. Key cards didn't work on room 904.

Entering the room, the mirror staring me down like a demonic eye, I thought about how there were things you just had to do. No matter how much dread the event held, no matter how tired you were, no matter how much loss was at your back. They were in front of you, a wall of impenetrable darkness.

I checked the equipment, and set out what I'd brought, which wasn't much. Everything was humming along, as if this were just an average hotel room, on an average night, full of ghost-catching equipment. I thought again about what was ahead of us, how intimidated I was, how guilty, and sighed heavily. There was something I'd learned, though, over the years. It was that no matter how overwhelming a task seemed, if you were humble, if you took it piece by piece, if you spent your time practicing and researching, if you asked for help from the right people, and if you let yourself grieve the losses along the way, you could pretty much do anything.

I steeled myself.

Alejandro sat down on the couch facing the mirror and I joined him. I pulled the *Handbook of Ceremonies* out of my satchel and flipped to the proper ritual, turning the pages down at three sections. The key had been a perfect fit for *Ghostland,* which had promptly turned into the *Handbook of Ceremonies.* And the ceremony that Luella Stillwell had certainly used to trap Carlenna in the mirror was in the book: the book itself was divided up into three parts: natural rituals, celestial rituals, and, lastly, ceremonial rituals. I wished I had time to pore over its pages, evil as it was. Perhaps another time. Though I was keeping the book for reference, Dorian had helped me to rewrite the relevant ceremony, of which there were three parts, if one knew what one was looking for, one in each section of the book.

"Ready?" I asked, though I wasn't sure I was.

"I am," Alejo responded. He smiled and took my hand. "It's going to be okay. It's going to turn out exactly how we want. You've got this, bitch." He squeezed my fingers gently, and I nodded.

We'd talked a lot about when to recite and lay out the different aspects of what was less of a ritual and more of an exorcism. We assumed that the closer to the time of the reappearance of the women, the stronger it would be, but I'd also not wanted to take any chances. I didn't need my mother reappearing, compelled to kill herself before we had even done the ritual. Mom was with my friends at my apartment, and I'd told them to call me if anything seemed strange on their end. But I knew that if things didn't go as planned, I'd know.

"I'd still love to know where she got this ritual. The base is ancient Mayan, with a lot of contemporary flourishes, mainly from the southeast of the United States," I said, laying the Popol Vuh down and ringing it with black candles.

"Really?" Alejo asked. He was laying sweetgrass at the foot of the mirror at my behest, and I lit each flowered black candle, said a prayer for the trapped spirits, my sister and Mrs. Stillwell, telling them that I was here to help them move on to the other world, that there was nothing but love in this room.

"Yeah. It's a very complex layering. I've never seen anything quite like it." I glanced down at the *Handbook,* which seemed almost to be throbbing. I shuddered.

The atmosphere began to grow arch, heated, the air thick. I could feel the tiny hairs on my arms and back of my neck begin to prick.

I sat down. "Ready?" I asked, a nervous flutter to my stomach.

"I mean, no? But yes," Alejo said.

"Hunahpú and Xbalanqué, hear me. Lift this cursed spirit," I said. There was a sound like glass cracking, as if the glass had frozen fast. I looked up at the mirror and I thought I saw something deep in its recesses.

"Take them from Xibalba, let them win their battle, let them lift back—"

The mirror began to grow black, to smoke, the cracking noise growing louder.

"To this earth first for healing, for completion," I continued, Alejandro repeating the lines behind me. We were almost yelling, the shattering sound had become so intense. The room had grown freezing, and my skin began to prickle with the cold.

The smoke was now piling out of the mirror in a swirl pattern, becoming a kind of thick, wet mist, a low-pitched wail coming from the surface, the wind gusting straight out of the mirror, blowing the candles out, lifting the book from the table, slamming it against the wall.

"Jesus," Alejandro said, and I silenced him quickly, both of us shivering in the icy air.

"Do not use any god's name. Not one," I said. "The power in this room is electric. I don't know what could happen. You could conjure them by naming them."

Alejandro's eyes grew wide with either excitement or fear, I couldn't tell, but either way, he understood. I thought then about where we were standing, that it had once been a site of powerful spiritual gathering for the Cheyenne. Just why had this hotel, which had so much power, been built right on this spot?

I switched tacks. I had to stop whatever entity was trying to inhibit the ritual before I could continue. There was something else here, behind everything. I could feel it as deeply as my own skin. I searched my mind. Yes. There was a song a curandera I was loosely related to from Idaho Springs, a town thirty minutes from here, had taught me to sing when this kind of thing happened.

"Entidad negra, negra, con respeto, regressa al luagar de donde vienes. Con respeto. Con respeto," I said, asking Alejo to speak it with me. "Just repeat after me, call and response."

"Careful, Olivia. I'm not sure you want to do that," Alejo said, his mouth moving into a line of worry. "What if changing this thing fucks it up?"

"I can control this," I said. I spoke the words, over and over, the icy wind swirling around the room, almost lifting first me, then him off the ground a few times. I had to hold on to the couch to keep my balance, and I could hear the clack of Alejandro's ring on the coffee table as he almost fell forward.

The wind began to weaken, then swirl at our feet, and there was a kind of electricity to the air. A small storm building. I could feel it at the back of my neck, the hair on my arms rising, Alejo's hair spiking upward just a touch. There was quiet. Then the whoosh of wind and water rising to the ceiling, small cracks of thunder, tiny lightning bolts. I braced myself against the couch. I repeated the words. There was an anguished scream that made the hair on the back of my neck pull further. It almost felt like the entity was behind me, and I worked to stay on track, not look at it, not give it the attention it wanted, but now I could feel its hands on me, sharp, skeletal, male. I could barely quell the nausea in my stomach, its energy was so assaultive.

I pushed everything I was into the next repetition, my head splitting, my voice box growing rugged, my focus complete. I could feel the heat radiating around me, the sparks of pure energy, and went all the way in, screaming the words again. Again. I felt the dark pressure on my shoulders unclench, and I opened my eyes. There were eddies and whirls of the mist breaking up, becoming airy. Falling apart, retreating into the mirror. I sighed a rough, shuddering sigh. "Okay," I said, mainly to myself. I put my hands over my eyes and then took another breath.

"You all right?"

"I am. I think we're good," I said.

"Do we need to start again?" he asked, smoothing first his clothing, then his hair down. "That was intense. Like, crazy."

I nodded. I was tired. But we were running out of time.

My sister looked out at me from the mirror, her expression imploring, her long black hair floating as if underwater, a wild, otherworldly background behind her, full of dark, and shadow, and strange oblong objects that floated into almost consistency, then back into amorphousness again. "What can I do?" I asked. "What am I doing wrong?"

She sobbed angrily. "Dorian," she said.

"Tell me," I said, and she began to vibrate, the edges of her preternatural reflection going feral, her mouth cracked into an angry wail.

She howled so sharply, I felt my ears began to ache, and then she disappeared, as if she'd never been there.

I closed my eyes, pulled from whatever reserves I had, and relit the candles, set the book open to the proper ritual. Took a breath. "Then let them win their battle, let them lift back to their true home."

"To the south," I said, and Alejo repeated.

"To the west," I said, Alejo echoing.

"To the north," and he echoed once more.

"To the east," I said, "where everything is born, and dies, and is reborn. Flow home."

Everything stilled. The air grew a touch warmer, the mirror began to clear.

Alejandro and I looked at each other.

"Did it . . . ?" he asked, stopping the sentence before he could complete it.

Silence set in, and I felt a modicum of hope. I took a deep breath. Maybe my mother was safe, maybe we'd broken this thing after all these years. We had found the *Handbook of Ceremonies,* repeated the right ritual.

"I'm not sure. I hope so," I said, reaching for my phone. I thought I'd call Dorian, ask him what things looked like on his end.

"Olivia," Alejo said, his voice sharp.

I glanced up. He was pointing to something in the air. I squinted. I thought I saw a glimmer in the air above the divan.

"No," I said, "please, no."

The air in front of us shimmered further, and I heard a sound like a pop.

"Oh God," I said, slipping my phone into my back pocket.

My mother appeared, an expression of terror on her face. She must've been sitting in my apartment because her body was at a right angle. She collapsed to the floor, a single small scream escaping her mouth as she did, and I rushed to help her up, taking her hands in mine.

"Oh my God," she said. "It didn't work."

The air began to grow cold again.

I pulled her up.

"Let's not give up yet, okay?" Alejo said, but I could feel my heart seizing with fear, with guilt. I'd been the one responsible, when it came down to it, for my sister's death. I was the one she'd called. Now I'd be responsible for my mother's death. And then I'd be alone. I could feel my face trying to break open in grief, and I shook my head violently. I had to stop this. I had to make it work.

"I don't feel right, Olivia," she said, tears in her eyes. She wiped at them, pushing her hand over her blue jeans. "I don't feel in control."

"Don't worry. We've got this. Sit down."

"I know," she said, taking a breath. "I know . . ."

We began again, repeating the words over and over, until my throat was raw. Naiche pierced the air with a scream, my heart in my throat. She was back, returned from that other world, wailing, gnashing her teeth, tearing at her ghostly hair.

"Dorian," she said.

She was so close to the glass I could see every detail of her face, the lines I remembered, the ones that had barely began to form when she was taken from me. She pressed one pale hand to the glass, and I could hear it slap as I did. I jumped back. Could she come through?

"No," she said.

The dagger appeared on the divan, a star and the sign of eternal life carved into it.

"No," my mother whispered, her hands going to her throat.

# Chapter Fifty

My mother rose from the couch. "Olivia—" she said, her expression twisting, her arm shaking as she reached for the dagger. I could see how hard she was fighting it, her brow breaking into a sweat, but it was as if she was two halves in one body, and the demonic half was winning.

I tried pushing her away from the dagger, but a great, angry squeal came from the mirror, and something whooshed me from my feet. I fell straight on my ass, feet from my mother.

She reached for the dagger, her other hand gripping the one that was reaching and, straining, pushed it back with all her might.

"Call Dorian," Alejo said, desperation lining his voice, tears streaming from his eyes.

"Dorian," my sister echoed.

I pulled my phone out of my pocket and dialed. He picked up on the first ring.

"It's not working!" I said, my eyes closed.

"I know, Olivia," he said, his voice breaking. "I know."

My stomach plummeted. "What do you mean, you know?"

He sighed. "I couldn't"—and here, he was unable to speak for a moment—"I couldn't tell you. Your sister and I tried and failed.

Worse, we trapped her. So, for the next cycle, I put the items the 36 had on eBay, knowing they'd find the other descendants of the perpetrators of the Massacre. And that those objects would draw you, the only person powerful enough to break the curse. And that you could find a way to change *Ghostland* into the *Handbook*."

I was so stunned that for a moment, I couldn't speak. I shook my head to pull myself out of it. "You knew about the key in the golem, and the book, the entire time?"

He sighed heavily. "I actually didn't know the key was in the golem, and the book wouldn't change for me—hell, the box wouldn't even *open* for me, though it was my ancestor who put the spirit of the person he killed in the box, my ancestor who put a glamour on the book, hoping for someone as powerful as you to come along, to create a link between this world and the other one. Luella wasn't the originator of the 36. It was Chivington. But Luella and her husband, and the other descendants, kept it going."

I closed my eyes, shook my head. This was too much.

"But they didn't count on *their* descendants betraying them," he said with a small, dark chuckle. "In fact, we made a pact to undo the damage."

A scream split the air. I opened my eyes. My mother had hold of the dagger, and she was working so hard to let it go, I could see the veins in her arm.

Dorian kept going. "Every one of the original 36 wanted power. They understood that Native people—their land, their bodies, their spirits and spirituality—were a way to get it. Not just land that wasn't theirs or money. Immortality, as I told you earlier. In fact, Luella and her husband adopted a survivor of the Massacre. And used her to create the portal."

I closed my eyes. Carlenna.

"You know why the women reappear in three weeks?" he asked, his voice full of pain. I let him continue. "Because she tortured Carlenna for *three weeks* in room 904, often with a dagger—the one you're seeing right now—that was used to murder Cheyenne and Arapaho at the Massacre. That's what created a portal. Her pain."

Good God.

"At least with Carlenna's death, she was able to trap Luella behind the mirror when she died," he continued. "I altered the ceremony enough this time, I think, to break it for real—with you instrumental in that process, of course. But not without a sacrifice. Not without a Native sacrifice." He broke off then, sobbing.

"And Jenny?" I asked.

"I set her up too, I'm sorry," he said, sniffling. "Though I had no idea how far she'd go. That she'd get Josh to plant that dagger, frame Alejandro for murder. I should've never given her the dagger. She's even more attention-hungry than I realized."

I would've laughed if the situation weren't so dire. I'd thought she was so clever. But it had been Dorian pulling most of the strings.

My mother was walking toward the mirror now, straining, my sister screaming, my stomach turning into a garbage heap of revulsion and fury. My mother's hand slowly descended toward her arm, her wailing a song splitting the air.

I shot up again, hoping to somehow pry the dagger loose.

My sister emitted an ear-shattering scream of pure rage, of agony. And then—

There was something in my periphery, but when I went to look directly at it, it wasn't there. And then again. And again. A black hole at the edge of my eye, a stillness that shouldn't be there. And then a vibration that hit my body like a bomb. My legs were dissolving. I was dissolving.

I was being pulled into the mirror.

## Chapter Fifty-One

I felt like I was falling through an Escher painting; there were pieces of mansions, their stairs leading to black, whirling holes. Doors opening and shutting. Upside-down tipis, their fires burning bright, the smoke piling downward into blackness. Sounds of wailing in Cheyenne all around me, of laughter filtered through birdsong, of objects being dropped into vents that led to basements full of unthinkable wet things. Animals were skittering in the dark, spider-like, the feathers of their arms tickling me, my mouth opening to scream and then closing, the sound sucked back into my throat.

It was endless and yet it was quick, and then I was on my feet.

All around me were doors. Doors to tipis. Doors to longhouses. Doors to enormous mansions. To shacks. Doors that barely looked like doors.

Doors that breathed.

*Olivia.* The voice was coming from behind me.

I turned, my body a firestorm of nerves.

It was Nese. I would've known them anywhere.

*I thought I helped you to move on,* I said, though it felt like a whisper in the dark. Like I wasn't speaking a human language.

*I was trying to aid you. To warn you. To prepare,* they said.

I thought back to what Nese had said when I first met them at Cleo's place, that they were going to give me the key.

Nese's body wavered in the strange air, their long black hair like a beautiful underwater hallucination. *The 36 coerced an old, powerful woman of the Hebrew tribe, trapping me in a spell box with an aspect of Mammon. They put me beside the key, which was buried in the golem. Powerful medicine,* they said, their eyes narrowing. *But we have been trying to break the curse at every generation, with the help of the prayers of our people and of yours. Of many.*

*We?* I asked.

*Carlenna and I,* they said, their chin turning up in pride.

*I see.* No wonder she hadn't moved on either. I shook my head, something that felt strange, surreal, as if I was submerged. *How do I stop this?* I asked. *Dorian couldn't.*

*There is a song they don't know. I can teach it to you,* they said, their face breaking into a smile, their hands turning upward.

*Why me?* I asked.

*Your gift is very strong. It was born from many generations of pain. And beauty,* they said, their eyes turning soft.

I was quiet.

*See these doors? They're the doors to every world. This is the place you go when you pass on, from the door to your world to the next. And doors to other worlds.* They pointed, and in the distance, I could see light breaking over a hill, a strange, crystalline song coming from the brightness that filled me with a wild, sad feeling, as if everything was going to be all right, but in an overwhelming, obliterating way. I turned from it. Nese continued. *The original 36 want access to this place. If they're able to gain it, their power will be terrible, endless. Dorian thinks he's stopped them. He hasn't. And they are waiting. They know they're close. And they have help, one of their gods.*

*Mammon?* I asked.

*Yes. He's very powerful. While you sing, you must watch for him,* they said, their eyes narrowing.

*Teach me the song,* I said. *Then send me back.*

One of the doors, a door to a tipi, quivered, and I wondered what might emerge in such a preternatural, interstitial space as this. The flap opened, and for a moment all I could see was shadow, and beyond, furniture that almost looked like it belonged in a turn-of-the-century mansion. But before I could be too puzzled by this, I saw the shadow coalesce. It was Carlenna, her clothing shifting from European dress of the same period to a dress and boots made of deerskin, elk teeth lining the top.

She stood by Nese and they sang a tune to break me, to break the world.

# Chapter Fifty-Two

Time came back.

There was a hissing noise coming from the mirror. The mist I'd seen in Sasha's office was flooding the glass, flooding the room. Behind it I could see figures, women and men in turn-of-the-century clothing, their faces gray, their mouths open and salivating, their eyes black holes. High above them was a tall figure in dark robes, his face hooded, his long white talons scraping the mirror. There was a small cracking noise and a bright flash of light. A finger pushed through.

The dagger pierced my mother's flesh. She began to scream as she cut, her muscles straining, the bright red blood running down her long brown arm, dripping onto the floor.

I opened my mouth and sang, the words blasting forth, a blinding light. The room was flooded with it, and the monster screeched so loudly I thought my eardrums would burst. My mother's steps faltered, her arm falling to her side, the dagger bouncing onto the floor.

The mirror made a cracking sound, like a slice of a great sheaf of ice splitting off a glacier. I kept singing, my own eyes nearly blind to what was happening around me, the words a mix from the Yucatec,

Tsis tsi'tas, Indeh, and Tawantin Suyu people. I'd never sung anything this strong. I felt like my body was vibrating with something otherworldly, the languages somehow blending melodiously in my throat, almost like Inuit throat singing but more, my chest bouncing painfully with each powerful syllable.

I could see Luella Stillwell, her father behind her, his hands on her shoulders, at the front of the mirror, her hands pressed against the glass, her smile wide, terrifying, her teeth as long as Mammon's talons. Her mouth cracked open, a whirl of something alien behind it. She began to sing something in a language that sounded like a wild combination between ancient Russian and Egyptian, something so old it had disappeared from the world, something Mammon had buried somewhere nasty, dank, secret.

My throat closed up like I'd never had one. The light faded.

I could hear my mother sobbing, Luella laughing wildly, and, worst of all, the screeching, backward sounds of Mammon entering the space. As my vision recovered, I could see Luella, her eyes black, rimmed with an unnatural blue light. It was like she was feeding off the song. She was crooning, and the sound of that was mixed with a kind of animal sucking sound, her hands, then head, then the rest of her extending out from the mirror, Mammon at her side, almost moving through her.

Alejandro was frozen.

I cracked open my throat, but there was nothing. The mirror split all the way, and Mrs. Stillwell was over me, floating blackly, her dress undulating, her face a jagged series of pieces of unearthly white skin.

I was stuck. Numb. Her hand brushed into my chest, and the viscous cold that followed made me retch emptily, silently. She laughed and began to push farther into me, the frozen wetness a living thing.

I tried to shake it loose but couldn't. I tried to open my mouth to sing, but Mrs. Stillwell had taken my throat.

"In a moment, you will give us access to eternal life, power beyond imagining. We'll have access to so many worlds," Luella said, her voice dying to a whisper as she watched my mother pick the dagger up again.

Mom set the dagger once more to her flesh, and I felt the world rupturing open with the kind of visceral pain I hoped I'd never feel again. Flashes of my sister's body, my father's funeral, my mother weeping to raise the dead came unbidden to my mind.

As if I were drowning, my mother's screaming became distant, a curl of sound in the wind. I went to the memory I'd been avoiding. Not the night Naiche called. Not the night Naiche died. The night she first told me about how she felt, not just about me, but about the world, her world. I had been so sure I could fix her, control the situation, by refusing to engage her at all.

*I'd come home from class. I was a bundle of nerves and exhaustion. She knocked. I sighed heavily. I told her to come in. Her expression was anxious, her freckled face knocked into the shape of sorrow. I knew something was wrong. But something was always wrong. I wondered if she was using again. If I'd need to go through her room, her car, her phone. She sat down on my bed, put her hand on my hand. I pulled away. She frowned. I'm sorry, I said, I'm just tired, I said. I know, she said. I just have to talk to someone. I was silent. Then, I'm not using, she said. Okay, I said, not believing her. You don't believe me, she said. I do I do, I said, still not believing her, too tired to do anything about it. I just want to tell you, she said. What? I was tired, so tired. I have a job, she said, smiling. I'm going to keep it. Good, I said, not believing her still. She was silent. I waited for her to go. I wanted to look at my phone. I wanted to look at the ceiling. I wanted to sleep. I just want you to know . . . she said. What? I said, still hoping she would go, still hoping I could sleep soon. That sometimes, I just . . . She stopped. She looked down. I could feel her pain. But I was too tired. Too annoyed. Too sure that if I just didn't indulge her, she would come to me for a real solution. She stood up. I'm sorry, I said. It's okay, she said. But tell me, I said, while she was at my door, half in and half out. Just tell me, I said. Sometimes, she said, I just need you to believe in me. Because I don't believe in anything. But I can when someone believes in me, when they listen and don't judge. Okay, I said, trying not to roll my eyes. I could feel her pain rushing outward, an oppressive cloud. I do, I said, looking down at my phone. As she left, I could feel her pain leave with her. And God forgive me, I was glad.*

I opened my eyes, pulled out of the ocean, and felt for the first time that I believed in my sister. That she had been trying to teach me how to open to others, even if it hurt. To not try to control everything all on my own. I opened my mouth.

I sang, and the light burst forth.

# Chapter Fifty-Three

Luella screamed a wild, deafening scream. I clapped my hands over my ears. She began to pulse, a dark, blood-filled diseased heart, her mouth contorting. I could see that she was trying to sing, to counter my song, but it was too late, my voice overpowered hers and it was as if she wasn't singing at all. Her body grew faint, then distinct again; it began to lose its grip on me. I sang to break my own heart, to mend my mother's, and to forgive myself, to believe in the love I knew my sister and my ancestors had for me, the sound like a thousand shimmering lights. It was pure. And crystalline.

Mrs. Stillwell burst into a thousand darkened points, my sister appearing in the mirror as she disappeared, her arms reaching toward me, her eyes full of beauty, her mouth turned up in that same sad smile I remembered so well.

The mirror cracked straight down the middle.

And everything was silent. And everything was still.

## Chapter Fifty-Four

I set the mirror into a holder I'd bought at a Michaels, standing back to make sure that it was secure. I'd performed a powerful ritual on that holder, not that it needed it. The mirror was split, to the Brown's great happiness. And though I always covered my bases, the mirror had also blackened in room 904, not long after Mrs. Stillwell had disappeared. I set it next to the *Handbook of Ceremonies*. I shut the door.

"Martini?" Alejo asked me, and I smiled and sat down on the divan.

He settled in next to Sam, who'd been spending the night often enough to mainly call our place home. He was kind. And he was good to Alejandro. And when the time came, I would be happy if he wanted to move in with us, or if they wanted to get a place on their own. I just wanted Alejo to be happy.

A knock at the door signaled the rest of the party, and I got up to get more martinis as Victoria and Brett, Sara and her new girlfriend, and my mother filed in. They'd been off at Target, getting cupcakes and chips and more martini and margarita supplies.

"Bitch, I need a martini with about a dozen olives, stat," Victoria said, slapping my arm, and I laughed and asked Mom if she needed anything. Painkillers. A bandage change. She told me to stop fussing and let her get a drink. I could hear a knock at the door. I was sure it was Sasha, and despite myself, I could feel my heart lift.

I felt, as I joined everyone in the kitchen, the noise of chatter surrounding me, as if my sister was with us. Not in that cheesy way; in that warm, real way. In a way I hadn't felt since she died. She'd always been with me. But in a way that hurt. It would always hurt. But now I felt like there was beauty there too. There was love.

I went to the window with my martini and sipped. I thought of Dorian.

It was slipping, finally, into summer, the leaves bright, the flowers brighter, the wind moving through the branches.

I could never forgive Dorian. But he had joined with the other women who'd had ancestors at the Massacre, and they were planning to petition the Colorado Senate alongside a local Native organization that handled issues around Missing and Murdered Indigenous Women, concrete movements toward LAND BACK, and—most pertinent in his case—a widespread movement to educate Coloradoans on what had happened at the Massacre.

I sighed. While I appreciated these efforts, and even what he'd tried to do to fix the sins his ancestors had perpetrated, as mercenary as it had been, what had been missing was something he could never have provided: a song only two Cheyenne knew.

I blinked, coming out of my reverie. I could see two tiny finches flitting in and out of the branches, singing to each other, their faces lit up. It was so momentary. But really, it was everything.

## The Massacre, Part IV: Epilogue

Nese tried to drive him mad, this soldier who said he was a man of God.

They were with the soldier at night, whispering and whispering in his cold white ear. They scratched his arms, gave him nightmares, frightened his dogs, took his hands and gave them knives and pulled them up to his throat and made him wake in front of the mirror, blood running down his skin.

Nese enjoyed the way Chivington screamed and screamed.

Nese wanted to show him the seed of just one tiny life, the life of a boy who had been training to be a medicine man. The life, the face, of the boy who had smiled up at them, handing Nese a small brown root, one they'd taught him to dig for, his hands close to the One who lives in the ground, in the dirt. The root was medicine for women. He'd loved to help; he was pure love, he was pure pure. They lifted the day they'd spent with the boy gathering medicine, so close to the Massacre, and placed it in the mind of Chivington. Nese showed this soldier of the Vehoc, this bad reverse medicine man these good things, these human things, these things that had been such a good, sublime part of their life as one of the Heévâhetaneo'o.

But Chivington only sneered, only turned over petulantly in his sleep, only pulled his lip up in scorn, batted at them as if they were a mite, called this sacred child who was gone forever a savage. Smiled when he thought of what he'd done to this good, sweet boy with the shy, bright eyes, the wind ruffling the feathers in his hair in Nese's memory for all eternity.

Nese's heart grew sick.

How can you work upon the soul of a man who kept the fetus of a woman who he murdered? He has no soul. He is proud. He kept it in a box. A box of power.

The soldier's house was so large Nese wondered at the spectacle of it: the marble, the wood, the large, round columns, the scale and grandeur Nese had only heard of the people of the Maya having before the invasion of the Vehoc. And then Chivington learned something: that the Heévâhetaneo'o were power, that all those the Vehoc called Indians could give the Vehoc immortality through their deaths.

Nese grew quiet.

Chivington found a woman who could conjure a ceremony. Nese could feel their spirit being pulled into the box, next to the golem that had been formed to trap a key that went to a book that was building strength, a book with so many twisted ceremonies in its pages it was too powerful to allow in its natural form until there was someone powerful enough to use it, though the daughter of the soldier tried. The book then took the shape, the name, of something else.

Nese was imprisoned.

For many years Nese despaired, their spirit twisting and twisting in the box.

But then there was a glimmer of light. They saw it through the edges of the box, through the edges of the world, and they began to feel something wild, good, like they had been searching for a vision for the camp and an elk had blessed them by walking through the forest at midnight. And it wasn't just an elk, it was a spirit, a good one come to bring hope to the camp, its antlers glistening with sacred moonlight, its head bowed down to grant a vision.

This spirit of moonlight was a girl who had survived the Massacre. The soldier's daughter had tried to use her to get to another world, this world of power, but she had eaten their ceremony and made it something else as she died. And trapped the daughter.

She called to Nese, and they began to crack open again, to crack open with hope.

Her name was Carlenna, though it had not been so when she'd lived with the Heévâhetaneo'o. She was powerful, and she had a secret: one was coming, the one whom the boy had told Nese about, one whose ancestors had been traditional enemies of the people but who had come to honor all their ways, their ceremonies.

Though Nese still tore at themselves with rage, their spirit grinding like teeth against teeth, Carlenna told them the one who was coming would heal them, would break the curse through ceremony, would sing the song that their ancestors were making for them in that other world. A song that was filled with the light of every one of the children who had died at the hands of the Vehoc on the day of the Massacre. Of all the massacres. That, actually, there were many like her, waiting to be born.

Nese sighed in their prison. Nese thought of that good, sweet boy who'd been cut down, his hair now ruffling in the wind of eternity, his precious gifts not a waste after all, his small, dark hands holding moonlight, cupped like water, holding magic. His name: He whose light is reflected back.

## Educational Resources

Sand Creek Massacre: www.sandcreekmassacrefoundation.org/history

People of the Sacred Land: www.peopleofthesacredland.org

Suicide in Indian Country: www.nicoa.org/national-american-indian-and-alaska-native-hope-for-life-day

## Acknowledgments

First and foremost, I want to thank my editor, Zachary Wagman. I can't tell you how much I appreciate your insight and your willingness to go through so many versions of this novel with me. I also want to thank my agent, Rebecca Friedman. You're a jewel; I've said that exact phrase so many times, but it's true. Not only did you work with me through so many versions of this novel, but you listened to countless crises of confidence.

An extremely special thanks to June Dempsy, beta reader extraordinaire. This novel would've been a hot pile of garbage if it weren't for you. And big thanks to my copy editor, Nicole Hall, who did so much to make this book shine.

I also want to thank my partner, David Heska Wanbli Weiden. Our conversations are really everything for me. Simply put, I'm deeply glad to have you in my life.

This novel was written during a time in my life where the outside pressures were intense. More intense than I ever could've imagined. But there's one thing I've learned: No one can stop you when you love to write. No matter how hard they try, no matter what happens in your life, if you want it, you do it. So, I guess this last part is dedicated to every Native person who felt that they didn't belong and to every nerd who was told that what they loved was silly. You belong. What you love isn't silly. And art is everything. It makes us able to love the world.

## About the Author

**Erika T. Wurth**'s novel *White Horse* was a *New York Times* Editors' Pick and a *Good Morning America* Buzz Pick and an Indie Next, Target Book of the Month, and Book of the Month pick. She is both a Kenyon and Sewanee fellow and a member of the Kenyon faculty. She's published in *BuzzFeed, McSweeney's Internet Tendency,* and the *Writer's Chronicle* and is a narrative artist for the Meow Wolf Denver installation. She's an urban Native of Apache, Chickasaw, and Cherokee descent and lives in Denver with her partner, niece, stepkids, and two incredibly fluffy dogs.